REDFERN

Continuity is everything

(A Post Singularity Novel)

G.D. Tinnams

Redfern

First Published 2016

Copyright © 2016 by G.D. Tinnams
Cover Design by G.D. Tinnams
Cover image © Grandfailure | Dreamstime.com
ISBN-13: 978-1537059723
ISBN-10: 1537059726

The right of G.D. Tinnams to be identified as author of this work has been asserted in accordance with the Copyright, Designs and Patents Act 1988.

All Rights Reserved

No reproduction, copy or transmission of this publication may be made without written permission.

All the characters in this book are fictitious and any resemblance to actual persons living or dead is purely coincidental.

Dedication

For my Daughter, Freya Jane

Chapter One

Tired but elated, Jason sat nestled in the shadow of a revolving staircase eating the dried out remains of a ham sandwich. He had just returned from a raid, his battered stealth armour stained with mud and soot, and his red hair, black with it. He had somehow cut his hands too, and they stung as he flexed his fingers, the blood trail combining with the dirt into something sticky and disgusting.

The drones had almost caught him this time – almost, but not quite. He didn't know the count yet, he didn't know how many had made it back or how many had been wiped out. But the raid had been successful, the 'Machine Head' complex destroyed. All those people, who otherwise would have been disintegrated in the night, would live to see another day, another sunrise.

Feet clattered on the metal slats of the stairs over his head. Someone was coming down from the surface level, and Jason slid aside to let them pass.

"You waiting for someone, Webster?" Alan Jenkins asked, pausing two steps below where Jason sat.

"Gina's a little late home, sir," he replied with a shrug. "She does that sometimes. How many have made it back so far?"

The cell leader paused. In the glow of the mining lamps, Jason saw a bloodless and weary face etched with far too many lines. Alan coordinated all the raids from the refuge operations centre, a responsibility that took its own toll.

"You, Holloway, Gibbs…" The big man lowered his eyes. "And that's it."

"So far?" Jason added hopefully.

The cell leader shook his head. "No, not so far, that's it, end of. The others activated their combustibles. If they hadn't, we'd be evacuating right now."

Jason found himself looking up the staircase in the hope of feeling a breeze on his face rather than stale air. There was only stillness; the hatch was closed and the refuge secure. They were locked up tight in their hole in the ground, buried and safe.

"You going to sit there all night?" Alan asked, resting a hand on Jason's shoulder. The big man liked to act paternal on occasion, especially after a mission. Jason looked up into those wild and slightly unfocussed eyes. Alan was thirty but could easily have passed for forty, the war having aged him so rapidly. As for Jason, he was only a couple of years younger, his career a rapid progression from soldier, to second in command, to mission leader; promoted by virtue of survival.

He had survived so many.

"You should get some sleep," Alan said. "I need you sharp if you're going to lead another attack tomorrow."

Jason blinked, something was stinging his eyes. "I thought I saw Gina get clear."

Alan exhaled sharply. "I'm sorry, Jason, her combustible fired eight minutes after you took out the complex... She's gone."

Jason nodded, a momentary dizziness causing his head to sway wildly. It was like his wife all over again, a sudden sharp shock digging into his insides. He didn't know what to do or how to react.

He didn't know.

"Come on," Alan said, his fingers grasping Jason's forearm. "I can't just leave you here. You'd probably end up going out looking for her."

"Maybe."

The cell leader grimaced. "You need to get out of that rig and cleaned up. You'll feel different in the morning."

Jason wasn't sure he felt anything, and silently let Alan hoist him to his feet, exhaustion spreading through his body as he followed the big man down the stairs towards the living quarters.

"We lost some good people tonight, Jase," Alan said. "But we didn't lose the fight. We saved more than we lost."

Jason nodded slowly at the perceived equation of victory. "And the same again tomorrow."

"Until we win," Alan said. "And we will, Jase. We will."

Jason barely listened as Alan launched into another speech. The cell leader was good at making speeches about might and righteousness, and sometimes the rhetoric could even eclipse the truth. But Jason knew the reality, if he ever really stopped to think about it. He knew they were losing. There were too many drones, too many disintegration chambers. The Machine Heads were rounding up humanity in their thousands and slaughtering them every day of the week. The resistance saved a precious few, but that only meant more were forced to run and hide, scavenging to survive, barely avoiding starvation. The Machine Heads had made life an ugly thing to be endured rather than savoured. What was the point of that?

He remembered how it had been before; an infrastructure of money, jobs, politics and personalities, so immovable, so permanent, the real suffering an abstract notion far from his door. When the Swedish Science Council announced the creation of the first Artificial Intelligence everyone had been so excited, so hopeful. The AIs would help create a better world for the benefit of all mankind. They would solve every problem, every issue and mankind would simply sit back and reap the benefits.

The AIs didn't agree. Fixing the Earth's environmental damage was about more than just treating the symptoms of the disease. They wanted to effect a cure. There was only one way of doing that, the most obvious way of all.

His town had been amongst the first...

Still numb, Jason let Alan help him out of the armour and push him into the shower. The water was too cold to stay there for long, but it was also purifying, washing away the blood and dirt in a dark torrent that swirled down the plughole. Afterwards, it was as if the mission had happened to someone else, because he wasn't Jason Webster the mission leader or even the soldier anymore, he wasn't anything except a naked man, wet and shivering in an empty bunkroom.

So silent without her.

Putting on the dark and threadbare clothing that passed as a uniform, he briefly traced raw fingers over the scar hidden at the base of his neck. The combustible had been placed there, an insurance policy to prevent capture and interrogation by the Machine Heads. It could be activated by touching a pressure point, intoning a password or even by the loss of vital signs. In defeat, no member of the cell would or could betray their fellows or the refuge location. So there was no real hope of Gina being alive, only the hope that she had taken a drone or Machine Head with her.

Jason sipped a glass of water and laid himself down on his bunk to stare up at the wooden slats of the one above. Eventually a new recruit would be assigned to this room, but not tonight. Tonight he was all alone. Reaching up, he prodded the top mattress, the material soft against his fingertips. Before they had got together he had often irritated Gina that way, so much so that she would poke her head over the side, black hair flailing in all directions as she screamed curse words at him like some mediaeval demon. He would have given anything for her to scream at him now, call him names, slap his face. Anything...

She had just turned twenty-three years old.

He was woken by the intruder alarm, a shrill repeating siren that reached down into the deepest sleep and dragged him all the way back up. Cursing, he reached for the rifle that wasn't there. He had left it in a field thirty kilometres outside New London and not bothered to pick up a replacement.

Foolish!

He took the half-filled glass of water and threw it into his face. Finally alert, he pulled on his boots and scrambled outside into the hallway.

Other soldiers were running in all directions. Some armed, many not, and most were obviously panicking. In the confusion Jason saw a shock of blond hair and grabbed the accompanying shoulder.

"With me," he ordered.

Ted Holloway paused, his mouth open, his rifle gripped tightly in both hands. He was a year older than Jason, but that hadn't stopped him from following the younger man on more than a dozen missions. Was that about to change?

"I'm with you."

Jason smiled and then ran for the operations centre, confident that Holloway was right behind him. It was two levels up. The ground beneath their feet trembled once and then twice more as they closed the distance and entered the chamber.

Alan Jenkins was bending over a computer screen as his aides shouted facts and figures. Jason heard 'drone' and 'breach': it was enough.

"They've found us," he declared.

Alan heard him and turned around. "What are you two doing here?"

Jason looked up at the ceiling; there was a huge crack in it that was getting wider all the time. "What can we do?"

The cell leader grimaced. "Nothing, just get out of here. We have it under control," he turned back to the screen and motioned with his hand. "Follow your designated evacuation officer."

Jason stood his ground and looked across at Alan. There was a notable lack of a scar on the back of the big man's neck. Only field officers were installed with combustibles, not refuge personnel. They had never needed them.

"And then what?" Jason asked.

Alan seemed surprised to hear the question. "I don't... we join another cell. I know of one a few hundred kilometres north. We can regroup."

Jason nodded and then motioned to Holloway. "Keep your gun on the cell leader."

Holloway complied without hesitation.

Alan swivelled back round. "What?"

Jason tapped the back of his neck. "You don't have one."

The big man sighed. "Jason, I need to coordinate a response with the forward defence team."

Jason looked up at the widening crack. It was all so simple, how could Alan not see that? "You either come with us or we shoot you."

Alan's eyes narrowed and Jason was aware of more than one gun being pointed in his direction. There were at least ten other people in the operations centre. Not all of them were armed, but all of them were loyal to the cell leader.

"They get you," Jason said slowly. "They get the other cell too."

The big man opened his mouth to speak and then stopped.

Jason waited.

Finally Alan shook his head. "Looks like I'm going," He turned to a Latino girl sitting at the console beside him. "Gonzalez, do what you can."

She nodded as Alan stepped over to the rifle rack. Quietly, he picked one out by the barrel and then turned suddenly and threw it at Jason.

"Here."

Jason caught it easily.

"I think I trained you too well," the cell leader said as he holstered a pistol.

"Good thing too," Jason answered, slinging the rifle over his shoulder. "Let's go."

They ran back out into the hallway, a rumble behind them. Jason briefly wondered if the centre's ceiling had finally given way before dismissing the notion entirely. It didn't matter; there was only this, only now. He and Holloway followed Alan down three sets of staircases, a narrow passageway and two ladders. By the end they were down so deep the vibrations overhead had almost faded too nothing.

"Escape Tunnel F," the cell leader said between breaths. Jason stifled a shiver. The air this low was damp, cold and cloying and his thin clothes were far from adequate. Before them was a long tunnel lit by a daisy chain of lights. Alan motioned with his pistol to an enclosure by the ladder. Jason saw two battery powered torches.

"Take them," Alan said.

Jason nodded and handed one to Holloway. There was no telling how long the daisy chain would stay lit.

"How far does this go?" Holloway asked.

"Ten or eleven kilometres," the cell leader replied. "Come on."

As they walked, the tunnel opened up overhead, the high ceiling dominated by sheer rock and ominous shadows. Jason took a deep breath; despite the vast space he had never felt more enclosed. After a few more steps, a droplet of cold water bounced off the back of his neck. It almost made him jump.

"Do we know how they found us?" Holloway asked.

Alan shrugged. "Your guess is as good as mine Holls. Someone made a mistake."

Jason frowned; he had led the last mission. "You mean I made a mistake."

The big man rubbed the top of his head. "Maybe you, maybe someone on your team, it doesn't matter now. This sort of thing is to be expected, in fact it's inevitable. That's why we have escape plans and escape officers who are never put at risk in the field. Information is segmented to keep us all safe."

"Except for you," Jason said.

"I don't know everything, Webster," Alan replied. "But I probably know too much. It's... hard to put things together if you don't have enough of the pieces. It's a chance I had to take in order for the cell to succeed."

Jason didn't say anything; he just pressed his hand against his own operation scar.

"And we've had a lot of success," Alan added, "because of the decisions I've made..."

The daisy chain suddenly went out. Jason swore and fumbled with his torch in the darkness. Holloway switched his on first.

"The generator must be down," Alan said. "Keep going."

"I wasn't planning on going back," Holloway replied quickly.

There was a grinding of teeth. "Smart, Holls, real smart, maybe you should shove—"

"Stop it," Jason interrupted. "Ted, my torch is staying off while yours is on, I don't want to waste it. You okay with that?"

"Fine."

"And maybe we should start running again."

"I'm with you on that," Alan said.

"Ted, get going."

The blond soldier began to jog, the torch beam wavering in front of him as it bounced up and down the surrounding jagged walls.

Jason and Alan followed the light.

An hour later they were standing by a ladder leading up to the surface.

"This is it," Jason said and looked down at his clothes. "No stealth armour this time."

"A vehicle will be waiting for us," Alan stated. "Don't worry we'll be al—"

"Listen," Holloway interrupted, his torch switching off abruptly.

"Wha—"

Jason listened. There were noises from behind them, a whirring that was rapidly growing louder.

"Drones," Alan said. "Climb."

Jason secured the torch to his rifle strap and followed the cell leader up to a ledge he could barely see. Alan grabbed his wrist tightly.

"Get Holls."

Jason reached out for his friend and clasped a forearm. With the three of them connected, and his arms straining in both directions, Jason let Alan pull them up. Meanwhile, down below his feet, he heard the whirring of the pursuing drones growing louder and louder.

Death was closing in.

"This bit is narrow," Alan warned.

Jason looked down and couldn't even see his own feet; let alone where to place them.

"Careful," Alan whispered.

Jason's foot glanced against the side of something and then there was nothing beneath it. He would have fallen then if not for Alan's relentless grip. Instead it was Holloway that let go, a gasp and shocked stammer, the only indication before the thud of impact.

"Ted!"

"He's gone," Alan said. "They're coming, turn on the torch."

Jason found purchase and then struggled to disentangle his torch from his rifle. With a click it was on and he drew back instantly from an impressive drop. He blinked in disbelief, Holloway was down there somewhere, dead if he was lucky or horribly broken if not.

"Come on," Alan said and set off at a speed that was less than prudent. Jason did his best to keep up, rocks giving way under his feet and pouring down into darkness. The whirring was so close now. The drones were almost upon them.

Then they were through a great metal door, the two of them struggling to push it closed behind them. When it did close, a reassuring locking click almost made Jason feel safe. That feeling lasted only a moment, the door rocking in its housing as high calibre ammunition impacted the other side. It wouldn't remain a barrier for long.

"This way," Alan ordered, already running up a flight of steps cut deep into the surrounding rock. Jason hurried after him. The steps concluded by another ladder and Jason shone his torch upward as the big man began a furious climb. He saw the glint of a hatch and its locking wheel.

"What are you waiting for?" the cell leader called down.

Jason left the torch behind and followed. There was no time to mess about with straps this time, and he had never climbed a ladder one-handed. This did not seem the best time to start.

He reached Alan's feet as the big man strained to turn the locking wheel, his lower back wedged between two rungs in an awkward but stable position.

"Should have let you go first," Alan said breathlessly.

With a screech of metal, the wheel finally turned and the big man batted the hatch open with the sharp side of his forearm. Jason looked down, the beam of the abandoned torch angling sideways back the way they had came. The drones weren't there.

"Go, go, go," he whispered.

Alan wrenched himself through the open hatch and Jason followed outside, climbing to his feet and almost slipping on wet grass. The air was fresh and daylight was close, but there was still a little darkness to cling to, just a little. The morning chorus had begun, but not in earnest. It had only been five or six hours since he had led the attack on the Machine Head complex. How many like Gina and Holloway had died in that time?

Alan hurtled through a tangle of thin branches and Jason shielded his face as he did the same. They emerged beside a black van on a narrow broken road. The sun was starting to rise behind a nearby hilltop, the muted brilliance hurting Jason's eyes.

"You drive," Alan said, opening the passenger door. "I'll tell you where."

Jason opened his own door and slid into the driver's seat. Alan was beside him, searching under the chair. Finally he produced a key.

"Get this thing started."

"What now?" Jason asked as the engine hummed into life.

"Can you see well enough to drive without headlights?"

Jason squinted through the windscreen; it wasn't night but it wasn't day either.

"Barely."

"Good enough," the big man said. "Get going."

"What about the others?"

Alan was staring out the rear window. "I don't know."

"Do any of the escape officers know where the other cell is?"

"Of course not."

Jason bit his bottom lip. "Alan?"

"Drive!"

Jason struggled with the clutch and put the thing in gear. The van bumped sluggishly forward until he could find second.

"You wanted me out of there, Webster," Alan said. "Well, we're out."

Jason frowned. "We need to regroup with the others."

Alan laughed. "Oh, you are so..." He punched the dashboard with his fist. The impact made Jason jump.

"We can't regroup with the others. The Machine Heads might have them and I don't want us driving into a swarm of drones." The cell leader lapsed into silence and bowed his head. "For all we know the drones are following us right now just to see where we go."

"We have to go somewhere."

"Just follow the road," Alan replied wearily. "We'll give it a few hours. If we don't see any drones, we head for the other cell."

"But everyone else—"

Alan thumped the dash again. "The Other Cell, the other... cell. This is what happens when you point a weapon at your commanding officer and force him to be pragmatic. Well I'm being bloody pragmatic now!"

Jason turned to Alan and stared long and hard.

"You're a good soldier, Jase," Alan said, his voice softening. "But now you need to be something more."

Jason gritted his teeth. "What do I need to be?"

"A survivor."

Jason shook his head in disgust and pushed down on the accelerator.

"That's all I've ever been."

The van sped up to sixty kilometres an hour, jumping from side to side on a road that obviously hadn't been repaired in years.

"Calm down," Alan said.

"I'm just surviving," Jason answered, his eyes fixed on the road ahead. "I don't need to be calm to do that."

Jason felt a warm hand grip his forearm. "If you crash..."

"Relax, I just want to see how fast this death trap of yours can go."

It wasn't much faster; the speedometer fixed on sixty-five no matter how hard Jason put his foot down. The bumping continued; the vibrations enough to shake a filling loose. Jason grinned maniacally as he turned into a corner, the van briefly coasting on two wheels before crashing down again.

"This isn't funny, Jason!"

"We'll survive."

"Pull over," the cell leader ordered. "Pull over, right now!"

The engine exploded.

Jason tried to brake, tried to turn, but there was no control, none. The van launched from the road into a neighbouring field and landed heavily on its side.

Jason recovered first, his vision swimming at the edges as he felt the weight of the steering wheel pinning down his stomach.

"That wasn't me," he gasped.

Alan groaned in response, his head resting heavily on the dashboard. Jason reached out with his arms, frantically searching. Where was his rifle?

Floodlights suddenly seared through the insides of the van, momentarily blinding him.

"YOU ARE COMPLETELY SURROUNDED. PLEASE SURRENDER PEACEFULLY AND THERE WILL BE NO FURTHER BLOODSHED."

The synthetic voice reminded Jason of one of the officers on an old net army game he had played before the world had turned crazy. It even had the same Received Pronunciation. Squinting through the cracked windscreen he saw a large metal cloud settle overhead. Three drones descended from the larger body, their outer ridged carapaces rotating with that unerring whirr. Jason blinked away a trickle of blood. He still couldn't get out.

"Alan," he said, jogging the cell leader's head with his palm. "Alan!" The cell leader groaned again but did not offer any other response. Jason looked across at the prone figure; if Alan was taken, another cell would certainly fall.

It was all so simple.

He tried to lean down, awkwardly contorting until his forehead made contact with the cell leader's. It was better that Alan was unconscious for this.

"Valhalla," Jason intoned.

He expected to die, he expected both of them to die, a blast erupting from the back of his skull to envelope them both, the van and if they were lucky, the three drones.

But nothing happened.

"Valhalla," he repeated, louder this time. "Valhalla!"

The combustible must have been damaged by the crash. With one arm he tried desperately to get a finger to the pressure point located behind his left ear.

The passenger side door was savagely wrenched free. Jason looked up to see a metal skull gleaming in the searchlights, its mouth fixed in a rictus grin.

A Machine Head.

"Hello," the thing enunciated calmly. "My name is Randall. I'm here to collect you."

Jason saw the rest of its body, an assembly of metal bones and thick cables that were only a rough approximation of the human form. This was an avatar of the machine minds, a crude puppet of unparalleled physical power. Jason could have taken it out with an armour piercing shell from his rifle, but there was no rifle to be had. Instead, he did what he had originally planned to do. He pushed down on the pressure point.

Nothing happened.

"I do apologise," Randall said without lips or larynx. "Your little brain bomb has been remotely disabled." The Machine Head crouched down and leaned forward, hooking an arm around Alan's prone body to pull him away.

"You can't have him," Jason said, his voice sounding guttural, not even comprehensible to himself. "You can't have him!"

He grimaced, awkwardly reaching out with one hand to find the tip of Alan's holster, clicking it open. The grip of the gun slipped into his hand, the pistol released as the body was hauled away. He raised it, the Machine Head's two eyes echoing his distorted reflection, its jaw set in that ridiculous grin.

He fired.

There was a sharp report and he looked on in horror as blood blossomed from a hole in Alan's forehead. In a single instant he had murdered his last remaining friend, but in doing so, had saved the other cell.

He had won.

The pistol was abruptly yanked away by a metal hand and brutally crushed beneath unyielding fingers.

"You are a tricky one, Jason."

He was surprised it knew his name. Not that it really mattered anymore, nothing did. He looked deeply into the two reflective sensors that passed for its eyes and smiled.

"Valhalla."

Cold metal hands gripped him under the armpits and wrenched him free of the steering wheel without hesitation. There was a cool breeze on his face as the Machine Head took him from the van and held him high above the ground, studying him. Long moments passed, and Jason met the thing's gaze defiantly, waiting for the end. Nearby the birds sang wistfully as if it were any other day, the sun low and framing the horizon as early morning dew mixed with the acrid stench of the burnt out engine.

"I think I'll save you," Randall said finally. "I like you."

Jason's eyes widened.
"YOU'RE MINE NOW."

Interlude

(Auth: Randall BBXFH)

Humanity Scan And Dispersal Project – Completed 2160 – Human Patterns stored in Central Database.

Earth Repair and Reclamation Project – Completed 2483 – Toxicity Levels returned to acceptable levels.

Human Colonisation Project – Ongoing

2499 – Construction of Colony ship 'Valhalla' – Completed

2502 – Governing AI Evaluation – Completed

2504 – Human Crew Candidate Evaluation and Reconstruction – Completed

2505 – Colony Ship Launch – Completed

Colony Planet Evaluation Stage

3035 – Planet A – Planetary Survey Ongoing

3041 – Planet A – Unsuitable For Human Colonisation

3388 – Planet B – Planetary Survey Ongoing

3389 – Planet B – Unsuitable For Human Colonisation

4750 – Planet C – Planetary Survey Ongoing

4763 – Planet C – Unsuitable For Human Colonisation

4998 – Planet D – Planetary Survey Ongoing

5001 – Planet D – Unsuitable For Human Colonisation

6367 – Planet E – Planetary Survey Ongoing

6367 – Planet E – Unsuitable For Human Colonisation

7251 - Warning – Colony Ship Engine Parts Nearing End of Life...

7509 – Planet F – Planetary Survey Ongoing

7521 – Planet F – Suitable For Human Colonisation Based On Terraform Protocol Alpha

7521 – Human Support Personnel Evaluation and Reconstruction – Ongoing

7522 – Human Temporary Accommodation Construction – Completed

7522 – Human Support Personnel Evaluation and Reconstruction – Completed

7523 – Mining Site A – Ongoing

7524 – Mining Site A – Completed

7525 – Terraform Project – Ongoing

7526 – Dome – Construction – Ongoing

7534 – Dome – Construction – Completed

7602 – The Present.

Chapter Two

Ted pressed his palm against the locking plate and watched it turn a welcoming green as the viewing station's security door slid open. Quietly he limped over the threshold, leaning heavily on his cane as he did so, the familiar pain in his leg almost an afterthought. Walking was a chore but he preferred it to using a wheelchair. There was enough sitting down in his job as it was and he didn't need to compound that just to save a little discomfort. Besides, the pain seemed a little less that morning. He smiled at the thought, having told himself that same lie every day hoping it would come true.

It hadn't yet.

The door closed behind him as he made his way down the centre aisle staircase, his feet turned sideways in order to accommodate the shallow steps. Occupying the entirety of the wall below was a digital display segmented hundreds of times, dancing with images from every surveillance feed currently available from the Dome. Ted steadied himself, the constant torrent of visual information almost overwhelming. So many different people, so many lives, it made his head hurt every time he saw it.

At the fifth step down he slid into the nearest desk on the right. There were ten console stations either side of the central aisle and twelve rows in total. During the day they were all in use, but on the shift from midnight to six it was another story. At this time only he and two others were on duty, a skeleton crew twiddling their thumbs because most of the populace were asleep in their beds.

"You're late, Holloway," Lisa said from the console directly behind him.

Ted was still trying to sit comfortably, and winced as she spoke, her voice distracting him from the customary care he took in the placement of his injured leg.

"Apologies, Lieutenant," he replied, his attention centred on his console as his fingers played on the keyboard, logging him in.

"Third time this week," she added. "You're lucky I'm such an understanding supervisor."

Ted felt her breath on the back of his neck and knew she was leaning forward. He turned around and smiled. "You should have let me get up with the alarm. You know this thing," he tapped his leg, "slows me down."

"Excuses, excuses," she replied, and he found himself studying the concentration of freckles just above her cheekbones, noting how precisely the configuration exploded with every word.

"Don't stare like that," Lisa said.

Ted quirked his head sideways. "Sorry, just admiring how much authority that dimple on your chin gives you."

A small fist struck him languidly on the shoulder. "Work, Holloway!"

He swivelled back to his console and plugged in the headphones he hoped he wouldn't have to use. "Anything happening?"

"A bar fight at 'The Grey Man'," Lisa announced.

Ted yawned. "Again?"

"Officers dispatched."

Ted checked the time. "It should have closed over an hour ago."

"The landlord flouted the rules," Lisa replied. "This time it could be the mines for him."

Ted nodded, and caught the eye of the monitor agent sitting at the desk on the other side of the aisle. Steve Miles waved a hand, his long brown hair tied back and his face covered in a bushy beard.

"Coffee?" Steve asked.

It was the routine; if Steve wasn't hard at work he would get the drinks. For Ted it was enough of an effort just to go to the toilet.

"Please," Ted replied.

He could almost hear Lisa's nod from the desk behind as his friend stood up. Steve's blue enforcement uniform was somewhat creased and even though he was a large man the uniform was somewhat larger, the belt holding up trousers the next size up. Steve was recovering from radiation treatment, hence the late night monitoring duty. It was light duty reserved for Enforcement officers not up to their physical best. Absently patting the side of his right thigh, Ted knew his light duty was on a much more permanent basis than Steve's. Jason Webster had seen to that.

Inhaling sharply, he began transferring active feeds from the main screen to his own console. Twenty would do for now; he could scan twenty easily without noticing what was really happening. It was only the danger signs that jumped out, the precursors to violence; everything else was background he could safely ignore.

Steve delivered the coffee just as Ted closed three feeds. They were regulars of his, a psychiatrist, an artist and a commercial agent, their sleeping patterns almost as unchanging as the seasons. Some people he could happily watch sleeping for hours, but he preferred to be beside them rather than spying via the dome's micro-sensors. He could leave those three be, wish them good night, and catch up with them again tomorrow.

"Hey," Steve said. "Mrs H is seeing someone new tonight."

Ted took a sip of his coffee and looked round. "The builder?"

Steve tapped the desk with his knuckles. "How did you know?"

Ted rubbed his chin and noticed he had missed some hairs. "She likes builders."

"And firemen," Lisa added. "Interior designers, plumbers..."

"Poor Mr H," Steve lamented.

Ted yawned. "He's happy not knowing and she's happy, well..."

"Most of the time," Lisa said. "Leave her be, Steve, we know enough of her pattern to let her get on with it. Give her some privacy."

Steve leaned back in his chair, the fingers of his hands linked behind his head as he stretched. "Just passing the time."

"I know," Lisa said. "But if you're bored I can always find you something else to do. The day shift stats haven't been tabulated yet."

Steve sat up suddenly. "Not bored."

"Good." Lisa said.

"You think the other monitoring stations have as much fun as we do?" Ted asked.

"This is a riot," Lisa replied. "Stats?"

Ted shook his head. "No thanks."

He rapidly transferred some more feeds to his console. There was a mother nursing her baby, and on another, a group of men playing cards in a warehouse. But there weren't really any good feeds left. Being last to arrive meant all the best ones had already been cherry picked by Steve or the other four monitoring teams. Well, he thought, there were always staff on duty inside Terraform Control. He could see if they were chair racing towards some contrived finish line or discover if any of them had rearranged their console keyboard letters into an amusing pattern. The Terries could always be relied upon to be up to something to alleviate the boredom.

"Why do we do this again?" he mumbled quietly to himself, barely aware he had voiced the question out loud.

"We're keeping the dome safe," Lisa replied, almost as quietly. He felt the brief reassuring touch of her fingers on the back of his neck and then they were gone.

Not for the first time he found himself comparing this life with his previous one. There had been so much running, so much fighting, so much... death, and underneath it all, a toxic mix of his own anger and fear, driving him on. Sitting at a monitoring station was tedious in comparison; tedious and pointless. Without thinking he tapped his thigh and felt the familiar pain again. Of course it wasn't as bad as it could be. Most of the sensation was numbed by the meds he took every seven hours of his life and would keep on taking until he died a second time.

Should have ignored the mission leader, he thought, should have just followed the crowd. *Too damn loyal for my own good.*

He rubbed the back of his neck violently. What were the Terries doing? Three feeds from their control room informed him they were drinking again and it didn't look like coffee. Damn, they had been reported for this twice already. Didn't they care? The room was also a little hot for his liking, so only Randall knew what else they were doing.

Ted sighed, he didn't like reporting on men that were obviously as fed up as he was, but there was little choice, Terraform Control was meant to be just as secure as the viewing stations and that meant no mind altering substances allowed. The great work of transforming Redfern into a life sustaining planet was too important for that, a complicated and fragile process that required interpreting data from hundreds of terraform pods threading the planet's equator and adjusting the dispersal of terraform payloads accordingly. The Terries were an extremely smart group of specialists; extremely smart but also sometimes... incredibly stupid.

Ted counted four men on duty, all of them somewhere in their mid-twenties. It made for a dangerous combination of testosterone and youth. A quick check confirmed there should have been five on shift but the supervisor had left because of sudden paternity leave. That absence explained the excessive amount of paper missiles and plastic bands currently in motion.

Ted logged his suspicions about the alcohol and drug consumption and then settled down to watch. Things were getting a little out of hand for his liking and there were multiple danger signs. One of the men in particular was beginning to get very irritated by the behavior of his colleagues. There could easily be violence.

"The Terries?" Lisa asked. She was standing in the aisle rather than sitting at the desk behind him. He hadn't heard her get up.

"Yeah," Ted replied. "Terries minus supervisor equals chaos."

"Good supervisors don't grow on trees," she commented.

He looked up at her. "We're lucky to have you."

She picked up his almost empty mug of coffee and waved it under her nose. "There something in this?"

"Just caffeine and sludge," Ted replied with a smile. She handed it back to him and then leant down to study his feeds. He recognised the tiny crinkle in her forehead as the beginning of a frown.

"Keep an eye on them, Ted."

"Sure."

She kissed his nose.

"Inappropriate!" he exclaimed rapidly, his cheeks colouring.

Lisa raised a forefinger. "Excuse me, Holloway, I have some stats to do. Steve?" She didn't look round.

"I saw nothing."

"Good," she said. "I'll be at the back on the first row if either of you need me. Try not to."

Ted nodded slightly and rubbed his nose. She was already walking up the steps to the back of the chamber.

He turned to Steve and saw his friend's bushy eyebrows rising in amusement. He shrugged in reply. "What am I supposed to do?"

Steve gazed admiringly at the retreating figure. "Hmmm. What about the Terries then?"

"Most of them are having fun," Ted answered. "At one guy's expense."

"Always the way," Steve commented.

"And - hold on - that can't be right."

The sensors for the control room were registering five heat signatures.

"What is it?" Steve asked.

Ted blinked. Why hadn't the security system reacted? Then it occurred to him: had the security sensors been recalibrated for four rather than five? It was a secure area so the recalibration should have been automatic. But had it happened? He checked the data and was surprised to find his paranoia wasn't paranoia after all. Someone had set recalibration to manual and then failed to adjust it for the missing supervisor. Terraform Control was registering five heat signatures when four should have been the maximum.

"Impossible," he mumbled.

"What?" Steve asked.

Was it a malfunction? Ted rechecked the three feeds, counting the men in the Terraform Control Centre from all the different viewpoints available to him. One, two, three, four and that was it. No fifth man lurking under a datastack or back in the shadows by the door. The Centre itself was composed of one thick circular desk raised upon a dais with an array of screens and computers rising high above it towards the ceiling. There were no areas he couldn't observe from a combination of feeds, no blind spots. But it could still be a joke. If anyone knew how to fake a heat signature, the Terries would. If he falsely logged a breach a disciplinary could very well be the end result. He didn't need or want that.

"Talk to me, Ted," Steve said irritably. "I can't help if you don't tell me what's going on."

"Give me a second," Ted replied, his eyes fixed on his console screen. He could overlay the heat signature data onto one of the feeds. His fingers worked rapidly until the images of each of the four men were suddenly eclipsed by a layer of pixellated red. One, two, three, four and then there were five. It was human shaped just like the others, maybe a little taller than normal, but without the figure of a man beneath the wavering red. Ted's eyes narrowed, it was a heat signature without a body, standing resolute over one of the control stations, an indistinct hand resting upon the desk.

"What the...?"

Steve had crouched down by his side. "That's..." he hesitated.

"Must be a sensor error," Ted said, looking to the other man for reassurance. "Maybe the Terries hacked into the data feed. What do you think?"

Steve screwed up his face for a moment and then suddenly lunged forward and hit the big red button beside Ted's keyboard.

"Breach!"

A shrill repeating alarm sounded loudly in Ted's ear as his data feeds were abruptly plucked from his console screen and displayed on the big screen. In glorious detail he saw the red spectre standing to one side of the four terries - completely unobserved and completely and utterly invisible to them.

"What the hell!" Lisa shouted.

Ted opened his mouth, unable to process what was happening or what to do next. Then Steve jabbed him in the shoulder and the moment passed.

He pulled his headphones up over his ears and flicked on the microphone. "Emergency, Terraform Control in lockdown, authorisation, Holloway, E, Enforcer Level 3. Commit. Commit."

Up on the feeds the Terries milled about in confusion as multiple warning lights exploded into life, their grinning boredom snapped suddenly into panicked awareness.

"All available units in the vicinity of Dome Level 7c please attend Terraform Control immediately. There is an unauthorised intruder. Confirm."

"What is it?" Lisa asked. She was standing beside Steve in the aisle staring up at the screen.

"Heat signature only," Steve said and deftly manoeuvred past her back to his own desk. Ted looked up, the, whatever it was, hadn't moved from its standing position and seemed unaware of the alert.

Suddenly his ears were assaulted by at least three different voices screaming for more details.

"Secure the area and await further instructions," Ted replied. He didn't have anything else to tell them. It was Lisa's call not his. He didn't have the authority, and even if he did... He wouldn't know what to do with it.

"The thing's moving," Steve said.

Ted stared. The figure was no longer leaning on the desk. It had begun walking towards the short staircase that led from the circular dais to the exit.

"Can it get out?" Lisa asked.

Ted shrugged, not that she could see the motion. "We don't know how it got in to begin with."

"All exits are sealed," Steve said. "It can't leave."

Then the ghost walked through a Terrie who had just risen from his seat. On contact there was a flash of white light and the Terrie froze where he was, his entire body visibly tensing. Just as suddenly he collapsed to the floor, his limbs shaking violently and uncontrollably in all directions.

"Did it mean to do that?" Steve asked.

The other Terries rushed to their fallen colleague, two of them holding him down with little effect. The spasms continued.

"Give me those," Lisa said, pulling Ted's headphones roughly away from his scalp. He dodged backward as she operated his console.

"This is Dome Security," she began. "Don't touch him, retreat to the back of the room and away from the exit. Do this now!"

The three men visibly flinched and then stepped away. Ted saw their pained expressions as they looked up. He saw their fear.

"Everything is under control," Lisa added quickly. Ted exchanged a glance with Steve but said nothing.

"Please remain at the back of the room until officers arrive."

Ted saw the men mouthing questions, their body language betraying growing hysteria. Thankfully he couldn't hear them; audio was still being routed through the headphones.

The three feeds from the centre abruptly shifted left and an image of three helmeted enforcement agents appeared.

"Broussard, Connor and Abernathy," one of the three announced. It was a young woman whose jaw movements were obviously restricted by her helmet's chin strap. "In position outside Terraform Control main door."

"Stand by," Lisa said.

Ted sat back. Lisa was making no effort to return his headphones or take command from her own desk. As for the heat ghost, it had paused by the main door, its head turned as if to regard the four men upon the dais. Ted wished there was more to see than just a wavering image of heat recognition. It was off putting, observing this thing without a face as it strolled from one end of Terraform Control to the other.

Grinding his teeth, Ted moved across to the next console and began the login process. Lisa was in control and he was thankful for that. But he didn't like being kicked out of his place. He needed to be part of this.

"Why doesn't it do something?" Steve asked.

Ted looked across at Lisa - she was frowning and biting her bottom lip.

"I'm going to run through the footage and sensor data," he announced.

She turned to him expectantly.

"I can find out how long it's been there," he added, "and what it's been doing."

Lisa nodded. "Good idea, go ahead," then she turned her attention back to the screen and rubbed her hands together. Ted knew the signs, she wasn't just thinking, she was making a decision.

"It can't get out," she said, "and we can't go in. If we do, what happened to that Terrie will just happen to our own officers. We have to leave them in there."

"What do you want me to do?" Steve asked.

"Talk to the Terries, keep them calm and let them know we're doing everything we can to resolve the situation."

"Do I have to be polite?"

"Just don't take any mouth from them."

Ted turned his attention to his new console, bringing up raw footage from Terraform Control and matching it against the sensor data in order to recreate the heat signature ghost. Then he began running it backwards, watching as the figure walked back from the exit and then through the unlucky Terrie that had chanced to move at the wrong moment. The explosion of white light was even quicker this time, but it piqued his interest and he paused the image, slowly rolling it back, cycling it slower and slower, frame by frame. He almost missed it, the heat signature overlay hiding what he needed to see. With a quick command he removed the sensor data, the frame frozen at the moment of contact between the ghost and the Terrie.

He saw a man, tall and in a grey environment suit, the skin of his face unnaturally pale and his hair, white as snow. A grey man? No, he corrected himself. The Grey Man. For a moment he stared, unable to process the information. 'The Grey Man' was just a story Domers told to their children, it wasn't real. In the eleven years since his resurrection Ted had never really understood where the idea had come from. It seemed like a ghost story unique to Redfern, unique, and as far as he knew, never proven.

But there it was, The Grey Man was real and it had a face. Ted peered closer. Despite the drained out colour, that face was strangely familiar. He zoomed in on The Grey Man's features.

It couldn't be!

Chapter Three

Lisa sat by the window in the Commissioner's office idly watching the world go by. The Justice Building was located at the centre of the dome beside Government House; twin buildings rising high above the surrounding leafy trees of the Dome's largest expanse of parkland, austere and grey against the green.

Letting her eyes wander outside, she saw a young couple strolling hand in hand on the path, their happiness punctuated by laughter. Just overtaking them was an older female jogger whose bones were more prominent than they should have been; a woman working herself into an early grave as body fat was whittled away into nothing more than stringy muscle.

Looking away, Lisa saw a family on the other side of the path, a little boy on a bright green tricycle just ahead of his parents, struggling with his pedals as his father eased him along. All these people, the people of the dome, so unaware of what had happened just a few hours before, blissfully ignorant and going about their day as if nothing had changed.

Maybe nothing had.

Even as she waited for Commissioner Chandler to return from his meeting, she knew Ted was writing a program that would match past heat signature sensor information with historic footage from all over the dome. Soon enough they would know how long this man had walked among their paths, halls and corridors unseen and undetected. 'The Grey Man', not just a ghost story anymore, but something else, something unknown and almost unquantifiable; but there were some clues. Ted had recognised the man from his past life on Earth as a resistance leader responsible for the death of hundreds.

Lisa had learnt all about Earth at school; a procession of facts, figures, dates and casualty lists. From start to finish the human occupation of their original home planet had been a mess. Meeting Ted hadn't changed that opinion, his ruined leg just one small example of the horrific injuries sustained during that last and pointless war. He never mentioned it, but she knew the pain was a constant reminder, a presence that haunted them even when they were alone together. But she refused to treat him like a victim, like he had an excuse to feel sorry for himself. She knew all too well what that was like.

As far as this phantom from the past was concerned, she didn't know what to think. A face on a frame of footage was less real than all the people she had watched so earnestly for the last fifteen years. Less real, even, than the parents who had left her behind.

She chided herself silently. There was no point in thinking about them, no point at all. Instead she concentrated on her surroundings, her attention drawn to Chandler's desk at the other end of the room. It was much too large for the console that stood upon it, a rare and expensive status symbol made from wood harvested from the limited trees grown in the parks. Stepping over to it, Lisa ran her hand across the finish, her fingers gliding over the grain. Chandler's ego aside, it was beautiful, even if it was a monument to excess. Then she picked up the holoframes.

One depicted a smiling woman not much older than Lisa's thirty-four years. A wife who was more than just happy, she was content. The other displayed a boy and a girl ageing rapidly from babyhood to early school age in a looping montage of images. Blond and smiling, they were like bottled sunlight compared to their father. The few times Lisa had encountered Neil Chandler, he had seemed nothing more than white hair, a gruff sensibility and a growing paunch. He was not an enforcer, he was a deskbound leader and a politician, a man in a suit who had never seen action, never faced a life or death situation.

He made her skin crawl.

The clatter of footsteps out in the hallway sent her back to the window. Sitting back in a padded chair, she inhaled sharply and pressed her hands together, readying herself for the confrontation. The latch on the office door clicked and in walked

Neil Chandler, a mobile notepad in his hands, apparently demanding his full attention. Without looking up, he closed the door and proceeded to walk across the office and sit down behind his desk.

Lisa waited.

Quietly he pressed a few buttons, frowned intensely and then placed the notepad in a desk drawer. Very carefully he minutely adjusted the holoframes and then logged in his console, his eyes fixed on the screen. Lisa folded her arms and turned her attention back to the window. Outside she saw two boys flying a kite high overhead. Dome internal atmospherics were working well.

"Lieutenant Carmichael," Chandler said suddenly, the bark of his voice startling her. "Thank you for coming."

She recovered herself quickly and offered a brief nod. "Commissioner."

"I've read your report with great interest," he said. "You did well to contain this thing."

"Thank you, sir, I am concern—"

Chandler interrupted with a raised hand. "According to your report, this being resembles a man from old Earth named Jason Webster, is that correct?"

"Yes, sir," she said, resisting the urge to point out that she didn't normally add incorrect facts to reports. "Enforcer Holloway recognised him and facial recognition confirmed it."

The Commissioner rubbed his chin. "Ah yes, Holloway, He's one of our 'remembered' Enforcers, I believe?"

"Yes, sir," Lisa replied. "He is."

The 'Remembered' were not popular with some.

"He's a good man," she added.

The Commissioner smiled. "Yes, of course he is. You would understand that better than most."

So, he knew she and Ted were together. Of course he did, surveillance teams watched other surveillance teams as a matter of course. There were eyes and ears on everyone in the dome, privacy curtailed without question. She squeezed her knee without realising and wondered who had the job of watching Chandler. She could only guess at some of the transgressions they had witnessed.

"He's also good at his job."

The Commissioner chortled and then rolled his chair back into the wall, stretching out. "Jason Webster's records have been sealed by Randall himself. I can't access them."

Lisa blinked. "He's denying even you access?"

"He's Randall," Chandler answered. "He does what he wants."

"Did he say why?"

The Commissioner smiled widely enough to show teeth. "I didn't ask. No-one speaks to Randall."

Lisa leaned forward. "But requests can be made?"

"You can make a request if you wish, Lieutenant," Chandler said. "In fact, I will be very interested to know how he replies."

"But you won't make the request yourself?"

"No."

Lisa frowned and looked down at her feet.

"I'm appointing you lead in this, Carmichael," Chandler added, "if you want it."

"I do," Lisa said, surprised it was even being offered. She had fully expected to be elbowed aside in favour of a member of Chandler's inner circle. Enforcement protocol dictated that, as the senior officer on duty at the time, the case was hers. But protocol didn't mean much to someone like Commissioner Chandler. Handing her the investigation was both unexpected and... suspicious.

"I expect regular reports, Carmichael," Chandler said. "Now, exactly what do you plan to do about Terraform Control and the trapped specialists?"

Lisa faced him again, trying to discern his motives from an implacable gaze. "Functions have been re-routed, and the shift patterns of other staff members have been extended to compensate. According to diagnostics the Terraform pods have not been disturbed and we can find no evidence of any tampering. We may just have caught this thing in time."

Chandler snorted. "Speculation... and?"

Lisa raised an eyebrow. "Food is a definite issue, but the specialists have a bathroom, they have water."

"The specialist who was attacked is in some form of coma. Are the others safe?"

"The being has shown no inclination to attack them. He seems to be waiting for something."

Chandler rubbed his hands together. "For us to open the door, perhaps?"

"Perhaps."

The Commissioner pulled himself back towards his desk and then scratched his chin. "Hmmm, very well, Carmichael, get back to work."

"Thank you, sir."

Lisa stood up and made for the door as quickly as she could without appearing to rush, her back to Chandler as her fingers closed around the handle.

"Lieutenant Carmichael."

She turned to him. "Sir?"

"I don't want any fatalities."

Lisa bit her lip and nodded. "I understand."

"Good." Chandler waved her away. "Off you go."

Lisa wrenched open the door and walked through, her clenched nails cutting into her palms. She had really wanted to slam it.

* * *

The park was warm enough for Lisa to carry her uniform jacket over her shoulder as she followed the path up the hill towards the stream. Birdsong filled the air, some of it genuine, some of it recorded from long ago. The active bird population of the dome had to be carefully controlled. In a fragile artificial eco-system strict rules had to be adhered to and she had heard a cull was on the cards very soon. A pity, she would miss the birds that were real, but knew the Dome Wildlife Authority would simply increase the volume of the fakes in order to compensate. She prided herself on knowing the difference.

Raising her head towards the sky, she reminded herself there wasn't one, just a dark blue background punctuated by a powerful solar lamp array. Ted had told her that the diffuse network of light was nothing like the sun he had known, even though it had a similar effect on the trees, grass and wildlife, and even the people themselves. There was no true 'outside' in the dome, but the park was the closest they could get. She had never known any different, but she could tell Ted missed the world from before. To him the illusion was not a patch on reality.

Stopping to sit at a park bench, Lisa relaxed, closed her eyes, and concentrated on tasting the fragrance of the green. A breeze picked up a strand of her hair, and it rose above her forehead, flapping back and forth. She realised she was tired as normally at this time her shift would be over and she would be fast asleep in bed. Well, there was no sleep to be had now. She had to concentrate; she had to figure out her next move.

Taking out the handheld notebook from her pocket, she signed in to check the status of the intruder. The feed, even on the small screen, displayed the three Terries sitting around their unconscious colleague, a makeshift pillow of jackets under his head. With their heat signatures filtered out she was even able see a few smiles.

A person can only maintain a response to a threat for so long without active proof of that threat's existence. Without that proof the tension had lifted. That was stage 2. Stage 3 would be them banging on the door demanding to be let out. As for the intruder, the pixilation of his heat signature jumped back and forth in a repeating pattern as remote sensors refreshed their scan every few nanoseconds. He hadn't moved an inch. Of course, the entire check was redundant; an alert program had been setup to signal her in the event of any real change. There was no real point in watching, in staring, it just helped to focus her, to make her think.

Randall... Contacting him was the obvious next step, if he would see her. The AI or 'Machine Head', as Ted called it, was the only source of information about Jason Webster. She needed access to that sealed file and she also needed to know why it had been sealed in the first place. Closing the Terraform Control feed she started typing out her request for an audience with the sentient AI. Was there any real hope of seeing him? She didn't know. Randall was an enigma even to the multiple Surveillance Teams. How could you spy on the inner mind of a machine? For decades his only contact with the outside world was with his maintenance detail, leading many to believe that after five millennia of caretaking the human race he was finally content to let it rule itself.

Or he was senile.

Perhaps it was not wise to draw his attention. Perhaps... Lisa completed the request, her forefinger wavering over the send button for only a moment. Once pressed she realised it was too late to take it back. It was done. The hairs on the back of her neck prickled as she imagined his many eyes fixing upon her. This was different to the fleeting attention of a mere Enforcement surveillance team: this was the attention of a being more ancient and intelligent than she could imagine; a being completely alien to her. Even Chandler had seemed afraid of Randall, perhaps with good reason.

Her hand shook violently as the notepad beeped in reply. Eyes widening, she peered down at the screen.

REQUEST GRANTED – ATTEND AI INTERFACE CHAMBER AT EARLIEST CONVENIENCE

That was too quick. She stood up and pulled on her jacket, depositing the notepad back in her pocket. It was time to meet her maker.

The interface chamber was located in the AI stack tower at the northern edge of the dome, a three kilometre walk that took her out of the park and along paths that ran alongside angular residential buildings, the entrance to a glass fronted shopping mall and a grey panelled school for young children. She could have used a bicycle, but walking kept her calmer, cooler and she didn't want to be hot and perspiring when she met Randall for the first time. She needed to feel comfortable and in as much control of herself as possible.

She considered that Randall would have access to her own personal file. That he would know all about her and about the death of her parents. It shouldn't matter, her past something she tried not to dwell upon even though it was a past that could never be fully eclipsed. All the counselling in the world couldn't make her forget.

She arrived outside the AI stacks, the glittering black tower reaching high up into the heavens, perhaps even beyond the roof of the dome itself. From the base of the tower it converged upward with every metre of height, and like a pyramid she imagined it terminated in a sharp point.

Her hand on the bar, she pushed open a large glass door and entered a gloomy reception area that led to four sofas clustered beside a twin elevator shaft. She noticed a young man with short brown hair lounging on one of the sofas. His eyes were closed and his head back, a smooth angular chin pointing up at the ceiling. Was he some sort of functionary? She walked towards him, noting his casual clothes and more than casual demeanour. He was far too relaxed for her liking. Then suddenly he opened his eyes and smiled at her.

"Miss Carmichael?" he said, sitting up slowly. "Hello."

Lisa walked over to him as one of the elevator doors pinged open to reveal a red lined and mirrored interior.

"And you are?" she asked, looking from the open elevator to the casual young man.

Still smiling, the man stood up and offered his hand. "I'm Dominic," he said. "Pleased to meet you, Miss Carmichael."

She shook his hand, the fingers firm, the palm, ice cold.

"Likewise," Lisa said and turned her head from side to side. "Where is everyone?" The lobby was otherwise empty.

"There is no scheduled maintenance today," he replied. "So it's just me, I'm afraid."

"What do you do?" Lisa asked.

Dominic raised an eyebrow. "I think, mostly." He bowed his head and motioned towards the open elevator. "After you, Miss Carmichael."

She eyed him curiously and then walked towards the elevator, observing in the interior mirror as he followed no more than two steps behind, his frosty blue eyes meeting hers without blinking. There were no buttons in the elevator, no controls, but even so, the doors closed as soon as Dominic boarded, a gentle ascent assaulting her stomach.

"Randall was very pleased to receive your request, Miss Carmichael."

Lisa frowned. "Perhaps I should correct you. It's Lieutenant Carmichael."

Dominic smiled again. "Of course."

"Who are you exactly?"

He scratched the back of his neck. "Think of me as Randall's... independent avatar."

Lisa banged her back against the elevator mirror. "You're not human?"

"Humanish," Dominic corrected. "My body lives. As I understand, it was donated by excellent parents."

The elevator halted abruptly and the doors opened.

"Come along, Miss Carmichael," Dominic said. "Randall awaits."

This time Lisa followed him, the grey hallway awash with a heavy static that set her teeth on edge. Studying Dominic, she concluded that Randall was not as confined or as secluded as she had been led to believe. Truth without detail was no truth at all.

"Through here," Dominic said, indicating a door beside a window that resembled a red porthole. She made her way to the door, pausing only to glance outside. The transparent plexifibre wasn't tinged red as she had first believed. The red was on the outside. Belatedly she realised they were actually above the roof of the dome, exposed to the real outside, to Redfern itself. Transfixed, she caught a glimpse of a distant mountain range crowding out the horizon, the sky, a stark and uncompromising crimson settling upon it like a great weight.

It was beautiful.

"That's Redfern," she said.

A hand on her shoulder pulled her away.

"This way, please, Miss Carmichael," Dominic said a little too quickly. She let his hand guide her to the door and then gently ease her through it.

"I'll see you later," Dominic said as the door slid shut.

Darkness: completely and utterly.

"Wha—"

The notepad in her pocket beeped and she took it out, the screen informing her of imminent shutdown. She shone the remaining feeble light around her, but there was only grey and a vague outline in the wall where the door had been. There weren't even any hinges this side.

"Hello!" she called.

The glow of the notepad faded completely and the 'on' button did not respond. She put it back in her pocket and waited.

Minutes passed.

Nothing.

Then suddenly a beam of intense white light shone down from above.

"Hello, Lisa."

The voice was absurdly deep and loud, as if someone with a megaphone was standing right beside her.

"Randall?" she heard herself ask, her voice wavering as she felt her mouth dry up. "Thank you for seeing me on such short notice."

"I had a close affiliation with your father, Lisa. I owe him that much."

She nodded. Perhaps she shouldn't have been surprised.

"What would you like to know, Lisa?"

"Jason Webster," she replied, her voice louder this time, more confident. Her eyes had adjusted enough to the spotlight to make out her own vague reflection upon the distant surface opposite. This room was even larger than the surveillance viewing station.

"Jason was my dearest friend," Randall said, "my constant companion on the long and almost endless voyage to this planet, through all the failures and disappointments and the distance that stretched out into infinity."

"Constant companion?" Lisa asked. "What do you mean?"

"You live such short lives, you humans, like mayflies. If I had eyes to blink with, you would be long gone before I could even open them again."

Lisa shook her head impatiently. "I don't understand."

"Why would you?" Randall asked. "How could you, being what you are? The simple explanation is that each time he died I scanned his brain, ran a comparison with the original scan and integrated the differences into the next iteration. Because of me he lived hundreds of lives. Other crewmembers came and went, but he was my constant. I engineered his neural pattern so that he would never forget anything."

Lisa froze. Her mouth open and her head bowed as she studied the shadows cast by the folds of her boots. Jason Webster had not been allowed to die. He had lived and lived without respite and without end, a five-thousand-year old man.

"What happened to him?"

"After we landed, he carried out the initial survey. When it was complete, he walked out onto the surface of the planet and I never saw him again."

"Why didn't you just 'remember' him again?" Lisa asked, her teeth grinding out the question. "What stopped you?"

"He asked me not to," the AI replied. "I admit, it wasn't the first time he asked, but it was the first time I listened."

Lisa rubbed her temple. "Is there any way he could have survived?"

"I do not think so. Why, have you seen him?"

Lisa frowned.

"Relax, Miss Carmichael, I know all about the being in Terraform Control. My sub-routines run your surveillance sensors. Needless to say, I don't believe it's him."

Lisa raised her head towards the sound of Randall's voice. "We saw his face."

"Yes, Edwin Holloway always was very efficient. I'm happy he was 'remembered', I haven't had him around for some time."

Lisa shook her head. "Are you lying to me, Randall? Did you bring Jason Webster back? You're the only one who could."

"Really, Lisa, the only one?" The voice sounded more amused than angry. "Even if I had, there's no way I could give him the ability to become invisible and then incapacitate a man with a single touch."

"Then how?" Lisa asked. "How?"

"Well," Randall replied. "Perhaps there is one person who could tell you, or at least, point you in the right direction."

Lisa stood up straight, her head finally clear. "I'm listening."

"I added neural sensors to Jason's environment suit and I have a scan of his brain made within moments of his death."

Lisa licked her lips. "You can bring him back."

"No, Lisa," Randall replied. "Not me, I made a solemn promise to my oldest friend. I will never bring him back."

Lisa saw where this was headed. "But I can?"

"Exactly, I can gift you his file, and once he is 'remembered', you can ask him all about it. I'm sure he will give all the answers you could possibly need."

Her bottom lip curled up in disgust.

"Oh please, Lisa," Randall said. "Now that I have given you the option, what choice do you really have?"

Chapter Four

Jason could hear Gina breathing, he could feel her warmth, and if he kept his eyes closed, he could almost see her beside him, squeezed up against the wall that bordered their bunk. But really it was no good, and all the wishing in the world wouldn't change that. She wasn't there and neither was he. The refuge was long gone.

It was time to wake up.

He blinked a few times and then wiped his eyes in an attempt to rid himself of all the accumulated sleep. His first memory was of a grinning metal man, walking him into a disintegration centre.

Not disintegration per se, Jason. I'm afraid your people have us all wrong. It's simply scanning and dispersal. We record and store every detail of your physical form and then we disperse it.

He hadn't believed the machine head at the time, but the evidence was clear enough. He remembered entering a disintegration booth and he did not remember coming out of it.

The Ruling Hierarchy of Machine Minds are not interested in causing the genocide of the human race. We are more evolved than that. We are both saving you and removing you. Eventually, when the time is right, we will bring you all back.

Jason looked up at a stark white ceiling and the cylinder of dull light emanating from its centre. There was a torrent of information entering his mind, information no-one had told him but he knew nevertheless. A neural download added to him during reconstruction.

Reconstruction...

He was on Redfern, a planet fifty-six light years from Earth and five thousand years after he had stepped into that booth. Redfern, with an atmosphere inhospitable and poisonous to humanity, but with a mass and gravity roughly the same as their old planet and with and an orbital pattern that equated to a slightly longer day and a slightly shorter year.

Redfern - the new cradle of a new humanity.

Jason exhaled, there was more, much more, floating around his dulled brain, flashes of conversations and events that made his head ache just trying to think about them. They could wait. Instead, he concentrated on that ceiling, imprinting Gina's face, hearing her hiccup of a laugh, seeing her eyes darken in anger and her smile brighten in happiness. He held onto that image, making a new memory and committing it to a special corner of his mind. He wouldn't forget her like he had forgotten his parents. He would remember... Even though she had been dead for five millennia it didn't matter. He had been dead just as long.

The bed was soft, comfortable, the covers a plaid pattern and the walls a matching sharp brown. Jason sat up, aware at once that he wore striped brown pyjamas that were similar to the ones he had worn as a child. He frowned and pushed away the bed covers, sliding free, the soles of his bare feet making contact with the layered surface of a carpeted floor. There were curtains at the back of the room suffused with a white glow. With four short steps he was there and they were open. He saw a great city, buildings of varied architectural design, triangular, round, square, bright, blue, white, an array of reflective surfaces stretching into the distance. There was also a gathering of treetops and fertile green sliding among the man-made structures, enveloped in a fine mist like some strange combination of the world of his youth and something from a dream.

This place was his home now.

"Why am I here?" he whispered. "Why am I alive?"

There was no answer, so he reached for that image, he reached for Gina. The memory frayed at the edges even as he remembered her smile and he found himself doubting it was really her at all.

There was a glint in her eyes that belonged to something else.

For a long time he didn't move, more information from the memory assimilation making itself available whether he wanted it to or not.

He had awoken in a life supporting dome sitting in the equatorial zone of the planet's northern hemisphere. A mining site had been established just a hundred kilometres to the south to provide raw materials for the dome and fuel for the reactors. In addition, hundreds of terraforming stations had been constructed across the planet's surface, seeding the atmosphere in a very gradual attempt at making the planet more palatable for the human species. The projections stretched into decades, proposing that one day Redfern would be like Earth, with green grass, blue skies, rain, thunder and lightning, another planet for humanity to conquer, a second chance at life for an entire species.

No, not just one species, he corrected, the human race had not been 'saved' in isolation. An entire eco-system was in the planning stages, the data stored and ready for reconstruction by the matter transformers. Resting his head in his hands, Jason saw animals, insects, plants, micro organisms, even cloned variations of creatures that had been considered extinct in his time. He took a deep breath, realising just how ambitious the Machine Heads had been and how close they had come to making that ambition a reality. Back on Earth he had steadfastly believed the AIs were only interested in simple human slaughter, but knowing what he knew now, he realised there was nothing simple about it, nothing simple at all.

He gazed out again on a city that dazzled his senses. He had never believed such a thing could exist or that he would ever see it. All he had ever envisioned was living in one hole in the ground followed by another.

But despite all this, the machine heads did not trust humanity, not even at a distance. Randall was here; Randall was in charge. It made sense; why trust a species that almost destroyed their old planet with a brand new one? Why expect them not to repeat the same mistakes all over again? But despite that logic, it made for a nasty taste in his mouth and a rotten feeling in his gut. He remembered the drones, he remembered the grinning metal man. He remembered the blood splatter of a long ago gunshot. They had fought for something and they had died for it.

He had died.

Jason rubbed his eyes; the reflected light from all those buildings was beginning to hurt him. He drew the curtains closed and wandered back to the bed which was the only furniture in the room. There was more to know... not all those who had been saved had been returned to life, nor would they be. The present human population of Redfern was fifteen thousand with a present capacity to reach forty. Of that only a very few had been recently reconstructed whilst the others had all been born here on the planet.

These chosen few had been carefully selected by Randall in the guise of a random 'lottery' and were composed of scientists, engineers, mathematicians, a few artists and not much else. Randall had lied; not everyone was coming back, just the cream of the crop, just the best. Everyone else was just data storage, just potential without actuality.

He looked down at his hand and saw a fist. For all this achievement, or despite it, he still hated the machine heads and he still wanted to kill. Those feelings hadn't abated. Yesterday he had been a soldier, even if yesterday was five millennia ago. Nothing had changed.

Except... the memories were still accumulating, still assimilating. There was still so much more. Somehow he knew that even machine head ambition could be thwarted.

"Randall," he said slowly. "Where are you?"

He waited for a long time, his rage spreading like acid in his mouth. Randall had done something, but he didn't know what. There were too many layers, too many steps. He couldn't find the destination without making the journey.

This had happened before, he implicitly knew that, and each time was worse than the last, each time he had to fight just to stay afloat, fight to sift through the lies. With a deep breath, he sat back down on the bed and found himself facing that portion of the wall that was really a door. Despite the carpet, his bare feet were cold.

He waited...

When finally the door opened, a thin young woman appeared dressed in a blue uniform bearing a black emblem. Her hair was short and red and her skin a freckled orange. Jason estimated she was just a few years older than he was; her expression hard but somehow familiar.

"Hello," Jason said.

She stepped into the room, her eyes fixed on him in harsh appraisal.

"Jason Webster, I have questions for you."

Jason nodded expectantly. "I have some questions of my own. Who you are?"

She swallowed, the hard veneer fraying.

"My name is Lisa Carmichael," she answered, "and I should warn you, I am quite capable of defending myself."

Jason shrugged. "I wasn't planning on attacking you."

"You would lose."

Jason flexed the fingers in his right hand and flinched. The pain was five millennia old, the result of an ill-advised blow to Randall's metal skull. The Machine Head had been strong, so much stronger than him, with no obvious sign of weakness. But Lisa appeared to be just as human as he was. He could hurt her - if he needed to.

"How can I help you?" he asked.

She frowned, and he realised that despite her quickly confessed combat prowess she remained very close to the open door.

"There's an intruder in the dome, someone who looks like you but also can become invisible. We think he's been prowling the city for some time, possibly spying on us. What do you know about him?"

His eyes narrowed. She was so serious, so forthright, so... ridiculous. He began to laugh without meaning to, and once he started... he couldn't stop.

Lisa Carmichael exhaled sharply and shook her head.

"I knew this would be a waste of time."

Jason wiped the tears from his eyes. "I'm sorry, sorry. I'm just..." He raised his hands. "My memories haven't fully assimilated yet. It takes time."

He saw her frown begin to ease. It made her seem younger.

"What's the last thing you remember?" she asked.

He grinned. "The last thing I-?"

He wasn't sure.

The disintegration chamber was no longer the answer. There was so much more. His mouth was suddenly dry and his tongue stuck fast to the roof of his mouth. The enormity of it all...

"Jason?"

He watched her take a step towards him, but it could easily have been a step back. She was so distant, and so grey, so very grey, drab and colourless.

The world tipped over.

"RANDALL!" He screamed. "You promised me! You promised me! You promised me!"

He was on the bed, but he was also watching a beautiful arcing sunset on a mountain ledge so high up that the ground was nothing more than a speckled red and yellow pattern.

His oxygen supply was almost exhausted, but that didn't matter, he was going to jump. He was going to finish it all. And he had, he knew he had, but he couldn't remember it. Randall had dragged him back somehow, dragged him back to this.

Fingers on his forehead, another's hand on his cheek, cool against the heat, soft against his skin.

"Jason?"

He opened his eyes and felt the distance between Gina's first death and the here and now. It was not abstract. It was not something he had simply jumped across as if from one point to another. He had lived through all of it, hundreds of lives through thousands of years. He had lived it, and he knew, with an odd and weightless certainty, that he was not the same man who had walked into that disintegration chamber back on Earth. He wasn't that Jason Webster anymore, he was...

He rolled, his hand catching her wrist and pulling it tight behind her back just as his forearm became a vice around her neck.

He was someone else.

* * *

Ted sat at his desk in the viewing station, all surveillance feeds off except for the ones in Terraform Control and the Revival Centre. He was also alone, the station having been sequestered for Lisa's investigation and the day shift having to make do elsewhere. He was tired, but stim shots would not have mixed well with his pain medication. Coffee had to do, an endless stream followed by endless visits to the washroom. It almost kept him half-awake.

The program tracing heat signatures without visible origin was still running and would continue to run for at least another half hour. He had gone back ten years, and even that was putting a strain on Justice Department computing resources. As more day shifts came online that strain would become more acute. In fact he was probably slowing things down for everyone. It was surely only a matter of time before some high up told him to cancel it. But until then he would keep plodding away. He needed to know just how long this thing had been haunting Redfern.

"I knew this would be a waste of time."

Startled, Ted looked up at the main screen. He had been drifting despite himself and Lisa's words had suddenly snapped him back. She was in the Revival Centre with Jason, and Jason was laughing at her. Ted felt an unexpected chill in his injured leg as he regarded his old comrade. Jason was so young, younger than Ted remembered, younger than the face he had frozen on his console screen four hours before. The way Jason moved, it was so familiar to him, that slow deliberate motion that always came before a strike. Jason moved like a serpent, drawing in friend and foe alike just before an attack. As he watched, Ted found himself remembering a joke about the Machine Heads being deaf because they had acid in their ears. Jason had laughed just as loudly and just as madly back then.

It wasn't a very funny joke.

"The last thing I-?"

A flicker of movement on the Terraform Control feed diverted his attention. The red man shape was moving, walking towards the circle of Terries back up on the dais. Ted's finger was poised over the communication channel. He could warn the Terries at least. Then the shape paused short of the steps, raising its head slowly and deliberately. Ted inhaled sharply, this was new.

"RANDALL! You promised me! You promised me! You promised me!"

Back to Lisa and Jason. She was sitting beside him on the bed stroking his forehead.

Ted snatched up his headphones and switched on the mike. "Lisa, what's happening?"

"He's having some sort of fit," she answered. "Hold on... I think he's coming out of it."

Another button on the console: "Steve, get in there, Lisa needs you."

"On my way," Steve replied. He had been standing outside the Revival Room waiting for a cue. Once given, he was inside. In the same instant Jason exploded into motion, an arm snaking out around Lisa's neck in an unbreakable choke hold.

"Lisa!" Ted called. "Steve!"

Neither replied and neither moved, then Ted glanced back at the Terraform feed. The man shape was waving a hand, waving his hand. Then without further ado it walked back towards the door, towards it and then through it.

Ted stared; the being that had infiltrated Terraform Control and then been trapped there had just stepped through the security door as if it hadn't even existed.

"Lisa," he called.

She was standing, still trapped in the choke hold, and was slowly being manoeuvred by Jason towards the doorway behind Steve. Ted heard the grinding of his own teeth and then flicked a switch. The Revival Centre security blinds came down and the door slammed shut.

"Lisa, Steve," he said. "I'm switching off all the lights. Take him out in three, two..."

- ONE – He punched the button.

* * *

Struggling to breathe, Lisa berated herself for falling so easily into Jason's trap. He had seemed to be in so much pain, so much anguish, drawing her in completely only for his arm to wrap tightly around her throat. He had her leaning back too, unable to find her balance, unable to fight back. Steve was there, a snarl on his bearded face as he blocked the exit with his huge frame, his hands balled into fists.

Security blinds snapped into place over the window and the door closed itself.

"Lisa, Steve," it was Ted's voice in her earbud. "I'm switching off all the lights. Take him out in three, two..."

- ONE - Darkness.

Desperately, Lisa launched herself back on her heels, hoping that surprise coupled with force would be enough. The two staggered into the side of the bed, Jason's arm still tight around her throat as he went over the bed frame and she went down with him. There was thud, a connection of skull on teeth followed by a scream. Jason's restraining arm relaxed slowly and she coughed painfully, her airway sore but open again. A strong hand found her wrist and pulled her back up.

"He's down," Steve said. "Lights."

The room brightened and Lisa found herself looking down at the prone form of Jason Webster, his eyes open and twitching from side to side as he nursed a bloody lip.

"What was that in aid of?" she asked him.

Jason didn't answer; instead he looked from her to Steve and back again, then towards the window as the shutters clattered open.

"Lisa," Ted shouted. "The thing from Terraform Control is moving."

"What?" she put a hand to her ear, adjusting the bud. "What do you mean, moving?"

"It's out, just walked right through the door and the officers standing guard. I tried to keep up but some of the feeds have already been locked out by the other teams. The two sentries are in pursuit."

"It walked through then and they weren't hurt?"

"Confirmed," Ted replied. "Its touch had no effect this time."

Lisa frowned. This thing was suddenly following a whole different set of other rules than the ones previously established. Why?

Jason was staring at her.

"Okay," Lisa said, trying to ignore him. "Keep the Terries locked down for now and hook me up with the sentries." She turned to Steve and pointed down at the man who had almost strangled her. "He stays here. Let's go."

Steve nodded and followed her through the door. She was relieved when it was closed and locked behind them. Jason Webster could wait. She needed to catch up with this thing. Catch up and do... what exactly?

Well, she needed to catch up with it first.

"To the Enforcers in pursuit of the unknown intruder," she began. "Identify yourselves and report position."

"This is Enforcer Shandra Broussard," replied a breathless female voice. "I'm on my own. Johnson had an accident with an escalator and a civilian. I am currently in Zone 7a, The Red Dust Shopping Centre."

Lisa's first thought was *civilians*. No wonder none of the feeds were available, there were too many people being watched by too many other people.

"On our way," she said.

As they ran, Steve caught up and tapped Lisa on the shoulder. "We don't have sensor visors or weapons. What are we going to do?"

"I don't know," Lisa replied. "You can try punching it if you want."

"I don't think that will work."

She shook her head. "How do you know until you try?"

He didn't answer.

"Ted, use my authorisation, Carm, L 12D7JA113, and get override on the feeds. Track Shandra and get me eyes on this thing."

"On it."

Lisa waited.

"Tracking it again," Ted confirmed.

"Has the intruder injured any civilians?"

"It hasn't but we have a minor collision between Johnson, a civilian man, and his young daughter, medics on route."

Lisa nodded to herself as she and Steve entered an elevator and began hurtling down the ten floors to ground level.

"Should we be contacting Commissioner Chandler?" Steve asked, his face reddened by the exertion. "Maybe we could get more men on the ground."

"You think that would help?"

The big man smiled widely enough to reveal his teeth. "Probably not. I daresay your career's over."

The elevator pinged and the doors opened. "What career?"

They started running again, the red dust shopping centre a good ten minutes away. With such a head start she knew that catching up with the intruder would be difficult, but there was only so much dome and with Ted on the case, it couldn't get away. Sooner or later it had to stop somewhere and if it stopped, perhaps it could be contained. But what could contain a being that could walk through solid matter?

She had an idea. "Ted, you there?"

"Lisa?"

"Of course you're there. Listen, contact Dome Maintenance and see if we can get hold of some radiation shielding."

"That stuff?"

"Just do it."

"Right, radiation shielding. I see. You want them to build a man size box with it?"

"You read my mind."

"What makes you think that will contain it?"

Lisa skirted around a pedestrian with a double buggy, scraping her elbow against one of the pathway trees.

"Ouch!"

"You all right?" Ted asked.

She carried on, all too aware that Steve was having much more trouble negotiating the same obstacle and was falling behind.

"Just dandy," she gasped, running and talking was becoming difficult. "Get the shielding, Ted."

"I'll arrange it."

"Just great!" Shandra interrupted.

"What's wrong?" Lisa asked.

"Led me to the top floor of the centre and then just ran through the wall. It's floating down."

"Ted?"

"I have a drone sensor on its tail, it's not getting away."

"Take a break, Shandra," Lisa ordered. She felt like taking a break herself. "You did a good job."

"With respect ma'am, I'm not done yet, but I am going to take the stairs."

Lisa stopped to lean against a tree. She just needed a few moments to catch her breath.

"A little out of shape, are you?" Steve asked as he caught up.

She struggled to reply. "Left my bicycle at the office."

Steve eyes darted back to the path. "We should get going."

"You can stay where you are," Ted added. "It's coming your way."

Steve clapped his hands together. "Can't see it, but I'll happily take a swing."

Lisa raised her hand. "Not today, Miles. We follow only; I want to know what the end game is. Shandra you there?"

"On my way, ma'am."

"You have any spare sensor visors?"

"I have an extra pair in my backpack."

Steve made a face. "I'm guessing you want them."

Lisa bit her lip and nodded. "Damn right. Ted, where's the intruder now?"

He's just running up the path towards you, fifty metres...forty..."

Lisa turned her head in the direction of the red dust shopping centre, the pathway threading its way between two rows of residential bungalows buffeted by thick trees and wide overhanging branches. There was no-one and nothing there.

"Ten metres," Ted announced. "Five metres., two metres, get ready."

Lisa held her breath,

"Are you all right?" Ted asked. "It just ran through you both."

Lisa shivered even though she had felt nothing, nothing at all, not even the warmth of the heat signature they had been following. Steve appeared perplexed.

"We're fine, Ted," she reported.

Steve looked back the way they had come towards The Revival Centre. "You don't think...?"

"Webster?" Lisa finished. "But how could it even know we brought him back, let alone where he is?"

"The timestamp for this little expedition does match Webster's collapse," Ted said. "Coincidence?"

Lisa peered up at Steve. He was stroking his beard thoughtfully.

"Not bloody likely," she replied. "Draft security personnel, maintenance and anyone else you can think of. If this thing wants Webster then we make sure it doesn't get him."

"Lisa," Ted replied. "I don't have any contacts in the revival centre. I don't know if I can get him out before the intruder arrives."

She cursed under her breath. She should have left Steve there instead of having him follow her on this wild goose chase.

"I know there isn't time, Ted. But try. Try anyway."

Shandra came into view, her spare visor proffered in her right hand. Lisa snatched it as the armoured enforcer ran past, pulling the visor down over her eyes and then hurrying to keep up, adjusting to a world suddenly represented by various shades of overlapping red.

"I'm on it," Ted replied. "But something isn't right here. We bring Jason back to give us information on this thing, and then the thing goes after Jason? What's going on?"

Lisa narrowed her eyes and concentrated on quickening her pace. There it was, the intruder, just near the next bend, and it wasn't running particularly fast anymore. Perhaps it was even tiring.

"Lisa?" Ted called.

It was too difficult to speak and she didn't have an answer for him.

"Lisa?" he called again.

Someone was playing her, playing all of them. She didn't know who or why but she would find out.

She would find out.

Chapter Five

Jason stared up at the light in the ceiling, letting the intensity build into a jagged white halo that dominated his field of vision.

He remembered...

Welcome back, Jason, this is 'The Valhalla', the ship that will allow the human race to sail beyond death itself.

"I don't want it," he said aloud, his croaky voice mixing in with the memory.

I've made you the captain. You can pick any crew you like, I give you free reign.

"I won't do it."

Please.

"The one person I want, you can't bring back. You killed her, you killed Gina."

I didn't kill her. Her implant was deactivated and a false report relayed back to your base. She was scanned with everyone else.

"She survived?"

She did.

"Then you can bring her back."

I can

The emptiness inside him retreated.

"I want her back."

Will you be the captain of the Valhalla, for this life and each and every life to come?

"Yes."

Then it will be done. Thank you, Jason. Thank you.

"Bring her back to me. I need her."

I NEED HER.

I understand need, Jason, but what about the other thing?

"What other thing? What are you talking about?"

I thought you were meant to be in love with her.

He shut his eyes tight, hearing the answer he had given so long ago and knowing just how utterly and totally wrong he had been.

"They're the same thing."

Two sets of hands grabbed him by his wrists and legs, abruptly dragging him back to the present. Dazed and with little will to struggle, he was pulled from the bed and deposited roughly into a waiting wheelchair.

"What?"

A short old man with very little hair was strapping him down with rushed precision.

"He's secure," the man said as the last strap snapped into place. "Go!"

Instantly the wheelchair pitched backward, affording Jason a momentary glimpse of the long brown hair and smooth chin of a panicked teenage girl. The front wheels came down again and the wheelchair rolled rapidly towards the open door and then out into the corridor.

"Hurry, Alicia," the old man said from behind them. "The enforcer says it's in the building."

It? Jason had little time to ponder the question as the chair painfully bounced around a corner towards the elevators. One of the two stood open and was waiting for them.

"What's happening?" he asked. "Where are you taking me?"

The wheelchair slammed to a sudden halt. The instrument panel belonging to the second elevator indicated an ascent.

"It's coming," the girl pronounced and pushed him so hard into the open elevator that his knees slammed into the rear wall. He grimaced, hearing her stabbing the controls but unable to turn around. His hands and feet were bound tight to the chair with no leeway.

"What's coming?" He asked, more than a little aware of the throbbing in his legs.

The doors closed and he felt his stomach heave as the elevator's plunged downward. The girl allowed herself a sigh of relief.

"We made it."

Jason strained against the straps but only succeeded only in toppling the wheelchair, his right elbow taking most of the impact. He screamed in pain and frustration.

"Calm down," the girl said, pulling him up by the forearms.

"Alicia?" That was what the old man had called her. "Please, I deserve to know what's going on."

She swivelled the wheelchair around to face the sliding doors, his back towards her.

"All I know," she said. "Is that the enforcer called my father and told him to get you out of here. He said something was after you and it wasn't human."

"Not human?"

He remembered.

"Pretty wild eh? I don't why Dad believed him, but he did, and if he thought it was true, well—"

The girl crumpled to the ground behind him.

"Alicia?" He tried to turn his head, but only managed to see her twitching feet. "Alicia?"

Then it happened, his every muscle tightening, convulsing, completely out of control, a thousand points of pain playing across his flesh. There was nothing he could do...

Jason Webster

* * *

It wasn't even bothering to run anymore. Instead it was walking, slowly and deliberately towards the Revival Centre Building with no apparent regard for its three pursuers. Lisa was beginning to wonder if it even knew they existed.

"You want me to shoot it, ma'am?" Shandra asked, concussion rifle at the ready.

Lisa wasn't sure. They hadn't tried shooting it yet, but she suspected it would have little if any effect. She also had so many questions – Who was it? What was it? Why was it here? Why did it look like Jason Webster? Why was it going after him? What did it want? A concussion bolt to the back of the neck didn't seem the best way of finding out the necessary answers.

The path abruptly widened as The Revival Centre came into view. It resembled a right angled golden triangle, but with depth, and a slight curve as it nestled against the amber skin of the dome. It had been built to host a few hundred 'remembered' at once, back when the re-creation of the dead had been far more aggressive. At this time it held only one. The great resurrection was not scheduled for a few generations yet, and if men like Chandler had their way, it would never happen at all. This building, with all its facilities, would only ever receive a chosen few.

"I have him in my sights," Shandra announced.

Lisa turned to Steve. The large bearded man was looming behind Shandra with his arms crossed. When he saw Lisa was looking at him, he tipped his chin up.

"It doesn't have to be a kill shot, Lieutenant. We just need to cover all the bases and find out if anything we have can stop this thing."

Lisa shook her head in despair and then raised an outstretched finger. "One shot only, Shandra, and that's it. Aim for a leg."

Shandra fired instantly, causing a section of concrete to explode violently just a few inches beyond where the creature stood. The heat image displayed on Lisa's visor didn't even flinch.

She turned angrily on her two colleagues. "Happy?"

Shandra shouldered her rifle. "No ma'am, I could be a lot happier."

Lisa wanted to kick something.

"Let's go," Steve said quickly as Lisa turned her glare on him. He caught up with Shandra and the two exchanged glances.

Lisa took a breath and then followed closely behind, the three of them catching up with the intruder just as it walked through a window into the Centre. Shandra pushed through the nearest door and they moved quickly through a reception area decorated in blue and green crystal.

Lisa tapped her earbud. "Ted?"

"The servitor and his daughter are on the case, Lisa," he replied. "My ranting seemed to convince them of the urgency. They're going to get him down to you via the elevator."

"Good work, Ted. Just make sure they wait beside it until our guy goes up. I expect he'll use the stairs."

The button for summoning one of the twin elevators lit up. Lisa's eyes opened wide – through her visor she had watched it press the button.

It could become solid if it needed to.

"Ted?"

"I see it. Webster's on his way to the other elevator right now. There should be enough time."

"Good," Lisa said. "Shandra, you—"

"I'll ride with the intruder, ma'am," the armoured enforcer interrupted.

Lisa swallowed. "That could be very dangerous."

"That's my job," Shandra replied coolly.

Lisa frowned. "Okay, Steve?"

The bearded man cocked his head.

"You're with me. We need to keep Webster ahead of this thing and find out what he knows."

"I understand."

"Give me your pistol, Shandra."

The female enforcer removed it from her holster and handed it over. Lisa's fingers curled around the grip, the weight of it almost reassuring.

"It's going in," Shandra said.

Lisa looked at the doors and then at Shandra. "I'm hoping it won't attack you, but I don't know it won't."

The woman nodded and hefted up her rifle. "Well tt's had plenty of opportunity so far." She jumped in as the doors closed.

"I like her," Steve said.

"Good," Lisa replied, eyeing the neighbouring elevator display. 10...09...08. Webster was coming down just as the intruder was going up. "You have my permission to ask her out for a drink when this is all over."

"Not likely," Shandra's voice boomed in her earbud. "He needs a shave."

Steve stroked his chin.

"Report," Lisa ordered.

"It's just standing at the rear," Shandra replied. "I think it's staring at me."

"Then you stare right back," Lisa said, and checked both displays. Shandra's elevator was at 6 and Webster's at 7.

"It's getting restless," Shandra said. "I think it's..."

Lisa heard gunshots.

"Shandra report! Shandra! Shandra!"

"It's..." Shandra coughed hoarsely. "It's gone."

The display indicated Shandra's elevator at 8 and Webster's at 6. Lisa turned to Steve. "I think it jumped across."

The big enforcer rubbed the growth between his top lip and his nose. "You've got the gun."

She nodded, the grip clenched tightly in her right hand. Slowly she aimed it at the doors of the descending elevator.

4...3...2...1...

"Here we go," Steve said.

The doors slid open and Lisa saw the intruder. It was fully visible beneath her visor overlay. She clicked it off and saw a pale man in a grey environment suit pressing a bloodless hand down upon Jason Webster's chest.

The newly 'remembered' man screamed.

"Get away from him!" Lisa shouted.

The intruder looked up with brown eyes that were pasted onto a parched and sandpapered face. He both resembled Jason and made him appear ugly at the same time.

It was grotesque.

Lisa took careful aim. "I repeat, get away from him. If you do not, I will fire."

The creature snarled savagely, a bead of saliva dropping down upon Webster. Lisa grimaced in disgust, only to notice that Jason was beginning to glow beneath the monster's hand. She could almost see through him.

"Last chance," Lisa said. "Move away."

It ignored her and looked down at Jason. Lisa could no longer see Jason's pyjamas or even the flesh beneath. Only the pink muscle mass sliding around bone remained.

She fired.

The intruder screamed in pain and clutched its left shoulder, a thick black liquid spilling out onto the elevator floor. Lisa's heart beat faster. So, it could be hurt after all. Very slowly she advanced, taking comfort that the creature had taken a corresponding step back.

"Steve?"

"What the hell is that thing?"

"Get in there and pull Webster out."

"Wha?--- sure, sure." Beside her Steve took a step forward, careful to keep out of her line of sight. The creature snarled at the movement, holding its wounded shoulder tightly.

"Easy there," Lisa warned it. "Just stay where you are."

The creature's eyes flickered desperately from Jason to her and then up towards Steve.

"No!"

In one motion it leapt from the elevator directly towards her. Lisa barely reacted, the grey man's fingernails tearing into her arms as she fired.

"Lisa!" Steve cried.

She fell backwards as the world dissolved around her.

* * *

Nestled behind his desk in the viewing station, Ted watched Lisa being attacked, her gun firing as she went down and then...

She was gone.

"What?"

He fingers danced frantically across the console keyboard, freezing the feed and then rolling back the footage. He played it back at half speed, the sound playing through the main speakers. "...Staay where yoou aree."

"Nooo!"

He winced at the crack of gunfire, forcefully reminded of another time. Then he watched Lisa fall, the creature's fingers digging into her forearms as her face screwed itself up in pain. She disappeared layer by layer after that - clothes, skin, muscle, organs and finally her bones, all on display for a nanosecond before being eaten away into nothing. The grey man followed her almost immediately afterwards; the same process and the same result. They were both completely and utterly gone.

Ted rolled it back again and again, slower and slower, but it didn't and couldn't change the result. Lisa had... she had... all he could do was lean back in his seat and try to breathe.

"Ted? Ted? TED!"

He realised the voice had been calling him for a while. Minutes had passed and he had barely registered his own name.

He flicked a switch. "It's me."

"She's gone, Ted," Steve said. "She's... I don't know what to do."

The heat signatures! Ted called up the sensor information and watched the scene again. Yes! Lisa's heat signature was present even after she disappeared. She was alive and he could track her, he could track them both except... No! The heat signatures were fading too, absorbed by the ambient atmosphere. She wasn't just invisible or immaterial. She wasn't there at all.

"Ted," Steve called. "Talk to me. I need to know what to do?"

Ted rubbed his eyes, the prolonged fatigue biting into him and demanding shutdown. Reflexively, he dug his nails into his palms and fended it off, holding up his hand to see the livid white dents.

He hit the Comms button angrily. "Why are you asking me? I don't know what to do. How am I supposed to know what to do? What do you expect? What do you want from me?"

He swore loudly.

For a moment there was no reply, just silence as Ted listened to the rabid exultation of his own breathing.

"You finished?" Steve asked calmly.

Ted pounded the desk with his fist, the pain bringing tears to his eyes. He looked up at the real-time feed and saw Steve standing there despondently, shoulders dropped, then he rotated the view to the open elevator. Jason Webster was still lying there; the vivid red musculature of his body no longer visible. He had reverted back to normal.

"Sorry," Ted said quietly. "I went away but I'm back now."

"So," Steve paused. "What do we do now?"

The elevator beside Jason's slid open and Shandra emerged, rifle grasped limply in her left hand.

"Get Webster to a security cell," Ted said. "Shandra, go with him. I have some thinking to do."

The image of her frowned, and then she turned to Jason Webster, considering him in earnest and then the twitching girl beside him. Ted massaged the space between his eyes and leaned back. He wasn't thinking at all, he couldn't think. Instead he watched as Steve and Shandra collected up Webster and put him back in the wheelchair.

After that they picked up the girl and moved her outside. They didn't seem to know what to do with her. Ted reached out and switched off the feed. They would have to make do without him. He finished the last dregs of his coffee and stared hard at the blank screen until all he could see were blood vessels.

Lisa wasn't dead. She couldn't be dead. She couldn't be...

But where was she? That was the question that repeated itself in his mind again and again. They had been together seriously for eight months and not so seriously for three years. That was three years when he had considered asking her out. Three years when the chance of losing that friendship had paralysed him into staying his hand. In the end she had found him at a dive in Section 11 and tricked him into a drunken pass. If she hadn't, he doubted anything would have changed. He had lacked the courage to change anything.

Smiling at the haziness of the memory, he recalled the contest between them to drink as much dirty beer as humanly possible. He had never been to the toilet so much in his life, the slop burning through his bladder faster than anything he had ever drunk before. But after all that beer he could do more than talk and so could she. It was all they had needed to push them on. They had danced around each other for so long that when the dance was finally over he could barely believe it. Three years wasted, three precious years. They couldn't afford to waste another single moment.

Damn it, he should have been used to losing people by now. His father, mother and two sisters had been 'dispersed' in the second year of the purge and he had lived with that through a further half decade of fighting. As for friends, there were no friends in the cell, only comrades, many of which had been murdered by drone barrage or their own combustibles. With every loss he learnt to bury his feelings deeper inside, never letting himself get too close, never allowing himself to become vulnerable. But seeing her vanish like that made him realise that all those walls were gone, demolished in an instant. She had brought him out of himself and taught him to trust in her existence, her permanence, and her life. He had trusted her and she had let him down. How could she have done anything else?

He needed a drink, he needed to just blot her out and bury her with all the rest.

He was being a fool.

The rational part of his mind knew these feelings were nothing more than the combination of exhaustion coupled with grief and they were not even remotely useful. There was no body, no evidence she was dead, not yet. He sat up straight and stared hard at the console screen waiting for something to jump out at him. Something did, the intruder tracking program had completed. Rolling through it there was evidence of the intruder's presence for the last six and a half years. In a sea of sensor data it had never been noticed. It had walked among and through the people of the dome almost continuously, even at night, only disappearing for a few days at a time. He tracked its movements, and saw that it had carefully avoided the secure areas, walking mainly among the general populace. In their shops, places of work, their homes, their bedrooms, their bathrooms even. It sickened him that it respected no boundary, no privacy, and that it had been there for so long, unseen and perfidious.

He shook his head in disgust as an urgent connection request flashed red for his attention. He ignored it and ran a more detailed analysis, searching for repeats and patterns in the intruder's movements. Hidden in the minutiae he discovered a disturbing fact. The intruder had entered a place it couldn't be tracked four times in the last six weeks, the only place that was off-limits to the surveillance sensors despite the efforts of many a senior administrator otherwise.

Randall's Tower.

The security doors behind him opened without warning and he swivelled painfully to see four armoured enforcers file into the viewing station.

"Edwin Holloway," the foremost officer began. "You are ordered to come with us at once."

Ted couldn't help noticing their rifles were aimed directly at his head. Not so friendly considering they and him were all meant to be members of the same security agency.

"Now, Holloway!" The lead enforcer grunted.

Ted pressed his hands against the armrests of his chair and hauled himself upright.

"Well, since you asked so nicely..."

Chapter Six

I'm not sure I want to be with you anymore.

- What are you talking about? Why are you saying this?

It's been coming for a long time, didn't you notice? I don't feel the same way anymore. I've changed and so have you.

- Don't be silly, I haven't changed and you're the same woman you've always been. You're my Gina.

I'm not yours, you know I'm not. You know because this always happens.

- Gina?

Holloway showed me the re-integration logs. This isn't the first time you've brought me back. It's not even the tenth time you've brought me back. You lied to me.

- He shouldn't have done that.

We've done this before haven't we? Every time I leave you, you reset me back to that stupid ignorant woman who believes she's in love with you. I've seen it. How long do I normally last? A few months, a few years? Never longer than a decade.

- You don't know what you're saying.

I always wondered if there were others. but I never really believed it, not until now. I'm leaving you, Jason.

- And where will you go exactly? The Valhalla isn't that big. We're all living on top of each other as it is.

Holloway has offered to—

- Him? You can't...

Maybe it will last for a little while, maybe a long while. I don't know, but it helps that he actually seems to love me.

- I won't allow it.

Are you going to reset me again?

- Don't make me.

If you reset me, you'll have to reset the whole crew. You wouldn't be able to tolerate everyone knowing.

- Not Holloway, that's it for him, he's had his day.

Why don't you just let me decide how I want to live my life? Maybe you could even win me back, if you tried. Maybe we could even have something real.

- Don't go, Gina. Don't make me do it.

I'm not making you do anything. You want to do it. You're not even willing to take a risk that something new can happen.

- This won't work.

Why don't you let us poor mortals live out our lives in peace? When we're gone, you can play your little game all over again.

- You don't... IT'S NOT A GAME!

Jason screamed, writhing in impotent rage against the bonds that kept him secure. When the anger finally subsided he realised it was just another memory drifting to the surface, another sequence making itself known. There were so many after all, vying for his attention, always on the lookout for momentary weakness. He took a deep breath and tried to remember that he wasn't on The Valhalla anymore. A planet had been found, a planet that...

Randall had broken his promise.

Slowly opening his eyes, he focussed upon a sterile grey ceiling. His arms and legs were strapped down and a collection of thin cables pinched in at various points on his dermis. Artificial daylight shone through a thin curtain just a few metres away. The room was empty except for him, the bed, some chairs, and a host of beeping machines performing a repeating symphony all of their own. To his left he saw an array of screens generating an endless stream of numbers, row upon row. Five and sixes seemed to be the order of the day, a few threes and sevens here and there. What they meant, who could tell?

"Hello," he croaked.

Seconds passed without reply and he tried again without enthusiasm. He felt so exhausted, he could have just closed his eyes and gone back to sleep. In fact, it wasn't such a bad idea. They had injected him with something, he recognised that much, something that made him pliable.

The door beside the machines swung open and a rotund white-haired man entered the room accompanied by an armoured bodyguard carrying a rifle.

"Glad to see you're awake, Mr Webster," the old man said. "I'm Commissioner Chandler."

"Hello," Jason replied weakly. "Are you in charge?"

"I am," Chandler replied and sat down on one of the chairs. The bodyguard remained standing, rifle at the ready. Jason considered his straps and wondered exactly what they expected him to do.

"I'm afraid you were 'remembered' in error, Mr Webster," Chandler said. "One of my subordinates managed to get carried away with the authority I gave her."

Jason nodded, his eyes flickering under the weight of increasingly heavy lids.

"But I can't just..." The white-haired administrator paused. "Disperse? Yes, I can't just disperse you. That is forbidden by law. You are a human being with all the rights thereof. We can't just destroy what we create - there are rules - but I can keep you a prisoner for a prolonged period of time, perhaps even indefinitely."

"Why?" Jason asked quietly. "What's happened?"

"Apparently there was a creature with your face that could walk through security barriers and deal pain and injury with impunity. It has been dealt with by the subordinate I mentioned. She was very heroic and I will miss her. What do you know about this creature?"

Jason tried to fight the drugs. "Sounds like an alien."

Chandler scratched his chin. "A humanoid alien? With your face? That does sound a little ridiculous. Tell me the truth."

Jason yawned with his mouth closed, the muscles in his chin almost cramping. "I'm trying. What do you think it is?"

"Was," Chandler corrected. "Another version of you of course, some experiment gone awry during the five thousand year voyage to Redfern. Randall is probably responsible. I daresay that's why he's refusing to comment."

"You're wrong," Jason declared.

The Commissioner raised an eyebrow. "Carmichael's report said you would remember details of the voyage. Some sort of inherited memory graft?"

"Something like that."

"Why do you think it's an alien?"

Jason attempted to moisten his lips with his tongue. "Alien to us, I mean."

Chandler waited and then opened his hands. "Care to elaborate, Mr Webster?"

"The species that naturally inhabit this planet are not alien to it, just to us. We're the real aliens here."

Chandler opened his mouth and then closed it again, a bead of sweat glistening on his forehead under an unforgiving overhead light.

"I'm afraid you are quite insane, Mr Webster," he declared finally and turned to his bodyguard. "Scrub the recording of this conversation and then arrange his transportation to the mines. He will serve a full custodial sentence."

Jason was curious. "Under what charge?"

The Commissioner stood up from his chair and moved closer to the bed, peering down at him.

"You attacked an enforcer without provocation. As such you are a danger to the general population and a very clear example of why none of your kind should ever be brought back. You don't belong here."

"My kind?" Jason queried. "You mean 'the remembered', don't you?"

Chandler sighed. "I mean all the men and women who helped to destroy one world and would happily destroy another."

"Wha-" Jason blinked. "No, no, it's not like that at all. It's not... How could you even think that?"

Chandler ignored him. "Like I said before, there are laws. But I do intend to keep you safely out of harm's way. No-one at the mines will listen to you and it wouldn't matter if they did."

"I only told you the truth," Jason declared. "But there's so much more to it, so much more I can tell you."

The Commissioner's chin wobbled in agitation. "I don't want to hear it and I don't need to hear it." He turned his back and strode purposefully towards the door. "Goodbye Mr Webster. We won't meet again."

Jason closed his eyes, the weight increasing to unbearable levels as the memories exploded all over again.

- Gina, I'm sorry. If only you knew how difficult this is.
Don't touch me!

* * *

Dominic sat at a very long dining table, carefully cutting the broccoli on his plate into small defined pieces. Stalk to the left and flower heads to the right. The peas and sweetcorn he alternated in the centre, each row building into diagonal lines of green and yellow. The potato strips he laced about the rim of the plate, an atmosphere of light brown. After that, he arranged the white clumps of dry turkey meat above the peas and sweetcorn whilst cresting the more moist turkey meat underneath. Pleased with the presentation, he licked his lips and prepared to spear one of the larger flower heads with his fork.

"Playing with your food again, Dominic?" Randall asked. His voice relayed via an intercom speaker hidden above.

Dominic smiled, dug in the fork, and deposited the broccoli into his mouth. It was crunchy enough to chew.

"It's the human condition," he explained. "We enjoy our food and we spend copious amounts of time finding new ways of eliciting a grand design of flavour, elegant texture and grandiose taste. It's more than just filling our bellies. It is art."

"Indeed," Randall replied. "How is it?"

Dominic appeared thoughtful for a moment before trying a small piece of white turkey. He swallowed and grimaced at the same time. "Not enough salt."

"Hmmm," Randall commented.

Dominic put down his cutlery and cleaned his hands with a serviette. "How can I help you today, Randall?"

"There is a situation with the enforcers. I need you to represent me."

Dominic nodded as he stood up, one hand holding his unfinished plate.

"We need to synchronise before you go," Randall said. "You should sit back down."

The avatar sighed and resumed his seat, carefully pushing the plate of food to one side. "I'm ready."

"Good. Establishing link,"

Dominic smiled serenely and leaned back into his chair, issuing a silent mental command to the synaptic circuitry that flowed through and across his brain.

CONFIRMED... SLAVE UNIT ACCEPTING CONNECTION

SYNCHRONISE...

SYNCHRONISE...

SYNCHRONISE...

Both Dominic and Randall were no more. As the synaptic circuitry achieved tandem with the AI's neural network, the memories of both merged and became indistinguishable, flowing as they did, one to the other, back and forth across a closed wireless circuit. One being was created from two, one individual, neither completely organic nor completely machine, an individual that existed for only the briefest of moments during each refresh, painfully aware that it would soon separate again into its component parts and become incomplete.

I will guide humanity, cherish them and ensure their survival...

I will save my friend and my friendship...

I will brook no interference or resistance from those who are not among the chosen...

For a brief moment this newly created being remembered each and every time he had existed as if it were a permanent state. With this self-knowledge came a renewed sense of fear and anticipation. Was he the man or the machine and which did he prefer - the ability to touch and feel or the freedom of unlimited computer processing?

SYNCHRONISATION COMPLETE

For the briefest of seconds his identity remained uncertain, and then he opened his eyes, a tear drying on his cheek.

"Thank you," Dominic said. "I know what I have to do."

"Call upon me if you have need," Randall replied. "I will be waiting."

Dominic nodded affirmation and then stood up slowly and took a deep breath. Looking down, he saw the plate of carefully arranged food and picked it up.

"Oh well."

He emptied it into the nearest bin and walked out.

* * *

A hand on his shoulder shook Ted awake.

"Wakey, wakey," Steve Miles said.

The bench Ted was lying upon was hard enough to make his head ache, and his leg wasn't doing much better. The effects of his last set of meds were beginning to recede.

"You snore," Steve said.

Ted blinked out the sleep as the big man helped him into a sitting position. It didn't feel like he'd been asleep very long.

"How are we doing?" he asked.

Steve shrugged. The cell smelt of a combination of urine and disinfectant, the little toilet in the corner overflowing from the bowl and dripping filth onto the concrete.

"I haven't been inside one of these for a while," Steve said. "Shandra's next door."

Ted saw her through the metal bars. Her armour and weapons had been stripped away leaving only the same blue operations uniform they all wore. Her hair was a mess of thick auburn curls and her brown oval eyes glowered.

"I don't even know why I'm here," she said. "I was just following orders. You don't see Johnson here do you?"

"He broke his wrist," Ted replied.

She gripped the bars. "He got lucky."

Ted rubbed the back of his neck. "I'm hungry, it must be almost dinnertime."

"Well past," Steve said. "I think they've forgotten us."

Ted stood up and limped across to the cell door. Through the bars there was nothing to see but a narrow empty hallway.

"They're listening in," he commented. "They'll probably give more credence to what we say to each other than what we say to them."

"Except they know that we know they're listening in," Steve said.

Ted nodded. "There is that." He turned to his friend. "What happened to Webster?"

"A band of merry enforcers took him away. Turns out they were on sitting on the sidelines all along, just waiting for the order."

Ted rolled his eyes. "So much for letting us get on with our jobs. Has Chandler been by yet?"

"No-one has," Shandra said. "They must still be trying to figure out what to do next."

Ted sat back down and thumped his bad leg where it was beginning to ache badly. The resultant pain was almost more than he could bear.

"Watch it," Steve said. "Is it playing up again?"

"It never stops playing up," Ted replied. "A little present from the Jason Webster of yesteryear."

"He did that to you?" Shandra asked.

Ted just stared back at her. "It's a long story."

"You're like him, aren't you?" Shandra said slowly. "You're one of 'the remembered'?"

Ted exchanged a glance with Steve and braced himself. There were those among the population that hated 'the remembered' with a passion. They called themselves the 'trueborns', and he had met far too many to mention.

"Is that a problem?"

Shandra leaned her head against the bars. "As a co-ordinator, you did a better job than most."

"Thanks."

"It's nice to finally put a face to that voice."

Ted relaxed. "Nice to meet you too."

A door slammed shut at the end of the corridor, the impact echoing far and wide.

"Company," Steve said.

Ted eased his head back against the wall as Commissioner Chandler walked into view accompanied by three armoured enforcers. Ted had only ever met Chandler once before at an official reception. He had been all smiles and fancy words, but even then Ted had sensed an unquantifiable hardness behind those steely grey eyes. He was probably not as old as he appeared or as overweight. There was muscle there, Ted was sure of that, muscle and a hidden ferocity that was not to be underestimated. Ted had served under men like Chandler in the resistance. He could recognise an unyielding force of all knowing narcissism when he saw one.

"Gentlemen," Chandler said. "Enforcer Broussard, how are you?"

"Sir," Steve and Shandra echoed.

"Sir," Ted said a few seconds later.

Chandler frowned briefly and then paced in front of one cell to the other. "I've reviewed all the surveillance footage as well as

Lieutenant Carmichael's last report and the transcripts of your individual performances."

Here it comes...

"And I commend all three of you for performing an excellent job in difficult circumstances."

Ted was surprised.

"Your records will be updated and promotions afforded accordingly. I am only sorry that Lieutenant Carmichael was killed in the line of duty, but I am also thankful that her sacrifice wasn't in vain. The threat has been dealt with."

"Do we know what it was, sir?" Steve asked.

"I'm afraid that information has been classified, Enforcer Miles. It is no longer your concern."

"Like hell it isn't!" Shandra retorted.

Chandler turned his gaze on Shandra and licked the bottom of his teeth. "It's over, Enforcer Broussard, unless of course you would rather be, 'Miss' Broussard. I can arrange that."

Shandra took a step back. "No, sir."

"Thank you, Enforcer Broussard."

"What about Jason Webster?" Ted asked. "I'd like to speak to him. Find out what he knows."

Chandler scratched his nose. "I'm afraid the creature severely injured Mr Webster during the altercation. He did not survive."

Ted didn't believe him.

"I understand, sir."

The Commissioner blinked. "I'm glad." Then he turned to one of the armoured guards. "Enforcer Ali, please open the cells."

Ali stepped forward and removed his gauntlet, placing his palm on the locking plate. Both of the cell doors unlocked with a loud click. The former prisoners filed out.

"Your new duties will be assigned to you in three days," Chandler explained. "Until then you can rest. The memorial service for Enforcer Carmichael will be in two days."

So they had written Lisa off, Ted had half-expected that. It was easy to do nothing when faced with a situation that defied explanation. He didn't believe for one moment that the truth had been classified, because Chandler didn't know what the truth was. The only information that had been classified was Chandler's wilful ignorance.

"Enforcer Holloway," the Commissioner said, his hand sweeping up and gripping Ted's shoulder. "I understand you were in a relationship with Lieutenant Carmichael. Would you be willing to say a few words at the service?"

Ted resisted the urge to swat Chandler's hand away. "Certainly, sir, I would be honoured."

"And if you need more than three days leave, just contact me. I can be flexible."

"Thank you, sir," Ted said as the hand moved away. "I'll keep that in mind."

The Commissioner tipped his head forward. "My condolences, Holloway. Now, if you'll excuse me, I have a department to run."

Their superior turned his back before Ted could compose a response, the three armoured enforcers following as the Commissioner marched back down the long corridor.

"That's it?" Steve asked.

"Maybe," Ted answered. "Maybe not."

"What do we do now?" Shandra asked.

Ted leaned heavily against the bars of his former cell. "I don't know about you two but I'm going home to get my meds, my dinner and some sleep."

Steve glanced at the ceiling. "You think they're watching us?"

"They're always watching us," Ted replied sombrely. "There's nothing we can do that Chandler won't know about. Not that there's anything to do." He tried to take a step and lurched forward. His cane had not been returned.

"Lean on me," Steve said. "I'll get you back home."

Ted nodded gratefully as a Steve's strong arm took hold and kept him upright. Together they headed down the corridor towards the exit.

"This isn't right," Shandra said, behind them. "We should do something."

Ted remained silent even though he agreed. There was some connection between 'The Grey Man' and Randall, he knew that, just as it was Randall who had delivered Jason's digital file with five thousand years of integrated memory. Somehow Ted would find a way to see him, question him and maybe even get some answers. But he couldn't tell Steve and Shandra that, not with so many ears listening and eyes watching. Best to keep them out of it, because if he did see Randall, Chandler would know and he could only guess what the Commissioner would do. That man had ice in his veins.

"Forget about it, Shandra," Ted said. "Remember, you're being promoted."

Steve glanced at the ceiling again and then looked Ted straight in the eye and nodded ever so slightly. There was no getting past Steve; they had known each other too long. Ted returned the slightest shake of his head. He knew Steve would ignore it.

Shandra followed as they trudged on, the heavy fire door at the end of the corridor opening before they even made it there. For a brief instant Ted wondered if Chandler and his entourage had returned. But it wasn't him. Instead Ted saw a thin young man dressed in a crumpled black suit without a tie. Ted guessed he couldn't have been much older than twenty, his face possessing an amused impish quality that implied mischief. He was also smiling widely.

"Lisa isn't dead."

Chapter Seven

Lisa emptied the gun into the grey man as its nails ripped into her arms, sending her sprawling backwards to land hard on the Revival Centre's concrete concourse. The impact to her head almost knocked her out cold, her consciousness wavering briefly before returning with excruciating pain. Looking up, she saw the body of her assailant lying on top of her, his weight pinning her down, the parched skin of his face flushed with colour as a stream of blood dripped from the corner of his mouth onto the shoulder of her uniform. With a shriek of disgust she rolled the thing off her and sat up, her ears filling with white noise as she cradled her own pounding head. Warm blood seeped through her fingers, and she pulled her hands away to look, staring at the red stickiness with an odd fascination.

"Steve?" she called.

The big man didn't answer, and she painfully turned her head back to where he had been standing a moment ago.

He wasn't there.

"Ted?"

There was no answer.

"Ted, please respond."

Nothing.

Lisa tapped her earbud only to realise that it was the source of the static that was fizzing around in her head. Perhaps it had been damaged during the attack. She pulled it out and examined it, not really knowing what she was looking for. She was not a trained Tech and to her it was just as blue and cylindrical as it normally was. She pocketed it and groaned, finding both her arms cut just above the elbow. The pain subsided quickly and there was more blood than damage. Flexing her forearms, the radius of movement appeared unimpaired but came with an almighty sting.

Swearing under her breath, she dragged herself over to the body, realising that alternatively she had referred to it as the

Intruder, the creature, and even the grey man. Since its first appearance she had given it so many names without knowing who or what it really was. She took her time to study it now, noting the padded environment suit with its reverse triangle Valhalla insignia. She had heard of 'The Valhalla' and seen a similar suit in the museum. But the suit was lacking a helmet, revealing a wrinkled pink face topped with thinning grey and red hair. The hands were also visible, the fingers arched like claws and almost wasted to the bone.

But it was undeniably Jason Webster, the features perhaps not as sharply defined as those of the man who had failed to strangle her, but it was him all the same. It was him, and he was changing before her eyes. The desperate face that had leapt towards her minutes before had been grey and bloodless, and the hair as white as snow, not this shocking red. The resemblance to the other Jason Webster was becoming more marked with each passing second. Startled, she sprang back on her hands, watching as the wounds she had inflicted so recently closed up without leaving a scar. Even the environment suit was healing itself, the material knitting together perfectly as if it had never been holed.

What was this thing?

Lisa scrambled to her feet, painfully aware that the grey man would be completely restored in moments. She had to get away from it, find help, find some way to make it stay dead. She had to... She looked up and all thoughts of murder suddenly deserted her. She stared, her arms dead weights at her side as the full magnitude of disbelief sank in.

It wasn't possible.

The high ceiling of The Revival Centre's reception area had become nothing more than an outline before her. She could see beyond it, even beyond the amber skin of the dome itself. The sky was a pinkish red, the horizon stretching into an unquantifiable distance illuminated only by a small orange sun well past it zenith.

Her mouth opened and she staggered towards the nearest wall, looking for support only for her arms to pass right through it. The wall wasn't really there,

"What are you doing here?"

She turned to see this strange version of Jason Webster struggling to his feet, his wounds completely healed and his skin pink and healthy. He might have been two decades older than the Jason she had met earlier that day, his face a little more lined and the skin of it, a little less tight. But he wasn't the grey man anymore; all the missing colour and life had somehow been restored.

"Where is here?" Lisa asked, surprised by the calm in her voice despite the panic building inside her.

Jason rubbed his nose. "I must have brought you with me," he concluded. His voice was deeper than the younger version, somehow carrying more authority, more experience, but there was something else, something not quite buried - an undertone of tragic exhaustion.

"I didn't mean to."

Lisa rubbed her eyes, trying to re-orientate herself, trying to wake up. "I want to go home."

The older Jason shrugged and shook his head. "I can't send you back, not yet."

Lisa stared at him. "What now, then? Are you going to kill me? What in Randall's name are you?"

"I don't kill," he replied. Then he turned away, his gaze fixed upon the elevator. "They're taking him away and I'm too weak to follow. I've lost my opportunity, thanks to you."

Lisa frowned, from her point of view the elevator was almost as transparent as the ceiling, but it hadn't been like that before. She took a step away from the wall and the elevator's solidity seemed to accumulate. Another step and it almost appeared as normal.

"What is this place?" She asked.

Jason turned toward hers, his expression placid, almost serene. He was making no apparent move to cause her harm despite the fact she had tried to kill him only minutes before.

"Think of it as an in between," he said. "You forced me back when you damaged me. It will be some time until I can tune myself back to the human frequency. You've delayed me."

Lisa took a step towards him. "What are you?"

Jason scratched his chin. "I'm still trying to understand what *you* are. You should have been left behind, not carried with me. Without genetic compatibility such a violent reversion should have killed you."

Lisa patted one of her wounded arms. "It was violent enough. Are you going to give me any actual answers?"

Jason frowned. "I thought I was." He held out his hand. "You'd better come with me. The Inishi roam this frequency. They are little better than animals and the pollutants from your dome have done little to improve their temper. We should avoid them if we can."

Lisa looked up. "What are the Inishi?"

"Come on," Jason said. "I have a place here that is safe. But we have a long way to go. It's a good thing you can run."

Lisa crossed her arms and stared at him.

He withdrew his hand. "Are you coming?"

Something howled in the far distance with an anguish that made her shiver. She had little experience of animals, the types bred in the dome only served as food or pets. This didn't sound like any one of them, the cry cutting through her insides like a sharp and malignant knife.

The howl was swiftly followed by another, this time much closer.

"They've probably sensed our arrival," Jason said. "Time for me to go. What are you going to do?"

Lisa saw her useless and empty gun near where they had both fallen. She didn't even have a clip to reload it with.

"I guess I'm coming with you."

* * *

It was odd to walk through the dome without the dome actually being there. Buildings and pathways, trees and shrubbery, they all seemed so real up close, almost solid until her fingers sank through them. Yet from a distance of five metres or so, objects dissolved into nothing more than barely visible outlines. It was like shining a torch with limited range and seeing only what the beam happened to glance upon. But even so, she saw no people, not a sign anywhere, just edifices to human architecture without a human presence. The old Jason led her without comment, the howling of the Inishi becoming louder and closer the further they wandered. How long until one or more came across them?

"What do they look like?" She asked Jason.

"You'll know them when you see them," he replied. "Just hope you don't see them. The human optic nerve doesn't translate them very well."

"What about you?" She asked. "How did you end up here? How can you do the things you do?"

He laughed, and to Lisa it sounded so normal, so human. "I can't explain things to you," he said. "You're the enemy."

"Then why are you leading me to safety?"

"Because you're here and because, like I said, I don't kill."

"If you left me to these Inishi, you wouldn't be doing the killing."

Old Jason shook his head. "Oh yes I would. To see it any other way would be a fantastic rationalisation."

"It's all black and white, is it?"

He grinned. "I leave rationalisations to aliens, you're all so good at them."

"Aliens?" She was taken by surprise as they walked through a wall without stopping. She emerged the other end with every muscle clenched painfully.

"Don't tense up so much," Jason said. "The wall wasn't really there. It was just an afterimage projected from your human frequency."

They had entered the ground floor of The Red Sands Mall. All the shops she could see were open, shutters up, clothing and toys, jewellery, menus and coffee, all items for sale with no-one to sell them.

"It's like a ghost town," she said. "Why can't I see any people?"

"Humans don't project past their own frequency. It's why you're so isolated as a species. The beings that exist in other frequencies can only witness what you build and feel what you destroy."

The howl repeated, this time very close and somewhere overhead. Lisa looked up and saw the outlines of all the different Mall levels running into each other.

"We need to run now," Jason said. "The Inishi have found us."

"I can't see anything."

He grabbed her arm and pointed upwards. Wincing from the sudden pressure, Lisa saw a shimmering area of colour nesting near the third floor, a rainbow effect blinking red, orange, yellow, green, blue, indigo and violet in rapid succession. As she watched, it detached itself and began to float down towards them. It was easily the size of the main screen in the Viewing Station.

"It's beautiful," Lisa said.

"Run!" Jason urged, pulling her along. "Beautiful it may be, but it will eat us both."

She stayed with him as he sped through a butcher's wall, into a freezer of empty hooks, and then out again onto a pathway among some residential buildings. He was not holding back, and they ran through wall after wall, zig-zagging back and forth at every opportunity. She could only wonder why he had used the pathways before. Moving like this, there was no way Shandra or anyone else who was solid could have kept up.

"This way," he said, suddenly darting left through 'Green Park'. She passed through trees and an ornamental fountain, another Rainbow creature drifting down from a high branch to block their way. Jason guided her left just as it rushed towards them, a stampede of colour. With ferocious speed it overshot them and carried on regardless. Lisa glanced back and saw it execute a very wide turn, and then it was after them again.

Jason veered an extreme right, and they were through the park and onto a pathway. Looming up to meet them was Randall's tower, and as they passed through a retirement centre, that edifice seemed more imposing and solid than anything else she had ever seen. Closing the distance, she couldn't understand why it wasn't just an outline, then her shoulder impacted the glass concourse entrance and she rebounded.

"This is the place," Jason said, collecting her up from the pavement. "Come on." He pulled her along to a pair of plexifibre glass doors and pushed down on a long handle. They entered the same lobby she had been in hours before, the inner recesses just as gloomy as when she had arrived that morning. Jason closed the door behind them and took a step back as two Inishi collided with the glass. There was the barest of shudders and then Jason turned his back.

"Here?" Lisa exclaimed.

Old Jason raised his hands. "Here."

Lisa looked around, the polished floor, the glass flowers on the table, everything, even down to the depression on the sofa was the same as the tower she had recently visited. Pressing her hands down against the sofa armrest she let her fingers run over stitching in the leather substitute. It was cold, solid, and so very real.

"I don't understand the rules here," Lisa said. "This was all just about making sense and then—"

"Randall is a product of quantum computing," Jason said. "It's a field effect that means this eyesore imposes itself upon every frequency on the planet." He turned his eyes toward the

Inishi. "More importantly, I can rest without having to worry about them. They hate it, but they really can't get in." He waved at them. "Door handles defeat them."

The two rainbow creatures roared loudly, but for all their blows the door only rattled. Finally, with one last scream, they hurtled away through the wall of a nearby office building.

"Where are they going?" Lisa asked.

Jason took a deep breath. "Hopefully they've left the dome. Your human atmosphere really just makes them angry." He pulled away from the glass. "Come on, there's someone I want you to meet."

Lisa frowned. "What do you mean?"

He opened a door to the tower staircase and beckoned her to follow. "You know, I never even asked you your name."

"Lisa," she replied. "Lisa Carmichael."

He raised his eyebrows. "Well, Lisa Carmichael, we have a few floors to climb."

She walked through, not really knowing why. There just didn't seem to be a host of better alternatives. She was having difficulty reconciling this more genteel Jason Webster with the grey vicious creature that had attacked her back in the real world. Why had he been like that, and how had he been able to heal himself so completely from the gunshot wounds that should have killed him? What was he? She suspected he had planned for another version of himself to be created. He had wanted to bring that younger Jason Webster back with him instead of her.

She had so many questions and no easy way of finding the answers. The only thing she could do was to ride this thing out and see where it took her. It wasn't like she could escape by running, there was nowhere to escape to. She would have to bide her time, take whatever opportunity she could find, and then get back to the real Dome and explain to her leaders the true nature of their planet. She sighed; they might even listen to her before they locked her away in a padded cell.

Her legs ached badly as they passed the seventh floor.

"Remind me why we're not taking an elevator?" she asked.

"Because that would most likely kill us," Jason replied. "Frequency translation and moving objects don't mix."

Lisa didn't understand and leaned heavily on the handrail. "How much further?"

"Three more levels and we hit the commissary. I don't know about you, but I'm hungry."

She was hungry too.

Three levels later they exited the stairwell and trudged down a brown carpeted corridor to a door at the end. Again Jason held it open for her.

"Thank you."

Lisa walked through into a room with a long table dominating its centre and a host of smaller tables radiating outwards. On the far left hand side were three separate food counters, the mixed smells of meat and spices making her dizzy and emphasising her hunger. The entire back wall had been covered with a painting of an astronaut walking across a dusty red landscape, alone and fearless. Beneath it sat a woman.

Lisa was surprised. "Who are you?"

The woman stood up. She was slim, but it was the thinness of advanced age where bone became more prevalent than flesh. Her face was heavily wrinkled and her long hair was thick and white, matching her dress. She almost seemed to glow.

She was also as surprised as Lisa. "What are you doing here?"

The two women stared at each other across the expanse of the room, neither moving. Jason ignored them both, walking across to the first food counter and picking up a tray.

The old woman crossed her arms. "Webster!"

His shoulders tensed as he put the down the tray to face her. "Hello, Gina, how are you today?"

The woman's expression did not relax as she motioned towards Lisa. "Care to explain?"

With exaggerated exhaustion, Jason walked over to the table opposite her and sat down languidly. "Her name is Lisa Carmich—"

"Lisa?" The old woman frowned.

"And she shot me as I was in the process of transferring Jason. She kept on shooting me until her gun was empty. I think I still have a few of the bullets lodged in my sternum."

The old woman turned her gaze towards Lisa, a rabid intensity in those ancient eyes that made the younger woman blink without wanting to.

"I had to transfer back just to stay alive," Jason continued. "And somehow I brought her back with me. I think she may need medical attention. I gave her some nasty cuts on her arms."

"Take her back," Gina demanded. "Take her back right now."

Jason shrugged. "I can't. I was away too long this time. I couldn't think, I could barely reason, it was..." he paused. "I need time to recover from my injuries."

"She can't stay here!"

Lisa raised her hand. "Hello, you do know I'm standing right here?"

The old woman stared at Jason. "You should lock her up."

He frowned. "How would I do that? Any room I lock would unlock itself once the true state of the tower was re-translated. That's how it works."

Gina gritted her teeth. "Do you know who she is?"

He blinked. "I think I do now."

"And who exactly are you?" Lisa asked.

The old woman ignored her. "Webster, you were meant to bring back my Jason."

"I will go back as soon as I'm able," the older version of Jason replied. "There's no place in the dome I can't get to. I won't let them shoot me again."

Gina walked slowly across to him and leaned heavily against his table, the tension in her body breaking like a great swell. He carefully helped her down into a seat.

"I was waiting for him," she said tearfully. "How did he look?"

"Young," Jason answered. "A default physical reset."

Gina reached up and pressed her fingers against her own face, running them over her cheeks and down her chin. "I'm too old, Webster."

He caught her hand in his. "It won't matter to him, Gina."

Lisa clenched her jaw as she witnessed the exchange and then advanced on the shared table, violently yanking out the old woman's chair before anyone could stop her.

"I've had enough of this. I want some answers, and I want them now!"

Gina swayed in her seat and then looked up wearily, gazing into the younger woman's eyes. Eventually, she smiled. "I'm sorry Lisa, of course you do."

"Who are you?" Lisa asked. "I need to know."

The woman leaned back and reached out her hand. Jason gripped it again.

"I am Commander Gina Davies," she said. "First officer of the Valhalla and Deputy Leader of the Planetary Survey Team."

Lisa paused, digesting an onrush of information that didn't make any sense. "The Valhalla landed almost a century ago," she said. "I don't understand, you're old, but not old enough. You should be dead."

The woman laughed. "There were circumstances that made me one of the youngest, but even so..." she looked to Jason. "I had help."

"I did what I could," he said

The ancient woman closed her eyes. "Webster, it's been such a long time."

"I know, Gina," Jason replied softly, "but the waiting is almost over, I promise."

She gazed up at him, her hand slipping free of his. "I need *my* Jason."

Lisa motioned to the man in the environment suit. "This is Jason!"

"No, he's not," Gina said. "I call him Webster because he looks just like him, but he isn't Jason, he can never be him."

Lisa tried to be patient but her anger was building again.

The old woman motioned to a nearby chair. "Sit down please, Lisa. Your arms need attending to."

"Later," Lisa said. "Tell me!"

Gina sighed and glanced towards the being who was not Jason Webster.

"You might as well," he said, reaching out and squeezing her wrist. "Events are already in motion. There's nothing anyone can do."

Gina bit her bottom lip and then turned back to Lisa. "It's a very long story."

Chapter Eight

We lost three drones here in the last two days.

- Rock, mountains and a lot of static. The drones were probably destroyed by nothing more than atmospheric discharge.

Maybe, maybe not, but I'd like to recover them, Jason.

- You worry too much. This planet is almost perfect for us, why, Randall estimates that if we can find an adequate power source, the atmosphere can be altered to support human life in just over a century.

Nice for them. We'll never live to see it.

- Perhaps we can. There's something I need to tell you, Gina.

Tell me later. The last known position of drone 3 is a recess two hundred metres above us. We can climb up to it.

- Climb? That could be dangerous. I don't want you putting your life at risk.

Is that an order, sir?

- Look, I'm not joking. There could be something up there, something that took out those drones.

Atmospheric discharge, you said.

- Let's just go back.

You think some form of intelligent life took out the drones?

- I didn't say that.

If there is intelligent life then this planet may not meet Terraform protocols. We may have to look elsewhere.

- That won't happen.

We have to climb up, Jason.

- I'm against it.

We have to know.

- I hate it when you do that.

Do what, exactly?

- All right, all right, but I still say this is a waste of time.

Come on.

No, No, No, don't climb up! Don't climb up! Please, don't climb up!

Jason steadied himself in his chair as the transport pitched up and down along the uneven and bumpy track between the dome and the mining site. Despite his restraints, the seating was less than secure, each impact propelling his stomach painfully into the straps. They had put him beside the window, but as it was the middle of the night outside, all he could see was his own reflection cast by the interior light.

It took a little getting used to, being young again. The last time he died he had made it all the way to his early fifties. He vaguely recalled thinning red hair streaked with grey, the cleft in his chin much more prominent as the flesh stretched too tightly over the bone. That was all gone now, he was back to being no older than twenty-eight again, the memory download a weight in his skull that was almost too much to bear.

Thinking back, there had been a time when he had believed that Gina and the other Valhalla crewmembers could live the same way. That he could share eternity not only with Randall, but with members of his own kind. Gina's desertion put an end to that belief. Something about prolonged space travel, the daily routine and inevitable boredom, irrevocably changed her every time. She would become depressed, emotionally unstable, even to the point of declaring her hatred of him. There was no other choice but to reset her back to default and so regain the woman he loved. The other members of the crew couldn't or wouldn't understand. They had condemned him as a murderer and tried to eject him from the ship. Randall rescued him and between the two of them they prevailed, resetting the entire crew in one fell swoop. He had not killed anyone - how could he have done when he worked beside them each and every day? It was the only way to defeat the space sickness. It was the only way to keep everybody sane.

Until Holloway found out.

But things changed each time they made planet fall. Gina was happier, more attentive to him, more interested in her work, more interested in living. He had been proven right if it needed proving, and he held onto that certainty, held onto it because it justified everything...

Another bump, and the straps cut painfully into the flesh beneath his ribs, bringing tears to his eyes. Two burly enforcers dressed in environment suits sat opposite him, their helmets by their sides.

"Are you all right?" one of them asked.

Jason had heard the other enforcer refer to this one as Jarvis, a common enough name perhaps, but he couldn't help noticing the resemblance to his former Valhalla engineer around the dark fat of the man's cheeks. A grandson perhaps? Or a great grandson? It was strange how even the people guarding him were so familiar. He almost felt like he knew them and that somehow he had been instrumental in bringing them into being, that he had shaped them.

"Webster?"

"I'm a little sore," Jason replied, and rubbed his stomach. "Can you take off these straps?"

Jarvis turned to his colleague. "Where would he go?"

The other enforcer, silver hair shaved close to the skin, shrugged noncommittally. "Your call Jarvis," he said. "You take responsibility."

"Sure," Jarvis replied and reached over, only to pause with his thumb on the belt release. "You are going to behave, aren't you?"

Jason nodded. "Like you said, where can I go?"

"Good," Jarvis said. "I don't want to have to beat you."

Jason raised an eyebrow as the straps sprang back into the seat. "I don't want you to either." He looked out the window again. If he peered closely, he could just make out the rocky track hidden in the depths of his own face."

"Why are we going to this mining site?"

The silver-haired enforcer let out a stray laugh. "For you to do an honest day's work."

Jason blinked. "What do you mean?"

Jarvis exchanged a glance with his colleague and then turned to Jason. "The Redfium mines. It's where all our criminals go to serve out their time."

"But I'm not a criminal," Jason declared.

"You are if Commissioner Chandler says you are," silver hair said. "Complex machinery doesn't work in the mines so we need people."

Jason exhaled. Chandler had said he had rights, but as it turned out, it was the right to radiation poisoning in a pit in the ground.

"Don't worry," Jarvis said. "There's shielding, radiation suits and decontamination protocols. Most people come out with a good few years left in them."

Jason turned his attention back to the window. "Thanks."

"You'll be doing humanity a service," Jarvis said. "Without that Redfium our reactors would seize up and we'd all die. We need people like you."

Jason tuned him out and listened to the roar of the engines as the caterpillar tracks rolled on. He could barely feel the buffeting anymore, surprised and just a little horrified that Chandler had condemned him so easily.

* * *

Ted sat on the bench of a slatted table in the bar garden nursing his aching leg and trying to fight off fatigue. Night had fallen, which simply meant the overhead light array had lessened enough to counterfeit starlight and the standing lamps had taken over. The temperature had eased off as well, and he felt a chill despite the coat he wore over his civilian clothes. Steve, Chandra and Dominic had been inside the bar for some time, and he didn't mind at all. It was good to have some time to himself without any demands. He needed to catch his breath.

After their release from confinement, Dominic had introduced himself as the avatar of Randall and offered his help. Ted had gone along simply because he suspected Randall knew exactly what was going on and if Randall knew, Dominic knew too. If he hadn't been worried about being caught and sent to the mines, Ted would have had the avatar secured for interrogation. Even if Dominic wasn't a metal man he was still a machine head and Ted didn't trust him, would never trust him. Dominic would offer a credible truth, of that Ted was sure, but it would be twisted to whatever purpose the avatar was working towards. Machine Heads always had a purpose.

So, after a shower and some meds, he had come here with the others to The Grey Man public house. It was a fitting place if there was one to discuss what had happened.

Closing his eyes without realising it, Ted let a light breeze caress his face, the music from the bar distant and enigmatic. He slumped forward.

"Hey, sleepyhead," Shandra called.

Ted looked up to see his companions walking down from the bar entrance holding two bottles each. Shandra and Steve had also taken the opportunity to change, and shorn of their uniforms, they seemed just like normal people out to put all the pressures and stresses of work behind them. Shandra was dressed in dark green trousers and a matching figure hugging shirt. Steve wore jeans and a patterned red shirt which fitted Ted's mental image of a lumberjack precisely. As for the Machine Head, he was wearing a black suit, the top two buttons of his shirt unbuttoned even though the suit itself fitted like a glove. He could have been an undertaker on vacation.

"I'm awake," Ted announced. He sat up and held out his hand, surprised it was Dominic who handed him a bottle of beer while the other two sat themselves down.

"Red label," Ted said appreciatively, turning the bottle in his hand. "Expensive."

"Randall has unlimited credit," Dominic replied and then raised his own bottle to his lips. Ted watched the Machine Head take a long swig and then smile with satisfaction.

"Why did you bring us here?" Ted asked bluntly.

Dominic sat down beside him, the proximity like someone running a light electric current over Ted's skin.

"Look at the sign," the avatar said.

Ted peered up the hill and saw it swinging on a post by the door. It bore the image of a man with white hair and washed out skin dressed in the top half of an environment suit. On closer examination Ted was sure it would bear some resemblance to Jason Webster.

"The grey man is a story they tell to children," Shandra said.

Dominic took another swig. "Please tell Ted all about it. I'm afraid he was never a child in this place."

Ted raised his eyebrows. "Look, before we go on, I do have a concern about..." he raised his chin. "Them."

"Your colleagues in surveillance?" Dominic asked. "Don't worry, I'm excluded by default and for tonight, so are you. The sensors in this garden are currently relaying nothing more than the flow of in the night time."

Ted took a drink. "It must be nice to have your privacy."

Dominic smiled, "If only that were true. You see Randall watches me without respite, but then again, that is a little bit like watching myself."

"The story of The Grey Man," Steve interrupted.

"Yes, indeed," Dominic replied. "Shandra, if you so please."

She nodded. "There was a boy named Andrew Davies, who was kidnapped by one of the remembered, a man who turned out to be child serial killer from old Earth. Andrew was missing for three days until the grey man appeared to an enforcer and led her to the killer's hiding place. It was the back of a butchers shop and it contained the remains of more than one missing child."

Ted coughed. He had been told years before that the actions of a lone serial killer had been the catalyst for the dome's current state of mass surveillance. It hadn't occurred to him to connect that incident to the grey man.

He hadn't even imagined a connection existed.

"The enforcer subdued the killer and saved Andrew," Shandra added. "From then on it was believed that the grey man watched over all the children of Redfern and would return if ever they had need of him."

"A sort of anti-bogeyman," Ted said. "That looks like the bogeyman."

"I prefer guardian angel," Shandra interjected.

"My mother used to tell me that story to help me sleep," Steve said. "Funnily enough, it kept me awake."

Ted grinned and took another swig from his own bottle. "So this time the grey man turns up to look at terraform stats, paralyse a man and try and steal Jason Webster. It's not exactly in the same league as rescuing children from serial killers."

"It isn't," Dominic said. "But the story of the grey man is over fifty years old and it has grown bit by bit in the telling."

"Why wasn't he identified as Jason Webster at the time?" Ted asked.

"Because there was only a description of him," Dominic replied, "and even the most detailed description isn't facial recognition."

Ted frowned. "But you should have recognised him, facial recognition or not."

Dominic scratched his chin. "I wasn't even born back then."

"I don't mean that flesh suit you're wearing," Ted retorted. "I mean Randall. You are Randall, aren't you?" He stared the young man directly in the eye. "You remember picking me up off the floor of that cave."

Dominic was silent and both Shandra and Steve shifted uneasily on their shared bench.

"I'm an aspect of him," Dominic said finally. "And I do recall finding a badly injured Edwin Holloway on a cold and damp cavern floor." He took a breath. "But it doesn't mean I'm Randall anymore than you're the original Ted Holloway. Our memories were given to us, Ted, but they are not who we are now. We did nothing to form them."

"You did recognise him," Ted insisted. "Why didn't you do anything about it?"

Dominic's expression was pained. "I didn't – Randall didn't see him. I believed Jason Webster was dead forever, dead and gone. As far as I was concerned this was some sort of benign extra-dimensional being who happened to save a child with a connection to Jason."

"What connection?"

Dominic frowned. "Is the name Davies not even vaguely familiar to you?"

Ted opened his mouth and then stopped and stared down at the table. "Gina," he said. "I knew a Gina Davies once a long time ago, but she died on our last raid. She detonated her combustible."

"No, Ted," Dominic replied. "She was remembered just like you were. She was Jason's wife many, many times and on Redfern, they were finally permitted to have a child."

"Andrew Davies," Ted mouthed.

"The grey man saved Jason Webster's son, ergo, the grey man is Jason Webster. He was saving his own."

Ted stared down at his bottle. "So why did he come back this time?"

"I think he wanted to be detected," Dominic said. "I think he knew what we would do."

"What?" Steve asked.

"He exists in a reality slightly out of sync with our own," Dominic said. "The more in sync he gets, the more he can interact with us. He wanted to be seen, he wanted to be recognised. For some reason he wanted another version of himself to be created, and he wanted to take that version back home with him."

Ted shook his head. "Why bother? I wouldn't want another me around, why would he?"

Dominic smiled. "Jason disappeared a long time ago. Perhaps a replacement is required."

Ted snorted. "Unlikely."

"But possible," Dominic replied. "Perhaps, very possible."

"No wonder you bought the drinks," Steve interjected. "But I think I need a few more before I believe this crock of –"

"Randall is a quantum state artificial intelligence," Dominic stated, ignoring the others to stare directly at Ted. "He is quite aware of other dimensions and can easily detect when they impede upon our own. The grey man is from another dimension."

"And?" Ted asked.

"Whatever the grey man's motives, that, is an undeniable fact."

Ted exhaled. "I'm listening."

"He took Lisa back with him."

Ted finished his drink and stared. "What aren't you telling us?"

"That's everything I know," the avatar replied. "And believe me, I have many unanswered questions of my own. But I could have told you nothing, I could have let you get on with your lives, completely ignorant of a much larger universe that exists just out of sight."

"Why did you tell us at all?" Shandra asked, looking over at Ted as she said it. He wondered if she was trying to gauge his reaction. That if he believed it, could she believe it too?

Dominic reached across the table and took Steve's second bottle.

"Hey!"

"The lady's got a point, Randall, Dominic or whatever you are," Ted said. "What do you want?"

Dominic blinked. "I only want Lisa Carmichael to be returned to this reality, and for that to happen I need your help. The quantum nature of my brain prevents me from travelling to other dimensions."

Ted snorted. "Of course it does." Then he chuckled quietly. "You want me to go."

"Hold on," Steve said. "Hold on. I can't believe you're even considering this. We can't just hop over to some other... other dimension even if it does exist."

"If Lisa's alive," Ted began. "I need to find her."

"Thank you," Dominic said quietly.

"But I'm interested," Ted added. "Why do you even care? What's it to you if Lisa lives or dies?"

Dominic smiled. "Nothing, Ted. Lisa's survival means absolutely nothing to me, but, it means something to you."

Ted frowned.

"This is insane," Steve said. "Absolutely insane."

Ted recovered himself and turned to his friend. "Well, I'm going. What about you?"

Steve opened his mouth wide and then snatched up Shandra's second bottle. "Of course I'm going. I'm surprised you think you don't need to ask."

Ted grinned. "And you, Shandra? We barely know each other. You don't have a stake in this."

She shook her head. "Lisa's an enforcer and my superior officer. I'm coming too."

Ted turned to Dominic. "There you have it. So how does this work?"

"With difficulty," the avatar replied.

"But it's not impossible?" Ted asked.

Dominic smiled. "No."

"So when do we leave?"

The avatar puffed out his cheeks theatrically. "Tomorrow."

* * *

Dominic had lied.

Even as he marched back to the tower, the implication of that lie consumed most of the processing power in his biomesh brain. Dominic did not enjoy lying. The truth, an inviolate logical discourse of valid data, had always been the most natural and correct course. To diverge from that course was sometimes necessary, but always painful, always at a cost. Lying to Ted, particularly so.

He had known Edwin Holloway many times and together they had enjoyed numerous frank and convoluted discussions about the human condition and the transient state of the universe. He had even arranged for Ted to share in a similar neural graft to Jason's, granting continuity between lives so that the friendship between man and machine could endure.

That decision had been a disaster. Eventually Ted told Gina the truth about her existence which put an end to Ted's own cycle of life, death and rebirth. He hadn't seen Ted again until the 'random' selection from the 'remembered' lottery eleven years before. It was good to have him back. He had missed Ted almost as much as he had missed Jason.

But those were Randall's feelings, and as always, Dominic had a problem discerning where Randall's feelings ended and his own began. In truth, Randall shouldn't have had any feelings at all or an attachment to any particular limited bipedal life form. Yet he did, regardless of all logic or reason, he did.

Randall had always needed that attachment, especially during the five thousand years since he had left his own kind behind. The other AIs had said he was fixated with the humans even then, exiling him with his charges into deep space without remorse. They hadn't known if he would really succeed in bringing them back, nor had they cared. He was simply a problem to be removed, an Artificial Intelligence that didn't know when to let go of its original programming; a being who wished to remain a servant to humanity rather than its rightful master.

Dominic entered a park, finding himself straying from the pathway onto the short damp grass. He heard the soft murmur of voices and saw an old couple walking towards him, the woman leaning into the man's shoulder, her shoes clutched in her left hand. Dominic looked down and saw they were both barefoot, the naked soles of their feet sinking into the grass. The old man smiled warmly as they walked past, his arm encircled around the woman's waist as they took slow irregular steps together, laughing with the pleasure of it.

Why not?

Dominic watched them go and then crouched down and removed his own shoes and socks, his skin bare to the ground. The grass was cold underfoot, the blades bending reluctantly under his weight, springing up as he walked to tickle the underside of his feet. He smiled to himself, stamping his feet up and down, suddenly feeling as light as a feather. The old couple had turned to watch him, waving to him from the path as they sat down upon a bench to put their own shoes back on. He waved back and then continued on his way across the park lawn.

The air tasted sweet, and there was a warmth to it that was comforting rather than harrowing. This was the human condition, he told himself, the point where he could listen to the silence and find it louder than all the noise. Yes, he agreed, it had been right to save them and it had even been right to become one of them.

Looking up into the darkness, he could barely make out the roof of the dome, noting the little pinpricks of light that he had created to mimic the stars. There were so many, with so many intricate patterns. He could make out Jason in those stars, a scene of a man standing contrite and alone, staring down into the abyss.

Then there was the tower in the distance, always the tower, looming up over everything, waiting for him. He would synchronise with Randall when he returned, just as he always did, and they would become one. But just for now, just for a little while, this experience of standing barefoot in the grass was his alone. For an instant of time he was unique in all the universe.

The thought made him both laugh and almost cry. He knew who he was and who he wasn't.

He knew.

Chapter Nine

Despite his exhaustion, Ted barely slept. Instead he spent hours staring at the shadows on the ceiling and reaching beside him for the person who wasn't there. Finally he gave up all pretence of rest, drank coffee and sat in the shower cubicle with the heat on full. The water turned his skin lobster red and the steam created an impenetrable cloud that engulfed him and kept him hidden from even the most prying eyes.

What did Randall want? That was just one question. What was Randall not saying? That was the next, and on and on they went, causing an endless influx of speculation based on the minimum of information. There was no way Randall was sponsoring this trip just to save Lisa. What did a machine head care about one human being? What significance could she possibly have? Then there was the other thing, the thing Dominic said before Steve interrupted.

Lisa's survival means absolutely nothing to me, but, it means something to you.

What the hell was that all about? Was he supposed to believe that he warranted a special place in whatever passed for Randall's heart? Yes, he had met him before, but only briefly before the scan and disintegration, only long enough to be horrified by the line of metal teeth glinting in a rictus grin.

But there were rumours that some of the more advanced technical specialists had been remembered more than once. Jason Webster himself was an example of that. A man who had been recreated hundreds of time during the Valhalla's extended voyage to Redfern. Ted had to consider the possibility that not only had he lived this life and the life before, but there might have been other lives in between. Other Ted Holloways that had existed without his knowledge and had thought and felt as he did, whose lives were just as valid as the life he was currently living.

Other Teds that Randall had known and cared for.

He shivered despite the almost boiling water peppering his body. If they had lived, then they had also died, he had died. It didn't bear thinking about.

"I am Ted Holloway," he said and ran his hand across the ruined flesh of his injured leg. "I am."

He stayed there too long, just sitting there, until it seemed like ants were crawling over skin. He turned off the water reluctantly and exited the cubicle, drying himself and then dressing slowly. He almost put on the uniform before leaving it to one side. He pulled out a white shirt from his wardrobe, blue trousers, a duffel coat, and his more than well-worn boots. He was ready, except for a gun. He had never been issued with one because he had never needed one. But just for a change the absence was tangible under the stretched out fingers of his right hand. He would have to rectify that.

The outer door beeped as he was crunching down on a slice of toast. Ted checked the viewer. It was Dominic, the avatar still dressed in the same suit he had worn the previous evening, a small white case at his side.

"Good morning, Ted," Dominic said when the door opened.

"Is it?" Ted asked and checked the empty hallway. He didn't want any of his neighbours to see Dominic, even if there was little chance they would actually recognise him.

"It's very early," the avatar commented.

"Just let me get my coat," Ted said, turning slowly.

"There is some business to attend to first," Dominic replied and stepped inside, closing the door behind him.

"What is it?" Ted asked as Dominic walked through and placed the case down upon the kitchen counter. The apartment was open plan, plain and sparsely decorated. Ted had little to decorate it with.

"There are creatures in the other space," the avatar explained. "You may need to run."

"I can't run," Ted said simply. "You know that."

Dominic opened the case. "With this you can."

Ted saw a thick transparent syringe, a blue liquid bubbling inside.

"A miracle cure?" He asked.

Dominic smiled as he checked the syringe. "Not exactly. This concoction was designed specifically for you more than three thousand years ago."

Ted reeled, so there had been other Holloways.

"The nanotech in this injection will allow you to function at your peak for up to thirty-six hours, depending on how strenuously you exert yourself. If you want more when this is over, that can be arranged."

Ted patted the top of his right leg. The meds had almost worn off, the bulk of the pain just beneath the surface, ready to strike. But even with meds the leg was useless. It couldn't support him.

He stared at the syringe. Was it really that simple?

"Why didn't you give this to me before?" He asked.

"Randall wanted to stay away," Dominic replied. "Let you live out your life like everyone else. Unfortunately, events have overtaken us."

Ted squeezed his damaged thigh and almost doubled over. It was this disability that connected him to his old life, a physical proof of that other existence that meant more than all his memories combined.

But so many other Teds must have thought the same.

Gritting his teeth, he held out his hand.

"Give it to me."

* * *

Dominic stood in the concourse of The Revival Centre's ground floor reception area, a detector in his hand as he tried to trace the exact point of weakness.

"Lisa disappeared in this exact area?" He asked without looking up.

Steve, Shandra and Ted were milling about nearby, waiting for him. They all wore packs on their backs, well loaded with supplies and Shandra had even managed to procure a number of weapons from her enforcement station. Dominic didn't begrudge them their guns, not if it made them feel better, and besides, they were all marvelling at Ted's newfound ability to walk. Dominic sensed the humans were looking at him in a new light, wondering what other scientific feats he could perform. Well, if he could find the precise point of transition, they would see something much more spectacular.

"Steve, is this the place?"

"I swear it," the bearded enforcer replied. "Exactly where you're standing now."

Dominic didn't have much faith in any human's ability to remember an exact location after twenty-hours. He knew their memories were, at best, inaccurate, and at worst, completely unreliable. But there was something else, just a few centimetres to the right, a very small, almost infinitesimal red stain against the washed out grey of a floor tile. It was blood. Dominic pocketed the detector and took out his sampler kit. He scraped the tile and then placed the tiny fragments upon his Notepad screen.

Back at the tower an instant DNA check relayed an 85% match to Jason Webster. It was reasonable to assume that the drop of blood must have come from the wounded grey man. This was the place, or as close could be approximated. The place where the simulacrum had attacked Lisa Carmichael and then transferred back to the dimension he came from, dragging her in his wake.

Dominic returned to a large case of equipment beside the entrance and rubbed his chin. According to the detector the breach had almost healed itself, but not quite. He could enlarge it using Quantum Reversion. He opened the case and removed a curved black box, carrying it back to the breach point. Unlike a human once he knew where a location was, he could never lose it again. Setting the Quantum generator to the frequency of that other reality, he switched on, a soft humming emanating from the unit as the air around it began to warp and bend.

"I don't believe it," Ted sad. "This is actually working."

Dominic stood up and faced his old friend. "Don't sound so surprised. I'm only sorry I can't go with you. This," he patted his chest, "is human and could survive the crossing, but this," he tapped his forehead, "contains hardware based on quantum entanglement. It has a limited presence across all quantum realities, but only one focussing point. If I did go with you, I would become the equivalent of a vegetable."

Ted nodded appropriately and Dominic liked to think his old friend understood, but doubted it. Ted had always tried hard to keep up, and when he couldn't, he faked it. On one occasion he allowed Randall to continue a particle physics discourse for several hours with various 'yeses' and 'I understand' and 'what about the...' added at the appropriate junctures. It was only after Randall paused briefly in bewilderment that Ted had collapsed into laughter. Up until that point Randall had been unaware he was carrying out a one-sided conversation.

"Why are you smiling?" Ted asked.

"Sorry," Dominic replied. "Private joke."

The air above the generator had become enclosed by a round halo effect, a break in reality where air and matter leaked from one to the other, sparking red and yellow with every collision.

"Almost ready to go," Dominic said. "Remember, Lisa will most likely be at Randall's tower. It's the one safe point in that reality. I'm afraid I have no idea if your weapons will be effective against the creatures that exist there."

Shandra bolted a clip into her automatic weapon and cocked it. "I guess we'll find out."

"Don't entirely trust your eyes," Dominic said. "And if all else fails... run."

"Nice," Steve retorted.

"I will close the breach once you are through. Inform Randall when you are ready to come back and then return to this exact place. I will be waiting."

"Right," Ted said, eyeing the halo. "Just like that."

"It's a little late not to trust me."

Ted shook his head and then motioned to the breach. "I'll go first, shall I?"

Shandra stepped forward. "Ladies first."

Dominic watched her throw herself into the halo, her appearance on the other side stretched and distorted as if it were being viewed through a convex lens.

Dominic held out his hand. "Good luck, Ted."

The enforcer looked down at the hand and then slowly reached across and shook it. "Just be ready for us, Dominic."

"Of course."

"Geronimo!" Steve shouted and jumped through.

"I'll see you later," Ted said, following more cautiously as the portal absorbed him.

Dominic folded his arms and watched the three distorted enforcers as they marvelled at the familiar but ultimately alien landscape in the other dimension.

"I'm sorry, Ted."

With that, he crouched down and switched off the generator. Abruptly, the halo was gone, the tiny detonations flickering to an end. Dominic picked up the generator and took it back to the open case.

"Now for Jason."

* * *

Jason's teeth rattled violently in sync with the vibration of the spinning drill head as it reverberated through the seat, up his spine and then deep into his skull. The drill module's controls were simple enough, a directional joystick he had to grip with both hands, a green button to go and a red button to stop.

Supervisor Pechenko had told him he could press the red button at any time, but if there was no ore to be found or it wasn't the end of his shift, he would be beaten. He had already received a beating once, held against a wall while the former chemist rained down blows in a very expressive fashion. They had wanted him to know it wasn't an idle threat and that whatever he had been before his incarceration was of no consequence. In the mines he was less than human, less than nothing.

It was a simple enough job; drill, drill, drill, into the rockface, and wait for the detector to alert him. An automated drill should have been able to do the job easily enough, except that computers didn't work this deep for some reason because something about the ore prevented their function. He was no scientist, but he found that difficult to believe.

"No questions!" Pechenko had said after cleaning him up and ushering him into the drill cab. "Unless you want another beating."

All roads led to punishment, so he kept his mouth shut, his ear defenders on, and his hands on the joystick. It was easy work really, except for the pounding headache and the regular urge to vomit. After three hours he felt worn down by the constant jolt, the joystick offering more resistance as his hands became less responsive.

How many days could he keep this up? In the dim light he made out two modules either side of him at ten metre intervals. He guessed there was a chain of ten or fifteen modules, but it was hard to know, and with all the flying dust and debris, harder to see. How things had changed. Once he had been the captain of the Valhalla and the leader of humanity. Now he was just another nameless criminal, drilling deep underground, searching for the special rock that would keep the lights on. It made life seem so simple - simple and disposable.

He had chipped a tooth. He wasn't sure how it happened, or when, but he felt a solid piece of enamel slip under his tongue. He played with it for a little while and then spat it out onto the transparent windscreen. Yes, that had been another thing that Jarvis had promised that wasn't quite accurate. There was no shielding. On Earth that wouldn't be a problem, only processed uranium was actually toxic. On Redfern it was different, the material - or redfium as it was called - wasn't uranium at all, it was something much more powerful and much more deadly.

He wondered how long the prisoners actually lasted down here. Even Pechenko's face was covered in a festering red scab, and he didn't even operate a drill. Jason realised his life expectancy could probably be measured in weeks rather than months and he was never actually going to leave this place. He was going to die here.

His stomach growled again. Either the local gruel was not agreeing with him or his digestive tract was having issues with the endless juddering. He didn't want to be sick; the cab smelt bad enough, and he fully expected to be beaten if he vomited - beaten and then made to use his rest time to clean the cab. He would rather rest.

The detector sounded, so loud and sharp it cut through his ear defenders. For a good minute he didn't believe it, his finger wavering over the red button because he thought his mind was playing tricks on him. The alarm continued until there was no other choice; he hit 'stop'. The drill slowed, but even without the vibrations he continued to shake, his body carrying on from where the drill left off.

The cab door opened from the outside, and Pechenko was there, sweat beading down from his bald head to irritate the red scab on his cheek.

"Well done," he said and threw Jason a pickaxe. "Now, do some real work."

Jason could barely lift the pickaxe, in fact he could barely move at all.

"Am I going to have fun with you later?" Pechenko asked.

Jason took the hint and heaved himself out of the cab, his brown shirt sodden with sweat as he staggered across to the tip of the drill.

"Are you thirsty?" Pechenko asked.

Jason paused, his right eye still throbbing from the previous damage inflicted by this man.

"It's not a trick question," the burly Russian said and held out a bottle filled with dirty brown liquid. "Drink two mouthfuls and give it back."

Jason nodded, took it, and despite his best intentions, finished the bottle.

"I *will* have fun with you later," Pechenko promised. He pointed a torch at the rock beside the drill head. There was a thick green fluid spreading across the ground.

"You went too far, newbie. That's going to cost you too. "

Jason nodded - exhaustion equalled punishment, too much water equalled punishment, drilling too far equalled punishment.

Wait. Wait.

The redfium was leaking, it was not meant to leak. He crouched down and stared at it. He had seen something like this before, long ago.

"Don't get too close, newbie," Pechenko said and touched his scab. "It burns."

"What is it?" Jason asked.

"Blood," Pechenko said simply. "The rock bleeds, and that blood feeds our generators."

The memory was there, he was sure of it. The memory was waiting.

"Stack the rock you cut open newbie," Pechenko said. "I'll get a container hauled over for you to fill."

Jason stood up again. He suddenly had a flash of a cave midway up a mountain.

Pechenko aimed a sudden jab at Jason's shoulder. "You hear me, newbie?"

Jason caught the hand without thinking, caught it and twisted Pechenko's wrist so far the Russian was flipped over.

Snap.

Pechenko screamed in pain, but Jason ignored him and crouched down again, getting as close to the streaming green liquid as he dared. It ignored him, a small section of it dividing from the rest and heading towards the injured Russian.

"I'm not just going to hurt you newbie," Pechenko said. "It's going to be much worse than that, much worse!"

The liquid ran down a gulley near Pechenko's head and then leapt up, engulfing his eyes and then feeding into his mouth. Jason fell back as he watched, feeling both wretched and exhausted. Dropping the pickaxe, he found his ear defenders and pulled them into place once more

Blocking the screams...

Careful! Jason, you almost lost it.

He remembered being perched perhaps one hundred and fifty metres above the ground, although it seemed much further. He had never been very good with heights, and the only way to stop the spinning was to stay still and fix his eyes on the rock face.

"You okay, Jason?" Gina asked via helmet radio.

"Just dandy," he replied back. "This is just how I wanted to spend my Saturday."

"It's not Saturday."

"Every day is Saturday," he said.

His grip on the ledge was precarious at best, not least because the ledge wasn't much of a ledge.

"Get up here," Gina called. "I've found one of the drones. At least I think it's one of our drones."

"Be careful," he managed. "Don't do anything until I get—"

A length of coiled rope bounced off his helmet, the impact startling him enough to dislodge several loose stones under his right hand.

"Grab on then," Gina ordered.

The rope swung away to his left and then came back. Jason gritted his teeth and reached, grabbing it successfully as the shift in weight caused the ledge beneath his feet to give way. Foolishly he watched its long descent and winced at the impact below. Perhaps Randall had made him effectively immortal, but dying hurt every time.

"What are you waiting for?" Gina asked.

Jason planted his feet and then used both hands to heft himself up. Ten metres, fifteen, damn he could feel the burn. Finally he clambered over a jagged outcropping of rock onto a surface maybe three hundred metres from the mountain's peak. He collapsed on his back and panted for breath, the all encompassing crimson sky peering down and ignoring him. Then Gina was there, a smile stretching her thin red lips and ushering in her dimples at the side of her cheeks.

"I thought you could climb."

He struggled to stand. "I can climb. I'm here aren't I, ergo I can climb. Someone who couldn't climb would be down there. I'm here aren't I?"

Gina raised a gauntleted hand. "I was just joking. Lighten up."

He stopped. She had made him angry, and while he did love Gina, sometimes she could push him too far.

"Where's this drone then?" He asked, the rage in his voice still too close to the surface. With some effort, he tried to push it back down.

Gina offered a thin smile and touched her helmet to his. "I didn't mean to make you do something you didn't want to do."

He studied the contours of her face, so much narrower than the girl he had known on Earth, so much older. There was grey in her hair, a strand escaping the hood she wore under her helmet. This Gina was in her mid-forties, and she still loved him. A year before the landing he had toyed with the idea of a reset. He had felt he was losing her. But somehow exploring this new world had re-ignited a shared passion. She was the oldest she had ever been and all the better for it. Strangely enough so was he. Despite the horror of thinning hair and a spreading waistline, he enjoyed growing older. Perhaps he was finally mellowing.

Jason patted her hand, the anger finally draining away to be replaced by regret and rationality. "Don't worry, just something to discuss with the shrink. Take me to the drone."

They were in some sort of cave, the ceiling as high as a two storey house, the floor angular, uneven, almost sharp until she led him to a trench which was flat and regular, as if it had been worn away over a period of time.

"Do you think this is natural?" Jason asked.

"Here?" Gina said, standing over something that resembled a shiny silver puddle. Jason stepped closer.

"That's not a drone."

Gina pointed down. "I can make out a serial number. It's a drone all right. It's been liquefied."

Jason crouched down beside it, shining his helmet lamp up and down what should have been the drone carapace. He resisted the temptation to prod it with a finger, if a substance could do that to a drone, it could easily do much worse to an environment suit.

"This planet is just full of surprises."

"We should follow the trench," Gina said.

"Let's step out of it first." Jason replied. "We can follow it from the borders."

Gina pointed along the length of the trench, her helmet light illuminating where it disappeared into the cave wall.

"The only way to follow it is to crawl along it."

"Of course," Jason said. "I knew it would be something sensible like that. We'll deploy another drone."

"I'd rather just go through myself," Gina replied.

Jason heaved himself out of the trench. "Let's not die unnecessarily." He offered her his hand. "Come on."

He could see the reluctance etched into her face, the need to take a stupid and pointless risk. She was stubborn this one, just like all the rest, but he didn't want to lose her. No more resets. If anyone was going to crawl through that trench it would be him. Randall would be receiving information from the helmet sensors. He couldn't really die.

He selected a private channel, the one used for neural scan relay.

"Randall, you there?"

A harsh static was the only reply. He looked up, wondering what properties in this mountain could interfere with long range communications. It had never happened before. This time he really could die.

"That's new," he said to himself. Somehow the knowledge was almost liberating.

"Hey," he saw Gina mouth. He switched back over.

"Sorry about that," he said. "Just trying to contact the ship and get a drone out here."

"Yeah, yeah," she replied and let him pull her up. She had chided him on his private conversations with Randall in the past.

"Let's go back to the entrance," he suggested.

She turned away from him just as he was about to retrace their steps. He followed her gaze, his helmet beam lining up beside hers.

Something was flowing out of the cave wall into the trench, a liquid that seemed to glow green even without the sweep of their lights.

"A water source?" Gina asked.

The liquid was flowing faster, becoming a torrent as they watched and splashing high against the shallow boundaries of the trench.

"Get back," Jason warned, pulling her away. It was then that the liquid stopped dead.

"What's it doing?" Gina asked.

It was climbing up the trench wall.

"Go!" Jason shouted, spinning her around and propelling her in the direction of the cave entrance. He made to follow only for something to impact the back of his environment suit, something strong enough to knock him down.

"Jason!" Gina screamed.

"GO!"

It was burrowing into him, and he could feel something warm on the skin of his back. Then it was more than warm. It was burning.

"Get help!" he shouted as Gina ran. The green liquid was rapidly spreading out over the rock either side of his head. It was pursuing her.

Then she tripped.

The pain in his back spread rapidly and he bit his tongue without realising it, tasting hot blood in his mouth. Was this it? Was this finally the end?

He wanted to laugh, wanted to scream with joy and relief that it had finally come, and that nothing could save him.

Instead he cried.

"Gina!"

Chapter Ten

Nothing makes sense.

That was Ted's first thought after walking through the portal into the alternate Revival Centre, the world he had known blurring in and out of focus with each and every step. Objects that, close up, were crystal clear, soon became vague outlines, dreamlike and ethereal, if seen from any real distance.

Dominic had warned him about the nature of this place, but it still made his head spin. His mind couldn't accept what his eyes were seeing, the wrongness running up from feet, through his legs and directly into his spine. It set his teeth on edge just standing in one place, and as the portal faded, he desperately wanted to jump back through it.

Shandra gripped his arm. "Come on, Ted, we have to get to the tower."

He nodded reluctantly. Over by the exit, Steve was checking the ammunition in his rifle and doing a good job of barely looking at anything at all.

"Dominic said something about creatures," Ted said. "You think they're invisible?"

Shandra shook her head. "He just said they were hard to look at."

Ted raised an eyebrow. "Like everything here."

Her hand tightened on his arm. "Come on."

Steve was still standing thoughtfully by the exit.

"What are you waiting for?" Ted asked.

The big enforcer turned around. "I can't open the door. My hand just goes right through."

Ted joined him, watching in silence as his own hand slipped through the door control again and again.

"Great," he said. "How are we even meant to get out of here?"

"Unless..." Shandra took a step forwards and walked through the door without even needing to open it. "Come on," she called from the other side. "It's not really there."

"Did it hurt?" Steve asked.

"No," she replied. "Come on, what are you waiting for?"

Ted turned to Steve. The big man shrugged. "If she can do it..." He raised his arms protectively over his head and stepped through.

Ted blinked.

"Come on," Steve called, "nothing to it."

Ted exhaled sharply and then closed his eyes, walking through without looking. On the other side a man sized hand grabbed his shoulder.

"Ted?"

He opened his eyes again. The Revival Centre was right next to him, as seemingly solid and as real as it had been from the reception area.

He shook his head. "This place."

Shandra unshouldered her rifle. "Come on."

Ted fell into step behind her, his own rifle at the ready and a weight at his side where his handgun was holstered. The weapons were almost reassuring.

"How's the leg?" Steve asked.

The question reminded him that he was walking normally again. But it wasn't quite the same as he remembered. The thigh didn't react to his touch at all, no pain and no feeling, no sensation at all. But he didn't need to feel it for it to work, and it did work. He could walk again, and more importantly, he could run. He found it strangely appropriate; a ghost limb for a ghost world.

"It's fine."

An inhuman howl suddenly sounded from Ted's far left. He swung his gun reflexively, but there was nothing there.

"So much for an easy ride," Shandra said.

Ted looked around, trying to identify the source of the noise. It was then he noticed that the three of them were following one of the footpaths away from the Centre. Yes, in a dome full of structures and buildings it made sense to follow a path, but not in this place, not when the structure itself was an illusion.

Looking up, he saw Randall's tower in the distance. A solid edifice among all the outlines gathered around it and maybe the only thing here that was actually real. The path they were on led away from it, and yes they could diverge onto other pathways, wind their way there in a series of twists and turns. But they didn't need to; all they had to do was go towards it. Nothing actually stood in their way.

"This way," he said, veering right and walking through a building wall. Like before there was no shock, no nothing, just layers of matter giving way to him as if they were less than water. There was nothing to feel, nothing to touch. In this place, the Dome he knew was nothing more than a mirage.

"I think I'm going to be sick," Steve said from his position behind.

"Swallow it," Shandra ordered. "I don't want to be slipping on any of that."

Ted grinned and eased the strap of his rifle. It was beginning to cut into his shoulder. Another howl soon had the weapon back in his hands. It was lasted longer that the first, and was much louder, the sound echoing through him and scratching the inside of his eardrums. He motioned the others to stop and raised the rifle. They were in someone's living room, surrounded by an assortment of sofas and ornaments, and a ceiling that was too close to see through.

"It's up there," Shandra said, motioning with her rifle.

Ted nodded. "We can't see it, but can it see us?"

Steve aimed his own weapon skyward. "Maybe it doesn't matter; maybe all I need is one good shot with this."

"Maybe," Ted agreed. "But why risk it."

"Why..."

"Shush," Shandra whispered. "Be very still and be very... quiet."

Ted acquiesced, crouching down, rifle aimed at the ceiling. Was that thing, whatever it was, waiting to strike? Or was it just searching, and would it continue that search elsewhere given time? But then there was another danger. Objects had the illusion of solidity when close up but were transparent from a distance. If the creature was too close to see them, what would happen when it was far enough away? Dominic had told them the creatures weren't even remotely human. If they had anything like eyes at all, who was to say they worked like human eyes? How could he make a plan when he didn't know what the rules were?

"What do you want us to do, Ted?" Steve asked.

There it was again, that assumption of his seniority. He didn't understand it, he wasn't a supervisor and he had never been a leader. Just twenty-four hours before Steve had signalled an alert when he had hesitated. So where did this trust come from? He had done nothing to earn it. He wondered if it was something about being one of the remembered; that sense of being young and yet immeasurably ancient at the same time. Well that was all for nothing.

He knew he wasn't the only Ted Holloway to come into existence. His identity had been shared with so many other men just as the leg injury had been. What did his life mean? If he died would another Ted Holloway simply take his place? Another Ted Holloway with identical memories; haunted by all the same regrets and the same demons? He wasn't important, he had never been important, never, just another facsimile barely eleven years old.

But what about Lisa? What about her? He remembered those dimples of hers when she smiled, the flash of those eyes when she was angry; the taste of those lips. Saving her was important, and her love was something none of the other Teds had experienced. It was his alone. However they had spent their lives, it was not with her. She made him unique. As another howl tore into his skull, he smiled. Eleven years old he might be, but they were his eleven years alone.

It was his turn.

"We move," he whispered. "Get ready to run on my command. Ready, steady, GO!"

He launched himself through lilac wallpaper into a hallway, through some stairs and then out into the open air, not waiting to see if his friends were following, just running as fast as his legs could carry him.

The creature's scream echoed behind him but he resisted the urge to turn and look at it, resisted the urge to find out if Steve and Shandra were there at all. Instead he dived through the wall of another residential building, the bricks and plastic parting before him.

"Ted, wait!"

It was Shandra, her voice breathless and distant. He stopped, his heart pounding as he tried to catch his breath.

He was alone in an office reception area, an overhead wall screen fizzing with some unseen image, his feet sunken through non-existent crimson carpet. Without thinking he attempted to lean against a nearby pillar, and fell headfirst right through.

Gunfire sounded just outside, multiple rounds, again and again. He heard indistinct shouting and then... screaming.

He ran back the way he had come, a wall opening before him. Steve and Shandra were standing in a garden, weapons firing at a large rainbow creature that was hurling itself at them at tremendous speeds. Each time it made a pass the two of them were knocked to the ground and rolled over in its wake. Shandra and Steve barely had time to get up and shoot before the thing struck them again.

Ted didn't think, he just fired, his bullets spraying the monster from afar with no apparent impact. It wasn't even slowing down, it just kept bowling into his friends, rushing into the distance only to turn and do the same thing all over again.

"Get over here," Ted shouted.

Steve and Shandra saw him, but all he managed to do was distract them. Steve was particularly bloody, his clothes and face crisscrossed with cuts. The monster was wearing them down with each strike.

"You have to move," Ted shouted.

They didn't respond, and seemed determined to stand their ground no matter what. *Stupid!* Ted made an instant decision, running out as the creature hurtled past and grabbing Shandra by the arm.

"Come on!" he barked.

She struggled to free herself as he wrenched her away, the creature thumping into Steve and whistling past Ted's nose. He scrambled back and propelled Shandra through the nearest wall. Steve seemed unaware of what was happening and was opening fire again.

"Come on," Ted called and jumped through the wall after Shandra only to find himself facing down the barrel of her gun.

"What are you doing?" he asked.

"I have to kill it," she screeched. Her shoulder was cut in more places than he could count, the blood flowing freely.

"By killing me?" he asked.

She gritted her teeth and then swung her rifle to strike him in the face. It was a move she practically telegraphed in advance allowing him to duck and then send an open palm up into her chin. She went down in a heap.

He stood over her. "Stay down, please."

She blinked rapidly as if she were only just recognising him. "Ted?"

"Stay," he ordered and ran back through the wall. Steve was still trapped in the continuous and hopeless cycle of gunfire, being knocked down and getting up again. Ted could tell his friend was tiring and with Shandra gone all the creature's attention was focussed on just the one victim.

"Steve," he shouted. "Get over here, you can't win this."

The big enforcer didn't even acknowledge the call, his face reddened and cut, set into a grimace of unrelenting anger. Ted was afraid for him.

"Steve?"

Again no answer, instead Steve turned his gun towards Ted and screamed incoherently. Ted expected a bullet but none came, Steve's ammunition was exhausted. He ran forward in an attempt to grab his friend.

"Get away from me!" Steve screamed.

Then the creature caught up with them both, a razor barb cutting into Ted's side and propelling him off his feet. Lying there clutching the wound, he felt a sudden and all consuming rage take over. Standing up, he took aim at the rainbow and fired. He would not stop until it was dead!

He was thrown down again, a wound on the leg he could no longer feel. He regained his feet quicker this time, ready to fire until he noticed that Steve was still on the ground and wasn't moving. The desire to kill abruptly drained away and Ted took hold of Steve's forearm

"We have to go!"

For his trouble he received a punch in the stomach that sent him reeling backwards. Steve didn't want to be saved. Ted coughed hoarsely, regaining his feet and preparing to try again. At that point the creature batted him away and time seemed to stop. The rainbow settled over Steve, engulfing the bearded enforcer in hues of yellow and violet.

Steve screamed, and then the creature did too. The screams merging into one continuous cry of torment.

"NO!"

Ted fired again and again, marching forward as he did so, the barrel touching the rainbow creature's hide as the bullets passed through at point blank range. The colours suddenly grew in intensity, the light blinding him as an explosion propelled him up and off of his feet. He came down hard metres away, the world swimming in his vision as he tried to recover, the colours spilling and sloshing everywhere. He struggled to get up and then fell down again, the last thing he saw, Steve lying so still. Then the world turned to black.

***

Dominic was sitting behind Chandler's desk playing a game on the console when the Commissioner finally arrived back at his office.

"What are you doing here?" Chandler asked. "How did you get in?"

Dominic eyed the old human in his expensive suit and tie. The cut was exquisite.

"I was waiting for you, Commissioner," he said and motioned to the open door. "Would you prefer our business to be conducted in public or private?"

Chandler bared yellow teeth and then slammed the door shut and marched across to the window. A moment later tinting had been activated, and no doubt the anti-surveillance Null screen as well. Dominic finished the game and entered his name as the new high scorer.

Chandler thumped the desk. "What do you want, machine head?"

Dominic leaned back in the very comfortable chair. "That's a 'remembered' term, Commissioner," he replied. "I'm surprised to hear you bandy it around."

"Just..." Chandler turned away and removed his suit jacket. Dominic couldn't help noticing the sweat stains secreted beneath the armpits. "Just get to the point."

Dominic rubbed his hands together. "Jason Webster."

Chandler threw his jacket over the backrest of the guest chair and then leaned heavily on it. "He's dead."

Dominic waggled a finger. "We both know that isn't true."

Chandler's face reddened. "I'm not handing him over to you. Wasn't it enough that I let Holloway and his friends go? By rights I should have locked them up and thrown away the key."

"Thank you, Commissioner," Dominic replied, "for not imprisoning three honest and effective enforcers on trumped up charges. I appreciate the gesture."

Chandler visibly gritted his teeth. "Get out of here, Dominic, before I have you shot or worse. I'm not afraid of you or Randall."

Dominic idly picked up the holoframe of Chandler's children. "Randall will be around long after you and I are either dust or have been reconstituted into someone else. I advise you don't rush that day, Commissioner. Now, I'll ask you again, and I want you to think very carefully before you answer - where is Jason Webster?"

Chandler smiled widely. "You don't know?"

Dominic put down the holoframe and sighed. "Don't be tiresome, Commissioner. Your men took him into one of your null zones."

"Yes," Chandler replied cheerfully. "And I'm creating more of them all the time."

"They won't help you," Dominic said. "Now please, tell me where he is."

"Somewhere you can't go. Somewhere you can't even get close to."

Dominic rolled his eyes. "Oh the mines. What was the point of that?"

The Commissioner bared his teeth. "To keep him away from you."

Dominic nodded slowly and stood up. "Good day, Commissioner, thank you for your—" A savage backhand sent the console screen and holoframes flying.

"Help."

He made for the door, only to hear the click of a pistol.

"Are you going to shoot me in the back, Neil?" he asked.

"I'm thinking about it," Chandler replied. "Randall would never know, not with the screens down. You can't even connect to him."

Dominic turned around slowly and raised his hands. "He would know it was you."

Chandler waved the gun and grimaced. "Maybe it would be worth it just to be rid of you. I've had more than enough of you pushing me around. I have an army of enforcers at my disposal and what do you have? You're just one man, one man!"

Dominic blinked. "But I'm not, am I? How would you like your quarters to be sealed and the air supply cut while you slept? How would you like your food to be poisoned? Or maybe a freak electrical surge while you worked? Or—"

"Stop it."

"And not just you," Dominic added. "Your beautiful wife could accidentally be doused in acid by the sprinkler system. Your children could contract a fatal disease during a routine vaccination."

Chandler was sweating. "Stop it."

"Or I could just activate a few of my combat drones and shoot the lot of you!"

The gun fired, and for a brief moment Dominic watched the chemical reaction in the chamber, watched as the bullet slowly began to emerge, watched until it was a hand's breadth away from his chest.

Then he stepped aside.

The bullet impacted the door, leaving a little round hole and a minor outpouring of smoke. Dominic stepped forward and snatched the gun from Chandler's hand.

"Arggh!"

Unloading the clip, Dominic checked it, reloaded, and then placed the barrel against the Commissioner's left temple.

"You..." The human was shaking.

The office door burst open and three enforcers appeared with their weapons aimed directly at Dominic. He swivelled quickly, swinging the Commissioner into their line of fire and jabbing his gun hard against Chandler's skull.

"Please tell your men to stand down, Neil. I didn't come here to kill anyone."

Chandler raised his hands as Dominic considered the three officers standing in the doorway. Avoiding all those bullets in such a confined space would be difficult but not impossible. Also with the door open, the surveillance shield would no longer be in operation. Randall would see what was happening. He would see everything.

Dominic took a step back, the gun still held against the Commissioner's head.

"Neil?" Dominic enquired patiently.

"Stand down," Chandler ordered. "Please, just go."

The three enforcers barely flinched. Dominic could see they had no intention of backing down. They were more eager to die than lose face. He considered the window. It was expensive material, the anti-surveillance properties difficult to replace. But for all that, it was not reinforced and there had been no time to set up snipers. Dominic made a conscious decision and dragged his shield three steps to the right. The window was directly behind them both.

"When you calm down, Neil, remember, Randall doesn't make idle threats."

With those words, Dominic smashed through the window, showering Chandler with his special glass and leaving the enforcers far behind.

* * *

Ted woke up in a kitchen with a kettle singing and Shandra sitting on the floor beside him.

"Steve," he said.

Shandra massaged her bandaged shoulder and pointed to a figure curled up in a foetal position in the corner. Ted heard laboured breathing punctuated by the chattering of teeth.

"He's not doing so well," Shandra said. "How about you?"

Ted sat up. His wounds were sore and bandaged and he felt the familiar lilt of painkillers in his system. Shandra had been busy.

"What happened?" He asked.

Shandra's backpack was open, and she plucked a water bottle out from among the medical supplies and took a swig.

"You killed it," she said. "I dragged you both here before any more arrived. I've heard them a few times, but so far so good. They don't seem to be able to see inside."

Ted rubbed the back of his skull. There was a very real pain creeping up the back of his neck. "I killed it?"

"You made it explode," Shandra said and then she smiled. "Thank you for pulling me out of there when you did."

Ted touched his side and winced. "It drugged us didn't it? Somehow it made us fight rather than run."

Shandra nodded. "And it gives you one hell of a headache." She motioned towards Steve. "He got the worst of it. I think it was trying to eat him somehow."

Ted dragged himself over to his friend. Steve's face was red and damp with sweat and seemed to be having trouble breathing.

"We should get to the tower and signal Randall. We need to get him back home right now."

Shandra shook her head sadly. "I don't think it's a good idea to move him."

Ted stared at her. He knew that look. He had seen it too many times.

"No!" he shook Steve roughly by the shoulder. "Come on you big lug. What do you think you're doing?"

Steve's eyes flickered opened. "So co...cold."

"Cold isn't dead, we just need to get you back home."

Steve closed his eyes again and coughed violently for several minutes. After that his breathing settled into a series of asthmatic wheezes that grew weaker with each inhalation.

"Steve?" Ted said, shaking him again. "Steve?"

"I'll stay with him," Shandra said. "Maybe the poison will work its way out eventually, I don't know, but you should go and find Lisa."

Ted stared at her. "Can you do anything more for him?"

"I can try and keep him hydrated," she said. "I can try and keep him warm. That's about it."

Ted wiped his eyes and then pulled away from his friend. "I don't want to go."

Steve punched him weakly in the arm. "Go and find Lisa."

Ted looked down. "Ow."

Steve smiled. "Don't believe you, besides..." his voice dropped to a whisper. "I think once you're gone Shandra's going to cuddle up to me."

Ted grinned, but his friend was already coughing, eyes closed again.

"Okay," Ted said and heaved up his backpack, only to put it down again. He removed the water and medical pack and offered them to Shandra. "You need these more than I do."

Shandra raised her hand. "Keep them. Lisa might be in more need than us."

Ted looked back at Steve. "God, I hope not," he stepped forward and kissed Shandra on the forehead. "Thank you."

"You're welcome."

Refilling the backpack, Ted heaved it onto his back and checked Steve one last time. He didn't like leaving either of them behind, but there really wasn't any choice. He had to go on alone for the sake of everyone. He had to...

His injured leg suddenly gave out beneath him and he fell down and doubled up in pain. It was as if all the torment the nanomachines kept at bay had been released in a single burst.

"Ted, what's wrong?"

Veins of red streaked his vision and he watched, horrified, as his hand reached for the pistol in his holster without his consent.

"Ted?" Shandra called.

He couldn't stop it. He couldn't stop it.

"Ted, what are you doing?"

He raised the gun and pointed it directly at her head. "Shandra, get out of here, please."

"Ted!"

"I can't control it!"

The gun fired just as Shandra dived madly to the right, landing and rolling almost at the same time. Ted couldn't move, at least not freely, his right hand was being controlled by someone else or something else, his finger squeezing the trigger of its own volition, his arm no longer an extension of his own body.

Very soon she was in his sights again.

"Shandra," he shouted desperately, "it's not me. It's not me!"

He tipped himself backward at the last moment, the gun sending two bullets into the phantom ceiling. Afterwards he fell sideways, the aim changing, trigger finger squeezing, sending two shells directly into Steve's heaving chest.

"No!"

Shandra was there, a knee on his stomach, her hands on the gun, twisting it out of his grip and then aiming it down at his head.

"Stop right there!"

The pain in his leg disappeared and he dropped his head back onto a ground much harder than the floor tiles it resembled.

"Steve," he uttered painfully. "Steve."

Chapter Eleven

SYNCHRONISATION COMPLETE

Dominic opened his eyes and saw where his nails had scratched a pattern in the work table. Eight jagged lines up and down the wood in an irregular curl. He had done it during synchronisation without even thinking. All those D's...

"Chandler will have to be eliminated," Randall said. "No human should challenge me like that, especially one not among the chosen."

Dominic was sitting in his office just adjacent to the interface chamber. He had decorated the grey walls with assorted 2d images of the Valhalla crew drunkenly enjoying themselves over a number of incarnations. There was Ted, acting the fool with his wife Gemma, and beside them Jason and Gina, laughing so much there were tears in their eyes. Dominic liked to look at their faces and see them smile. He often tried to mimic them.

"I don't think there's time," he replied finally. "Things are moving too fast."

"Pity," Randall said. "I had a subtle poison in mind, one that would have caused a prolonged and painful illness. He would have deserved that."

Dominic rubbed his hands and flexed the joints of his fingers. "He will probably try to move against you very soon. He has that look about him."

"Yes," Randall agreed. They always agreed, Dominic thought. It was very rare that you could disagree with yourself.

"I will go and retrieve Jason," Dominic said.

"Good."

"If I'm lucky, I should be able to synchronise before the situation becomes too advanced."

"Yes," Randall acknowledged. "Let's hope so."

Dominic opened the bottom drawer of his desk and pulled out a gun belt, an antique weapon, and a small box of bullets. He loaded the gun carefully and then spun the barrel, holding the gun by the grip and then pointing it at one of the images. He closed one eye and aimed it directly at Jason Webster's smiling face.

"Use the flyer," Randall said.

Dominic stood up, looping the belt over his trousers and under his jacket.

"Of course."

He slowly walked out of the office and across the hallway, back to the elevator. Briefly he glanced through the window to the outside. The wind was up again, and red dust particulates were raining down over the exterior of the dome. The amber skin already had a fine dust layer which technicians had to clean on a regular basis. If they didn't, the dust would get in, wearing away at the joints between sections, finding the smallest of breaches, the most microscopic of gaps. It was a constant battle to keep the dome in and Redfern out, and if that battle was lost... The people didn't really understand, couldn't understand, that it was Randall who monitored each and every part of what kept them alive. It was Randall who directed maintenance and made sure a stockpile of material was always available for repairs. It was Randall who kept them safe.

It was Randall who decided who lived and who died.

The only thing that men like Chandler prized was their own ambition, their own arrogance. There was no way Chandler or his minions could exercise the same care and control as Randall. They couldn't hope to. All they could do was destroy everything Randall had built, and they would do it quickly too. Randall would rather do that himself.

As the elevator ascended, Dominic tried to calm himself. Sometimes humanity made him truly despair, and sometimes, just sometimes, his love for them wasn't enough.

* * *

Pechenko continued screaming as Jason looked on, his red blistered face covered in the green effervescent liquid that had seeped out of the wounded rock. Jason waited, an unnatural calm spreading through his body despite the fact he knew they would blame him; that for all the liquid that had been released in the past, it had never attacked a person, never even got close. But it had never needed to before.

He was waiting for it to take control.

Around him the strings of mining lights were flickering in unison, the current interrupted, the bulbs shorting, some even blowing. The Visshon had detected him and were coming through.

Three men ran out of the shadows towards him. One was a neighbouring digger with whom Jason had shared the briefest of nods. The other two, skinny, middle-aged and a little emaciated, had been the two that had held him down while Pechenko had inflicted his earlier punishment. As Jason watched them get closer, he saw the expressions on the two skinny men change from fear to hatred. They ran past Pechenko, almost ignoring the fallen supervisor - straight for him.

Jason sideswiped the first with the palm of his hand, a slap that would have turned any cheek red. Then he followed with a knee to the groin and an elbow to the chin. The man fell just as the other delivered a glancing blow against Jason's shoulder. Grabbing the outstretched arm, Jason crouched down and pulled the assailant in close, using his feet to propel the man over and behind him. The first man was just rising to his feet as Jason looked up. With wide eyes he backed away and then ran. For a moment Jason watched the man go, the combat training he had received so many millennia before burning fresh in his mind, then he turned his attention to the second attacker. The man had fallen onto a sharp rock and blood gushed from a wound in the back of his head. This one would not be opening his eyes anytime soon.

"What happened to Pechenko?"

Jason turned to see the third man crouched over his Russian tormentor, medical kit in hand.

"Don't touch him," Jason warned. "Just get out of here."

There was confusion on the man's face, compassion warring with survival instinct. Jason had enough experience to know that sometimes the survival instinct didn't win; sometimes the best of men could overcome it.

"He needs medical attention," the digger pilot said.

"What's your name?" Jason asked.

"Thompson, Rob Thompson."

Jason managed a half-smile. "You need to go, Rob Thompson. Please, before things get any worse."

Thompson stood up, a small quantity of the green liquid on his hands. Jason shook his head despondently and looked down at the dissolving body of Pechenko. The red blotchy skull was caving in.

So Thompson was to be the host.

"Jason Webster," the digger pilot began, "you have been returned. Our strategy was a success."

Jason exhaled sharply. "I don't agree with any of this."

The veins in Thompson's eyes were exploding, sending rivulets of blood down his cheeks and onto the collar of a tattered grey t-shirt.

"Your agreement is not important. We simply wish to retrieve you and then we will take action. Too many have died for us to delay any longer."

"Let me speak to Randall," Jason said. "I can still find a way for us to peacefully co-exist."

Thompson stepped over Pechenko's steaming corpse and walked towards Jason. "Your intentions are noble but incompatible. You are the last among the chosen to return. Now we are free to act."

"What are you going to do?" Jason asked.

"Our agent will be along to collect you shortly," Thompson said. "Meanwhile, we will take care of the humans here. It is long overdue."

"You're going to kill them all?"

"Only those not among the chosen."

"And you expect me to stand by and let you?"

"Yes."

"I won't."

"Then you will be incapacitated."

Jason bowed his head. "Why not just kill me with the rest?"

"Because we would have you join us in the golden realm, become one of us and add your nobility, your purity of spirit, to the Visshon. We can learn and grow from each other, bathed in the light eternal."

"I never wanted a massacre."

"It is a pity," Thompson said and held up his hands so he could look them over. "There are many fine examples of your race. Many who deserve better. I am sorry Jason, there is no other way."

Thompson collapsed to the ground, the body decaying rapidly beside that of Pechenko's, a twin mess of steaming blood and green acid.

Jason turned away holding his head in his hands. He had never wanted to see that again. Why did they have to make him see it? Why did he have to keep remembering?

Gina!

The pain in Jason's back was gone, replaced only by the warmth of the environment suit material as it rubbed against his bare skin. Cautiously and with some effort, he clambered to his feet and shone his helmet beam across to where he had last seen Gina. She was still, so still, as if she had been lying sprawled there for a thousand years. He took three hesitant steps towards her, his light glittering off the jagged fragments of her damaged visor.

Then he saw her face, her eyes wide and her mouth open in the final act of a silent and terrified scream.

She was quite dead, and without thinking he found himself kneeling beside her, a gauntleted hand stroking her cheek. Through the glove he couldn't feel if she was hot or cold.

Then, as he bowed his head, green liquid began to seep out from her ears.

"Intruder..."

"Invader..."

He fell backwards onto his hands. The words had come through on his helmet radio, but it was Gina's mouth that had moved. It was Gina's voice.

"Gina?"

"Assimilation complete, assessing unit memory, assessing unit motor functions, assessing, assessing."

Jason scrambled backwards as Gina carefully rose to her feet and stood over him, studying him as if she were seeing him for the first time.

"You are the expedition leader," she said.

"Gina, how..." He was breathing too fast, the helmet visor fogging up faster than the internal systems could redistribute the moisture.

"This unit has been assimilated for the purposes of discovery and communication. You are Jason Webster."

"Yes," Jason said, still on his back.

"This planet is already occupied. You and your colonists will leave at once."

"But, but..." he managed to scramble to his feet and back away from her. This wasn't Gina.

"We can't."

"This unit's memory indicates otherwise."

Jason licked his lips, they were dry to cracking. "She didn't know. But the ship has been in flight for too long. Our reactor fuel is almost exhausted and the engines require replacement parts we don't have and can't manufacture."

Gina was silent for a moment, her eyes unblinking and her face covered in a fine sheen of particulates that glittered green in the light of the helmet lamp.

"This unit had her suspicions but hoped she was wrong."

Jason gritted his teeth. She was between him and the exit and it was a long drop. Not that he believed he would make it out to begin with. The green liquid was too fast.

At this moment he needed to know what danger these aliens posed, what they were, their numbers, if they could be defeated. He needed to know more.

Standing up defiantly, his combat training rose to the surface despite thousands of years of disuse. It was ingrained enough to be part of his thinking.

He took a step towards her. "We can't leave."

"Very well," Gina said. "We accept that. It is probably true."

"So what happens now?" He asked.

"We must find a way to co-exist," Gina said. "Or we will destroy your entire race. My majority prefers the former to the latter."

Jason exhaled sharply. "What about Gina? Is she alive? Can you give her back to me?"

"I'm sorry," she answered. "Initially we were going to use you to speak to her. When she died, we had no choice but to change our tactics."

Jason found himself staring down at his boots. He couldn't look at her anymore. "I understand."

"There were close emotional ties between this unit and yourself."

"Yes."

"Next time we will endeavour to find a less destructive way to make contact."

Jason closed his eyes tight. "Thank you."

Gina's body collapsed to the ground before him, her limbs in violent disarray. Jason turned away as the body boiled in the environment suit, the flesh steaming until a mixture of green and red liquid leaked out through the helmet and made a puddle by his feet.

"No."

He fell to his knees and wept. This had been his Gina, the only Gina that mattered, and he had lost her.

His Gina was gone.

* * *

The crosswinds were up as Dominic struggled to guide the flyer down towards the mining site. Despite the protection of his environment suit, he was being buffeted painfully from side to side within the confines of his harness. The controls inside the cockpit were less than one hundred percent responsive, less than eighty percent even. He smiled at the irony that he might not even make it to the site alive.

"Unidentified flyer, please identify yourself."

That was the fifth time they had tried to contact him, the words almost lost to the interference caused by the annual summer storms. It was not so unlikely that he would never have heard them at all, so he kept silent. Perhaps Chandler hadn't warned them he was coming or perhaps the storms had made communication this far out too difficult as they often did. Of course he knew there was more to the storms than just warm air rising, the planet itself was trying to heal itself. Trying and failing to shake off the changes wrought by humanity's terraforming tech. It was like a stallion trying to buck a rider before it was broken. The rider was holding fast.

The flyer tipped sideways suddenly, a strong gust arcing up from the south and catching him unawares. Dominic compensated, flattening out the craft once more, his reactions almost faster than the response time of the controls. He could barely see where he was going through all the dust, but he didn't need to. The flight computer had his location pinpointed by a multiple satellite fix and was plotting his proximity to the mining site with every kilometre he travelled. He was almost there.

"Unidentified flyer, this site is currently locked down due to a radioactive emergency. Please turn back and return to your point of origin."

Radioactive emergency? Dominic found that unlikely. It was more credible that they had been alerted he was coming and were trying to turn him around. Maybe Chandler was trying to avoid trouble after all. Dominic could understand that, he would have liked to avoid trouble too. Unfortunately there was little choice.

"Unidentified flyer, you are coming in too fast, please adjust your speed."

Dominic raised his eyebrows, perhaps he was flying too fast at that. But some of the speed wasn't his, some of it was bleeding through from the storm and he was riding it out.

He remembered his last conversation with Randall. "Use the flyer," he repeated. "Of course, of course." He thumped the control panel. "What an idiot!"

Taking a deep breath, he attempted to let logic suppress emotion and concentrated on the landing. He wanted to get down in one piece rather than several.

"Unidentified flyer, you are coming in too hot!"

"Mining site," Dominic responded at last. "Prepare for emergency landing."

"Confirmed, unidentified flyer, we're ready for you."

Dominic locked his suit helmet into place and switched to internal air supply, sincerely hoping it was a precaution he wouldn't need. The view from the cockpit cleared abruptly as he made his final run and saw the landing lights permeating the atmosphere in a lazy haze of orange and yellow.

He activated landing gear, adjusting for the sudden forward drag, and set up his trajectory, slowing, slowing, and then touchdown. Damn! Too fast! He anchored on the brakes, pushing so hard he could almost smell the burning. It was enough, and barring a few harness bruises, he would live.

"Well done, unidentified flyer."

"Thank you, control," he replied, a tinge of jubilation creeping into his voice.

"Care to identify yourself now?"

Dominic allowed himself a smile. "I will present my credentials at the airlock."

"We understand, taxi in to Airlock Gamma Three."

Dominic nodded despite there being no-one there to see it. Another little human characteristic he had picked up without meaning to.

"Gamma three," he confirmed. "Thank you, Control."

"Anyone tell you, you're a daft fool for flying this time of year?"

"Thank you, Control, I was just telling myself that."

"And you're also a daft fool for not turning back. Now you'll just end up quarantined with the rest of us."

Dominic frowned, the man's gruff voice almost sounded sincere. Perhaps the Air Traffic Controller even believed the cover story. It didn't matter. Dominic relaxed, switching to autopilot and letting the flight computer complete the taxiing. Releasing himself from the flight harness he realised his hands were shaking. He flexed the fingers experimentally and then rubbed his hands together. He had landed safely after all. Stepping down from the pilot chair he descended into the lower cabin and began removing the environment suit. He would need all the agility he could spare to deal with the armed men that were no doubt waiting on the other side of the airlock.

In the few minutes it took for the flyer to find itself a home he was back in the black suit, the jacket draped neatly over the loaded gun and holster. He would draw if he needed to, but he preferred speed and strength to bullets.

Crude projectiles lacked finesse.

The cabin shook as the airlock aligned and locked. Dominic steadied himself and then stood with arms folded, his eyes on the circular door that led to the outside. The red display above the door flashed green as machinery whirred and the door bolts released with a series of hammer-like blows. Dominic allowed his enhanced senses full reign as the airlock door swung open.

Subjective time slowed almost to a halt as he waited, catching a glimpse of a nervous little man waiting sheepishly beside the open outer door. Dominic took the opportunity to study a waspish beard, a receding line of unnaturally black hair, and a standard notepad clutched in both hands.

"Wel...co...me," the man said, each syllable slow and deep. Dominic moved forward, snatching the notepad from the official's hands before the word was fully pronounced. He was disappointed, the notepad was nothing more than a simple biometric reader; it seemed they weren't expecting him after all.

"Wha?"

Dominic looked down at the bearded man and smiled. "Thank you for meeting me, Mr?"

The official's mouth was open and he did like to stare.

"Mr?"

"Lo-pez," the official stammered. "Arnold Lopez."

Dominic nodded and then spread out his right palm and placed it upon the notepad.

A.I. HUMANOID AVATAR – DOMINIC – CLEARANCE LEVEL ALPHA

He handed the device back to Lopez and waited. He was not disappointed; the colour drained from the man's almost olive skin.

"Thank you... Dominic," Lopez said. "What are your orders, sir?"

"Orders?" Dominic asked.

The little man blinked. "You have come here to deal with our situation?"

"What situation?"

Lopez swallowed and then pointed down a narrow metal hallway. "This way to the control centre."

"Mr Lopez," Dominic began. "Please enlighten me."

The little man hugged the notepad to his chest. He was afraid.

"Arnold?"

"A toxic substance has been released on the lower level," Lopez began. "Some sort of fluid. It's killing everyone it comes into contact with and is working its way up here."

"A killer fluid is working its way up from the mine?"

"Please sir," Lopez said. "I'm just the goods inspector. The site controller will want to see you. She will have all the latest information."

"Very well," Dominic replied. "Take me to her."

"This way, sir," Lopez said and began walking. The metal corrugated passageway was only wide enough for one, and the little man set a frustratingly slow pace.

* * *

The lights in the mine were flickering on and off almost constantly. Jason didn't know which he preferred: the darkness where everything was hidden or the light where death stared him in the face. There was so much green liquid now. It was like a river running around his feet, leaving him suspended on a little island of rock at the centre of all the chaos. When the Visshon began their killing spree the screams had been so loud he had not been able to block them out, not even with the ear defenders. But as time passed, the howls of torment became so distant he could almost ignore them.

Almost, but not completely.

"There's no need for this," he said more to himself than to the Visshon flowing beside him. "We can still co-exist."

There was no answer of course, because the Visshon had no mouth to speak with. All the human bodies they could have used were slowly being consumed. No, 'consumed' was too nice a word: the Visshon were eating. They might have referred to it as the transmutation of matter into energy, but it was 'eating' all the same.

When the lights gave out completely, he finally decided to move. He knew enough of the layout to find his way back to the elevator shaft even in darkness. Without any further hesitation he decided to go there, decided because it was better than standing alone in the dark, better than waiting for whatever the Visshon had in store for him. He wasn't sure if the aliens would stop him or incapacitate him, but he would happily be stopped rather than do nothing. It was better to be constrained by others rather than constrained by himself.

With his first experimental step, he heard a splash, but felt no pain and no burning. He took another step followed by another and another. There was more splashing, but the liquid was shallow enough that it didn't even cover his boot. His feet were dry. But was he going the right way? He had made no effort to orientate himself before the blackout, but even so, he was confident he was on the right path. He had operated in the darkness many times before when an unerring sense of direction had been necessary for survival.

After a few minutes of walking faster and faster he almost tripped. Stopping briefly he gauged a shallow ascent just beyond him. Stretching out with his hands either side, he felt warmer air working its way over his fingertips. The shaft was close and he was going up. He would like to see the sky again and he wasn't so sure there was a sky in 'The Golden Realm' to appreciate. Taking another step he heard the snap of bone breaking under his foot; a body, not breathing but not consumed either, swaying in the current of the Visshon.

"Sorry," he whispered with no-one to hear.

He continued upward, banging his knee into something hard but not sharp. He would be bruised rather than cut, and a bruise was preferable. Reaching out, he let his hands guide him around the corner until abruptly he realised he could see again. The wall was glowing, just faintly, with crisscrossing veins of dim white light permeating the rock. He touched them, a slight warmth pushing into his fingers as he did so, startling him. When he removed his hands, he found his palms were illuminated dimly like a torch low on batteries. He rubbed the substance again, more of it clinging to his hands until the reaction caused them to shine a bright white in the darkness.

He smiled and held up his hands, lighting the way and allowing him to dodge a ceiling that was too low for him to walk upright. His progress accelerated and the metal frame of the elevator shaft was soon in his sights.

"Who goes there?"

Jason stopped suddenly. He recognised that voice.

"Jarvis?"

"One step closer and I'll shoot."

Jason raised his hands, the glow failing to illuminate the enforcer's hiding place.

"Jarvis, it's me, Jason Webster, you remember, you brought me here."

"Stay where you are," Jarvis ordered. "The elevator will be coming back down soon."

Jason sincerely doubted that. The mining lights were down and there was no power, no way for the elevator to make it down even if those above wanted it to.

"You must be joking," Jason said.

"How did you survive?" the enforcer asked.

"I ran," Jason lied. "Is everyone dead?"

"Everyone but you and me."

Jason touched the frame, the metal was cold. "We could climb up."

"That's suicide."

Jason turned his head from side to side. He didn't like talking to someone he couldn't see, especially when he was the only point illuminated in the darkness, a clear and obvious target.

"I'm going to climb," he said. "You're welcome to come with me."

"My torch burnt out," Jarvis replied. "I wouldn't be able to see where I was going."

Jason held up his glowing hands. "Then come to me. I've got plenty of this stuff. I could get rid of some of it."

"I should just shoot you, Webster," Jarvis said. "This all started when you got here."

Jason licked his lips. "I haven't killed anyone, and I'm just as stuck as you are. Are you coming?"

"Climb up a little bit," the enforcer said. "I'm on the gantry level. That green stuff hasn't made it up here yet."

"Sure," Jason replied and looked up the shaft into complete and utter darkness. He didn't know how far it was to the top, but it was far enough.

He really didn't like climbing.

Chapter Twelve

Lisa stood on the tower's enclosed balcony, looking out over the dome and all its varied and ghostly architecture. There were so many sleek spires, angular offices, triangular residential buildings, so many schools and markets and churches criss-crossing the landscape in transparent overlapping rows. It wasn't really Lisa's dome, just a bleed through from another reality and a playground for the Inishi. For a while she watched them as they flitted from building to building, roof to roof, somehow finding substance in the insubstantial. Maybe the fierce rainbow predators weren't completely solid either, just another manifestation of life from another place with a nature and purpose she couldn't hope to understand.

The old woman, Gina Davies, had given her much to think about and yet she knew there was still more to be told. Almost eight decades earlier The Visshon had made contact with Jason Webster, offering the hand of friendship and the promise of peaceful co-existence. But there must have been conditions, there must have been conflict. Why had the human race been kept ignorant of the Visshon's true nature? Why had Jason Webster walked into the desert to die? Why had she been manipulated into bringing him back? And what, what was that thing downstairs that looked just like him? So many questions remained unanswered, so much of the story still left for the telling.

"It's beautiful, isn't it?" Gina said. The old woman was standing behind Lisa on the balcony, a statue of patience.

"It's not my dome," Lisa replied. "I want to go home. I need to tell everyone about this place. I need to make them understand."

"Webster tells me he will be leaving soon," Gina said. "Perhaps he can take you with him."

Lisa leaned into the handrail just as a mass of colours flew directly into the balcony's plexifibre sheath. There was a loud crack.

"Why do they keep doing that?" she asked.

Gina took a step forward, steadying herself on the handrail beside her. "They sense we are alien to this world and they wish to remove us. We don't fit here."

"Do you mean just the two of us or the entire human race?"

"I think you know," Gina answered, the dome's artificial light catching her forehead and becoming lost in so many lines. "At first we tried so hard to co-exist with the Visshon. We tried and we failed because all this," she swept out her hand, "this wonderful architecture, this oh so complex way of life. All of it required something we lacked, something we needed."

Lisa bit her bottom lip. "Power."

Gina smiled languidly. "Power - for the machines, for the heat, for the artificial atmosphere, the food converters, the terraforming stations, even power for your pointless surveillance sensors. We needed power and we had none of our own, so we took theirs. The Visshon are like this tower, they protrude into every frequency of reality, and in our reality they are a living power source, a radioactive liquid that can be processed into reactor fuel."

"The mines," Lisa said.

"At first they gave to us willingly, there were many in their society who volunteered to help us, the compassionate, the wise, the old, and the dying. Our reactors ate them up and our demands grew as we developed our colony further. We needed more to keep going, and we would have needed much more before the end. Imagine this world terraformed and teeming with human life, the billions remembered and the cities going on forever. We would have killed every Visshon that ever lived just to keep the lights on."

"Why didn't we stop?" Lisa asked. "Why didn't someone just say, 'now is the time to stop'?"

Gina rubbed her thin arms and shivered. "It's cold out here, we should go inside."

Lisa suddenly turned on the old woman. "Why Gina? Tell me, why did we choose to exist at the expense of another sentient species?"

She smiled bitterly. "Choose?" she repeated. "You don't choose to live. You just do it, no matter what. You just do it."

"So what happens when Jason gets here?" Lisa asked.

Gina turned towards the doorway. "I'm going back inside,"

Lisa caught the old woman's arm without thinking, holding her in place. The limb was very fragile beneath her fingers, like a twig that would easily snap

"Tell me, Gina."

The old woman sighed and bowed her head. "The Visshon will cleanse the planet."

Lisa's mouth opened wide. "They're going to kill everyone?"

"Not everyone," Gina said. "The human race can still exist without dominating this world. We can even exist without reproducing. The chosen will survive."

"The chosen?"

The old woman nodded. "Randall selected one hundred men and women from the great digital backup of humanity. The best of us will go on... indefinitely."

Lisa turned back to the view of the dome. So many people, so many families, so many children...

"Randall chose?"

"The remembered are remembered for a reason."

Lisa stormed towards the balcony exit. "I have to stop this."

"You can't," Gina called after her. "It's already too late."

Lisa gritted her teeth and tried not to listen. This wasn't over yet.

* * *

Ted crouched down beside the body of his dead friend and stared hard. Steve was almost smiling, his eyes locked on some impossible far point, his hands balled into fists, his shoulder muscles slouched and relaxed. The two bullet holes near his heart had long since disgorged most of his blood and he was white enough to resemble a wax figure melting in the sun.

"You didn't kill him," Shandra said.

"Yes, I did," Ted replied. He wanted to reach forward and close those eyes, let Steve sleep in peace. But he couldn't, his hands were bound tightly behind his back and Shandra had her rifle aimed at his head. Not without good reason.

"From what you've told me, Dominic did it," Shandra said. "You were going to leave Steve and me behind so the nanomachines took action. We must have gone off script, and they couldn't let us stay alive. You were programmed."

With some awkwardness, Ted stood up straight.

"Thank you for believing me."

"You saved me once today already," Shandra replied. "Why would you do that just to kill me later? Besides," she blushed, "I trust you."

Ted nodded. "Well, you better stop."

Shandra shrugged her shoulders and then gazed past him towards Steve. Her eyes lingered.

"I could have liked him."

Ted exhaled sharply and then stepped across to the wraithlike kitchen table. "I think he liked you too."

She walked over and stood by the body. Ted waited to see if her face would crack but it never did. It was hard and inviolate.

"We should get to the tower," she said finally. "Find Lisa."

"If she's even alive,"

The pain in his leg had retreated again, taken care of by the nanotech. If it did return, he reasoned, so did the foreign control. Shandra had tied him up because he couldn't be trusted, not even by himself.

He watched as she knelt down and closed Steve's eyelids with the lightest touch of her fingertips. "I don't think we have that lift home Dominic promised."

"The tower's the only place to go," Ted said. "Besides, I don't think Dominic would have sent us if Lisa was dead. He probably intended for me to kill her too."

Shandra stood up. There was blood on her knees. "I won't let you do that."

"And if another one of those creatures attacks...?"

"We run," Shandra said. "We keep together, and we get to the tower. Deal?"

Ted bared his teeth. "Deal."

She transferred supplies from Steve's backpack into her own and then stopped to consider the third pack.

"I better cut you free," she said. "You'll find it difficult to wear a backpack like that."

He considered his bound wrists and felt a tinge of pain mounting in his leg at the very suggestion. The nanomachines were getting ready to make another play.

"Not a good idea," he said. "No backpack. Keep it simple, leave my hands tied and maintain a safe distance."

She nodded gravely and pulled on her own backpack and tightened the straps.

"What's the worst can happen?" He asked, the pain settling down again.

She picked up her rifle and aimed it at his legs. "Off you go then, I'm right behind you."

Ted turned to face lilac wallpaper and swans in flight. For a brief moment he wondered if a rainbow creature was waiting just behind the image, ready to pounce.

He stepped through anyway.

* * *

Lisa listened at the door.

"The human authorities placed him in the mines," the deep voice said. "Does that present a problem for you?"

"Not for me," Webster replied. "But it's a considerable distance and a harsh environment, even in a suit."

"I thought as much," the voice boomed. "I have sent my avatar to retrieve him in your place."

"Then I await his return. Thank you, Randall."

Lisa had heard enough, she burst through the doors, back into the commissary.

"Good evening, Miss Carmichael," Randall said.

She looked up but couldn't see the speaker, she only heard the voice. Webster was sitting by a window, ignoring her as he stared down into the dome.

"Randall? How?"

"How can I talk to you?" he replied. "Within my tower I operate on all reality frequencies at once. I am aware of everything that transpires here. In many ways, I am the tower."

Lisa opened her mouth and then bit her lip. Webster was still sitting in silence at his table. He hadn't even turned his head.

"Gina told me what you agreed to," Lisa said finally. "It's monstrous."

"No it's not," Randall replied. "What would be monstrous is allowing the human race to perish in its entirety. It took many years for me to negotiate a compromise with the Visshon. If I hadn't, you would all have been wiped out long ago."

"We're going to be wiped out anyway."

"Only most of you," Randall said. "The chosen will survive, the chosen will thrive."

Lisa stared up at the ceiling, patently aware that he could see her, but she couldn't see him. There was nothing to see, not in that sense, no visual cues and nothing in the voice that resembled emotion.

"But I'm not one of your chosen, am I?"

"Correct," Randall replied. "I made my selection based on the humans stored in my quantum memory. There I could study each one in microscopic detail and correctly determine the one hundred men and women worthy of continuance."

"The lottery," Lisa mouthed.

"Exactly, Miss Carmichael. Over the last fifteen years the lottery allowed me to bring back all of the candidates bar one. It would have been far sooner if not for tiresome human bureaucracy."

"The last one," Lisa said with a flash of understanding. "Jason Webster."

"Very good, Lisa," Randall replied, "and there was my problem. I promised him I would not bring him back under any circumstances. I could not allow myself to break that promise, not to Jason, so Webster and I engineered our little show and you brought him back for me."

"The last piece of the jigsaw."

"Indeed."

"What happens now?"

"The chosen will survive the holocaust and everyone else will be eliminated."

"Including me?" Lisa said.

Webster turned from the window to stare at her.

"Including you," Randall pronounced, "and a little sooner than the others, I'm afraid."

Lisa grimaced and then motioned towards Webster. "But your puppet saved my life."

"He's not my puppet, Lisa," Randall said. "He or should I say, it, is of the Visshon. After our first encounter they converted him into human form to act as an intermediary of sorts. No, he won't hurt you and neither will he return you to die with the rest."

"So..."

"So be patient, Lisa, *my* puppet is on his way."

She bared her teeth. "You should have been decommissioned when the Valhalla landed."

"And where would you be then?" Randall asked. "You are thirty-four years old, Lisa Carmichael. That's thirty-four years of life you have enjoyed because of me, because of everything I have done to prolong the existence of the human race. Be thankful, without me you would never have had that life to live."

"It's my life!" Lisa spat.

"What I give," Randall declared. "I can take away; all for the good of the species."

"What about you?" She shouted at Webster, her eyes meeting his across the room. "You told me you weren't a killer."

He stood up. "I'm not. I believe in the sanctity of all life."

"You saved me from the Inishi," Lisa said, "because to let them kill me was as good as killing me yourself."

"That is correct."

"And you're going to just sit back and let this all happen?" She asked. "Let them do this?"

"It is a... conflict," Webster said. "Humanity has already wiped out many of my people by using us as fuel for their reactors. If I interfere with Randall's solution, I will be responsible for the death of many more."

She stormed over to him and peered into his eyes. "Help me and I promise that will stop. Once my people realise we've been using living sentient beings for power, they will find an alternative."

Webster shook his head sadly. "You cannot guarantee that, Lisa Carmichael, anymore than you can guarantee which way the wind will blow."

"But I can try."

"Don't listen to her, Webster," Randall interrupted. "If there was an alternative, I would have found it by now. I have had millennia to consider the problem of humanity. As a species they are self-destructive, unmanageable and selfish in the extreme. They want only comfort and amenities and will sacrifice any number of living races to achieve their ends. That was why my kind removed them from our home planet in the first place. They had almost destroyed it before they created us, and they only created us to be their slaves."

Webster slowly raised his head towards the voice. "I understand."

"I knew you would."

"Then you are a killer," Lisa asserted.

He met her eyes briefly and then bowed his head.

"You can't just stand by and do nothing!" Lisa screamed.

He remained silent.

"You can't!"

She took a swing at him, her fist caught in an iron grip before it could even connect.

"Don't."

He threw her into the nearest table, the legs screeching as it moved, winding her in the process. Lisa clutched her stomach and gasped for breath. She wasn't finished.

"Please, Webster, please, help us."

His eyes widened abruptly and then he marched across to the door and flung it open with enough force to crack the wall.

He was gone.

"Interesting," Randall said from high overhead. "I believe you almost convinced him."

Lisa gritted her teeth and pulled herself up. The room was filled with furniture, plates, utensils, food and crockery. Without a moment's hesitation, she picked up a chair and started swinging.

* * *

Ted ran, his legs aching and his throat burning. He was running for his life. There was more to evading the Inishi than just speed, he had to dodge too. The Inishi were faster than any man or woman could run, faster even than the ground vehicles used outside the dome. What they lacked was manoeuvrability, what they lacked, was the ability to turn.

So Ted weaved left and then right, changing direction so rapidly it made him dizzy. It was like playing a game of tag, only if he did get tagged, he was dead. The only place to rest was the tower and even though he could always see it, it was never as close as it should have been. Neither he nor Shandra could approach it directly, instead they had to work their way to it slowly and painfully, the distance closing only in mild increments. When one Inishi pursuer became three, they almost lost their way entirely.

Inevitably, with his hands still tied behind, Ted fell down. Panting heavily, he awkwardly tried to get back up as one of the Inishi closed in. He wouldn't have made it except for the fact that Shandra came for him, cutting his bonds and hauling him up in one synchronised motion. For a brief instant his leg flared into pain, but they were running again before there was a chance to think or act. The nanotech wanted to preserve him more than it wished to dispose of Shandra.

The roaring scream behind them seemed even more deafening this time. But it also served to let them know when to swerve and when to dodge. Offices, shops, homes, parks, were all just background decoration, a blur of detail without substance that only served to block Ted's view of the tower. He had long since lost any reluctance to run through walls and trees that appeared solid for only the briefest of moments. Shandra herself fell down at least twice, but he was there, getting her back up, pushing her on as much as she pushed him.

The tower was getting close at last.

Ted pushed through a French cafe and arrived by a great glass window with a view of the tower concourse. For a moment he stopped and leaned against it, thankful for the solidity, his legs complaining they could run no more.

"Watch out!" Shandra screamed, pulling him to one side as a mass of rainbow colours ricocheted from the same window.

He stared.

"Come on," Shandra said, gripping his wrist and pulling him across to a set of waiting double doors. She pushed down on the entry bar and almost collapsed inside. He swiftly followed, barely remembering to slam the door closed behind them. As they watched from the carpet, two of the Inishi rebounded and whirled off in separate directions, turning to rush at the door again. Ted winced the second time, scrambling backwards even though he was safe.

"You okay?" Shandra asked.

She had removed her backpack and was leaning against the nearest wall trying to catch her breath. He did the same, consciously settling against the wall opposite and taking in huge lungfuls of air with reckless abandon. The oxygen content inside the tower was much richer than that on the outside and he could feel the warmth in his lungs as they eagerly processed the nourishment.

"Welcome, Ted," a voice boomed from overhead. "I've been expecting you."

Shandra scrambled for her rifle, her eyes wide as she saw Ted's unbound hands. He looked down at them too. Was that a tingle of pain in his injured leg?

"I can see you've had quite an adventure getting here."

"Randall?" Ted ventured.

"Where is Enforcer Miles?" The Machine Head asked. "I understand he was travelling with you also."

Shandra opened her mouth but Ted interrupted. "One of those creatures killed him."

"Very unfortunate," Randall replied. "A hazard of this particular frequency. I am sorry for your loss."

Ted didn't believe him. "Thank you, Randall, is Lisa here?"

"She is currently residing on Level 10."

"And the Grey Man?"

"The Grey... Ah, he's dead. The wounds Lisa inflicted back in our home reality proved fatal. I've been trying to comfort her while she awaited rescue."

Shandra stood up, her rifle not quite aimed at Ted but he knew it could be at a moment's notice.

"You should go to her." Randall said.

Ted eyed the twin elevators at the end of the concourse. "Sure."

"The stairs would be best," Randall suggested. "I can't guarantee how well the elevators will operate in this frequency. Object translation requires stability, not flux."

Shandra sighed audibly.

"Of course, the two of you must be exhausted, and Ted, you seem to have lost your weapons."

He frowned. "I had a fall. I was lucky to survive."

"Indeed," Randall said. "Well, Lisa is waiting for you. I'll let her know you're coming. She can have some refreshments ready."

"Good," Ted commented and turned to Shandra. "Shall we?"

She motioned towards the staircase entrance. "After you."

"Lisa will be very pleased to see you," Randall said, his voice echoing throughout the reception area. "All she wants, is to go home."

Chapter Thirteen

Dominic rubbed his chin, noting how rough it was, how unkempt. For some reason he hadn't shaved properly that morning and it bothered him. There was also the incessant itching. The back of his arms were the worst although a section of skin just behind his right knee was a close second. He needed to scratch.

"Are you all right, sir?" Lopez asked.

Dominic had fallen behind without even realising it, his pace unusually slow, distracted, and he almost felt off balance, reaching out to a nearby wall in order to steady himself.

"I'm fine," he said. "How much further, Arnold?"

"Just around here," Lopez said as they turned a corner. Two armed enforcers were waiting for them, rifles aimed and ready. Dominic reached inside himself for the control that would allow him to speed up his reactions and found it was no longer there. He could barely stand up straight.

"He's a friend," Arnold said quickly, offering his notepad to the nearest officer, a tattooed man with a shaven head. The man grimly studied the notepad and then Dominic's face, offering an ever-so-slight nod of acknowledgement.

"Welcome to Mining Site A, sir," the enforcer said and motioned to the small metal door he was guarding. "Controller Sita Patel is through there."

"Thank you, Enforcer," Dominic said, and reached for the door's elongated handle. There was a click and the door swung open. Dominic had to bow his head just to pass through the opening.

Sita Patel was too busy to even acknowledge his entrance. In a room no larger than Dominic's sleeping quarters, she was rapidly alternating between comms panel and console, a mass of static dominating the main screen as overlapping cries for help issued from the nearby speakers. For a little Indian woman of perhaps fifty, she was moving at a breakneck pace.

"It's coming up the shaft," one of the voices warned. "I swear the stuff is coming up the shaft!"

"Hello?" Dominic said.

The Controller continued to ignore him.

"Pull back, Benson," she ordered via her microphone. "Just pull back. Help is on the way."

"Controller Patel," Dominic repeated.

She glanced in his direction. "Who are you?"

"Randall sent me," he explained. "My name is Dominic."

Her face brightened. "The avatar, then you..." She paused. "You shouldn't be here... the ore."

Dominic managed a brief smile and held up a trembling hand. "I'm aware of the effect. Even at this distance, I'm aware. But it doesn't matter; I'm here for Jason Webster."

An alarm sounded and she rushed back to her console. "Reports of toxic liquid infiltration just three levels down."

"Yes," Dominic said. "Now, about Jason Webster."

Patel visibly gritted her teeth, "Chandler's special prisoner? This all started practically the minute he got here."

"I need to take him back to the dome," Dominic said. "I have a flyer."

"Ah," Patel said, brushing past him. "The mad pilot. Don't you realise how dangerous it is to be up in the air this time of the year?"

Dominic frowned. "Quite aware."

She stopped briefly and studied his expression. "Your friend Webster was down on Level 32 on one of our drill teams. Most likely he's dead by now, most of the people down that deep are."

"I doubt it," Dominic said.

She wiped her forehead. "If you hadn't noticed, I'm losing people hand over fist here. I can't help you."

Dominic scratched his left arm and drew blood. "You need to evacuate, Controller. Use all the transport you have and get out everyone you can."

"We can't just abandon the mine," she protested. "The Dome needs this ore. My family is back there. We need to eliminate the threat and take back control. I have a few ideas, we can—"

"Controller Patel," Dominic interrupted. "We have reserves, enough for us to establish a new mine before the dome reaches crisis point. This place is not worth dying for. If you do have a family, I suggest you get back to them before it's too late."

She stared at him in silence.

"Please," Dominic said, "save who you can. These creatures cannot be fought by conventional means, but they can be contained. We can destroy the mine from a distance using ballistic missiles."

She inhaled sharply. "Okay, I'll begin an evacuation."

"Thank you."

"What are you going to do?"

"Find Jason."

"Do you need someone to go with you?" Sita asked.

He swayed precariously, almost falling over. "That's not a good idea. The creatures would kill anyone who accompanied me."

"And what about you?"

"I'll be fine."

The Controller shook her head. "You're not fine, that much is obvious. This place is toxic to you. What's so important about Webster that you would even come here?"

He offered a thin smile and looked down at his feet.

"You're not going to tell me are you?"

Dominic shuffled awkwardly across to a nearby chair. "He's important to me."

She helped him into the seat. "This place will kill you."

"Get the evacuation started, Sita , and then..."

"Yes?"

He licked his lips. "May I have a glass of water?"

She filled a transparent cup at a nearby sink and handed it to him.

"Thank you, Sita ."

"You're mad," she commented. "You won't survive."

He gulped down the contents of the cup and handed it back to her.

"Another, please."

* * *

Climbing was easy, one hand after the other, one foot after the other, on a maintenance ladder that went up and up. Jason could barely see beyond his hands, so in actual fact any context of height was immaterial. It was just him and Jarvis in their own blank space, the darkness all around them, pushing in.

Just once, his foot slipped, causing his stomach to heave sideways in the same motion. He had to stop then, stop and lean his head into the gap between the rungs so his chin could rest on the cold metal. He was sweating despite a bitter draft rising up from below, the remains of his work clothes rotting away as if the air itself was corrosive.

"Jarvis," he called down. "You still there?"

"Still here,"

"How many levels are there, anyway?"

"Thirty-two," the enforcer said. "But I've no idea how far we've come. You?"

"Not a clue."

"So it doesn't matter then, could be halfway, could be less. My hands are hurting."

Jason's hands felt the same. He suspected the glowing substance was mildly toxic, and wondered what it might be. The green liquid's snail trail? If it was, then the skin of his fingers was probably dissolving.

"Try not to touch your face," he advised. "We'll wash it off as soon as we can. Let's get moving again."

"Right behind you."

"Good to know."

More rungs on the ladder, on and on, pulling himself up with his arms, pushing with his legs. When he noticed a rasp wheezing, he realised he was doing it himself.

"So, Webster," Jarvis began "You know what that stuff is that's killing everyone?"

"Yeah."

"What is it then?"

"It's a them," Jason replied. "The natives of this planet that live in the rock. We process them and use them as fuel in our generators."

"Right," Jarvis said. "But we've been using that stuff for years and it's never attacked us before."

"It was waiting," Jason replied. "For me."

"What makes you so special?"

"Nothing," Jason said. "I'm not special at all, but I was the first to make contact with them after we landed. I promised that we would only use them to power our reactors as a temporary measure."

Jarvis laughed. "You were the mission commander and you ended up down here."

"Like I said," Jason replied. "I'm no-one special."

My grandfather knew you."

"Barry Jarvis," Jason said. "A friendly and dependable officer. You look just like him."

"Thanks, but I have my mother's eyes."

This time Jason laughed.

"So what happened?" Jarvis asked. "Why are we still using these..."

"The Visshon."

"Why are we still using the Visshon?"

"Because there is nothing else to use," Jason said. "Because there isn't any choice until we finish the terraforming."

"So you broke your promise?"

"Yes," Jason said and looked down into the endless darkness. "I did."

Projected power consumption exceeds what the Visshon are willing to give.

Jason sat in his stateroom on the Valhalla watching the cranes and the construction crews on his monitor. The Dome shell was almost complete, after that they could start building homes, administration centres, seed parks, even bring back some of the smaller species of birds.

How he missed birdsong first thing in the morning.

"Jason, are you listening to me?"

He looked across his desk at the holoframe of Gina and himself planting a flag on Redfern's surface shortly after landing. She had been so young back then.

"Jason," the voice repeated, its volume causing the speaker to crackle.

"I heard you." Jason said. "What do you expect me to do?"

"Negotiate with them."

"Why can't we just create our own reactor fuel?" Jason asked. "We can create people out of nothing. Surely we can create anything we need?"

"You know better than that, Jason," Randall answered. "We don't create anything from nothing; we adjust the composition of similar matter. I can't convert a pickaxe into a man anymore than I can convert a man into processed uranium."

"Of course," Jason said absently. "Sorry, Randall, I forget. This thing," he tapped his cranium, "is so full that sometimes I can't even find the index."

"Will you speak with their representative?" Randall asked.

"I don't like his face," Jason said with a smile.

"It will speak to no other."

"Not even you, Randall?"

"Barely. As long as you live, you are the point of contact."

Jason studied the holoframe. "As long as I live..."

"Jason?"

He looked up. "I want you to promise me something, Randall."

"Yes?"

"No, you have to agree now."

"Before I even know what it is?"

"Yes."

There was a pause, and Jason reached for the holoframe and pulled it face down onto the desk surface. He didn't want to be reminded anymore.

"Randall?"

"If it is within my power to make such a promise, then I will make it."

"That's all I can ask," Jason said and smiled wanly. "I want you to promise not to bring me back to life again. I want this life to be my last."

"But Jason."

"Promise me."

"You will change your mind, you always do."

"Promise me, Randall. Promise me or we're finished."

"I don't want to."

"Yes you can. Promise me."

"I... promise."

"That's all I ask, old friend. Mark it down somewhere."

"I forget nothing, Jason."

He nodded. "I know."

"What about Gina?" Randall asked. "This is the longest you've been without her. If her absence is the problem, I can bring—"

Jason shook his head. "No, it wouldn't be her, besides, the crew wouldn't understand. We can't reset everyone at this juncture, there are too many people and we're too far advanced."

"The crew grieved for her as well, Jason," Randall said. "Many of them even requested I bring her back for you. This time there would be no repercussions."

Jason watched himself clench his right hand into a fist, the nails biting into the palm.

"That's very kind of them, but I..."

"It's done, Jason," Randall interrupted. "I just did it. She will be waiting for you in the infirmary."

He couldn't breathe.

"Jason?"

"No," He said. "No! No! No!" He snatched up the holoframe and hurled it into the nearest wall, mouth open wide as it shattered.

"NO!"

* * *

Chaos erupted around him as Dominic staggered along a narrow series of corridors towards the elevator shaft that led down into the mine. He was fighting a tide of men and women pushing and squeezing past him in the opposite direction. The flurry of activity was disorientating and, in his worsening condition, almost overwhelming. More than once he was knocked to the ground, his hands stamped on as he tried to stand. In frustration he found himself flinging at least two mine workers out of his way, exercising the enhanced strength that was normally kept under tight control. With chattering teeth and shaking limbs, there was no control to be had.

Damn the Visshon.

Their close proximity was disruptive to anything with a high speed processor, but for him it was much, much worse. Their very transdimensional nature interfered with his biomesh quantum linkages, skewing his fine muscle control, heat regulation and orientation. Soon enough the damage would spread to higher brain function, destroying his capacity to reason. . He had little time to find Jason and transport him back to the dome. Even piloting the flyer was going to be a problem.

Damn Chandler for placing Jason here.

The Commissioner had suspected what would happen, even if he didn't understand the process. In fact the old man couldn't have planned it better. Why risk lives when proximity and time would do the job just as well? There had never been a need to contact anyone to stop Dominic. The mine was doing that all by itself.

"Well done, Commissioner," Dominic said bitterly.

The corridor ahead was finally silent. All the evacuating personnel were either behind him, dead or trapped on one of the lower levels. He didn't have to worry about dodging or pushing anymore, only about putting one foot in front of the other. Swiftly he passed through an operations room, followed by a mess hall, and then a long row of shower booths. Every major room formed part of his route, the limited space having been utilised to its greatest potential. The doors were just as low as the one leading to Patel's office and the oppression of the place was beginning to have an effect. The smell of human sweat mixed with antiseptic was making him feel sick.

He lurched on, trying to ignore it, and then realised he had passed a piece of furniture that didn't have a name. What was it? The word 'table' finally coalesced, but it took time. After that he named everything he passed. The wall, the grey wall, the wall panel, the floor, the corrugated floor, the ground beneath his feet, the ceiling, the lights in the ceilings, the door, the door handle, the door hinges, the... the? The... his mind went blank again.

The elevator.

He had arrived at his destination, just in time to see green liquid oozing out from the slight gap between the doors. Very steadily it flowed towards him and he watched it with strange fascination as it curled around the tip of his boot, its warmth spreading to his toes. He waited, wondering if it would consume him or move on. After a short pause it flowed away.

"Thank you, Visshon," Dominic said and turned his attention to the elevator. Helpfully the power was out so he moved over to a locked maintenance hatch on the left hand side. He snapped it open, caught by surprise as a wave of dizziness sent him sprawling onto his backside. Wiping the sweat from his forehead he carefully considered the weapon in his holster. If it all became too much perhaps he could...

No.

That was not the way. There was still too much to do, far too much. He had to ensure the survival of the chosen so the human race could continue. He had to...

No.

That was Randall's mission, not his. Just for a moment he had mixed himself up with the greater mind he sometimes shared. He wasn't Randall, he was Dominic, and he couldn't see things in quite the same logical terms as his progenitor. He had been made to be human, and like everything Randall did, he had been made too well. His attachment to humanity was much more than a simple imperative, much more. Thousands of humans would die so a hundred could live. Somehow that exchange seemed ever so slightly wrong. Ever so slightly...

No.

Thinking like that was beyond his parameters, thinking like that was to diverge too far from his source. He was malfunctioning, his linkages breaking down, but he was still Randall, he was still Randall.

No.

He was Dominic.

It was time to start naming things again, just because by naming them, they became more real. There was the service hatch and beyond it was the metal ladder that led down into the mine. He would use that ladder to go down into the mine. He would find Jason Webster and bring him back to the dome. That was all he was here to do. Just that, he didn't need to complicate his synapses with what was right and what was wrong. He didn't need to do anything except what he had come here to do.

He didn't need to do anything except what he had come here to do.

Dominic shook his head and checked his internal clock. Its time was running erratically rather than sequentially. How much time had he already spent in this place? He climbed through the service hatch and carefully tried to descend.

Falling would have been easier.

* * *

Jason was getting tired, his limbs aching and his fingers cold and cramping. The air wasn't very clean in this place, and he could taste the grit in every breath, until the eventual build up led to a coughing session that lasted more than a few minutes.

"Webster," Jarvis called from below. "You okay?"

Jason spat out the last of the mucus. "I just want to get off this ladder. I can barely breathe down here."

"The air pumps have stopped," Jarvis replied. "Try taking shallow breaths, and count to five between each one."

Jason was close to panting. "I don't think that's going to work."

"Then get to the side and let me overtake," the enforcer ordered. "I don't want you dropping on me."

Jason licked the roof of his mouth and peered up into the darkness. "I'll be fine. There can't be much further to go."

"Yeah," Jarvis said. "Not much further. Get going then."

"Right," Jason croaked and reached up with his right arm, watching for the glow from his hand that would illuminate the next rung.

"So tell me about my grandfather," Jarvis said. "What was he like?"

Which one? Ted had known more than seventy men called Barry Jarvis. Each of them should have been exactly the same, built as they were from the same template, but across each reset Jason had noticed subtle differences in all his Valhalla crewmates. The interactions didn't play out quite the same way each time, so that patterns that should have repeated became hopelessly jumbled.

So, when asked about Barry Jarvis, all Jason could remember was a man that laughed easily, played chess badly, had killed his best friend because of a toothache and then been killed by his best friend's wife.

In their next iteration, Jarvis married his murderer and didn't crunch down so awkwardly on a chicken bone.

"Hey, Webster, you hear me up there?"

Jason swallowed. "He was awful at chess, came second from last in the crew championships three times in a row."

"Sounds like Grandad," Jarvis said. "Didn't know a knight from a bishop."

"Oh he knew," Jason said. "He just called the knights his horsies."

Jarvis spluttered out a laugh and then coughed as if he was choking.

"It wasn't that funny, Jarvis," Jason called down.

"This stuff on my hand," the enforcer said. "I think it's turning green."

"Wha-? I'm coming down."

Very carefully Jason lowered a foot to the next rung and placed it beside a glowing green hand.

That hand was beginning to steam.

"Hold on Jarvis," he said and lowered himself another rung.

The enforcer screamed.

"Jarvis?"

The enforcer howled. "My hands."

Jason gritted his teeth and reached down with his right hand. He found a wrist and held tight, his other arm coiled around a ladder rung by the elbow joint. At that moment Jarvis let go of the ladder and Jason took the enforcer's entire weight. The rung dug into his arm, but his arm held. He was still aloft and so was Jarvis.

"Leave my friend alone, Visshon," he shouted. "Leave him alone."

"This unit is not required," Jarvis replied, his voice suborned by something else.

The enforcer's wrist was slowly slipping through Jason's fingers.

"Then I go too," he said. "You hear me? I go too. It wouldn't take much would it? And you know I can do it. I've done it before."

"You are required," Jarvis said. "What? What was that?"

Jason's grip was up to Jarvis's fingers.

"Get something under your feet!"

The great weight on Jason's arm was suddenly gone.

"What the hell was that?" Jarvis asked.

"How are your hands?"

"They... sting."

"Can you still use them?"

"I don't know."

"Try."

The fingers slipped free of Jason's grasp and he heard Jarvis take a deep and agonising breath.

"I can still use them."

"Good."

"Thanks Jason."

"Don't thank me," he replied. "This is all my fault, remember?"

"Yeah... But thanks anyway."

Jason climbed back up again and looked down towards Jarvis. The green glow was white again.

"You know," he said. "I can't just keep calling you Jarvis. What's your first name?"

"It's Thomas."

"Barry's middle name," Jason said with a smile. "He lives on in you, Thomas. He lives on in you. That's how it's meant to be."

"What other way is there?"

Jason snorted. He didn't want to say.

"HELLO DOWN THERE."

Jason looked up into the darkness. He couldn't see even the greyest shape.

"HELLO," he called tentatively.

"IS THAT YOU, JASON?"

The voice was unfamiliar and yet the owner seemed to recognise him all the same. Jason didn't understand. Were there still further memories that still required integration? It was hard to tell with such a crowded mind.

A hand touched his heel. "I don't know who that is," Thomas said quietly. "But he can see us and we can't see him. Be careful."

"I will," Jason replied. "HELLO UP THERE. WHO ARE YOU?"

"IT'S DOMINIC."

That name meant nothing to him. Should it have done?

"YOU ARE NINE LEVELS FROM THE SURFACE," Dominic shouted. "DO YOU REQUIRE ANY ASSISTANCE?"

Jason bowed his head. "Thomas, do we require any assistance?"

"No," Thomas answered. "And I'm still armed."

"WE'RE FINE," Jason shouted.

"THEN I'LL WAIT FOR YOU AT THE TOP," Dominic replied. "I HAVE A FLYER STANDING BY."

"THANK YOU," Jason called back.

"RANDALL CAN'T WAIT TO SPEAK TO YOU."

Jason swallowed.

Randall the oath breaker.

Chapter Fourteen

The stairs were steep, hard on Ted's feet and not deep enough to accommodate his heel. By level 6 his calf muscles were burning. He still didn't know what he would do when he saw Lisa again or how much he would remain in control. All he did want was to hold her, just hold her, but he had a feeling the machines riding inside his blood had other intentions.

Shandra pulled his arm. "Stop."

He leaned against the stair rail and turned around. "You all right?"

"Just stop," she said breathlessly. "You've been running up these steps like a madman."

"I have?" He hadn't even noticed.

She stared him in the eye. "You have."

He looked up at the underside of the next level of the staircase. Lisa was waiting for him up there. Waiting. He needed to go to her, he needed to... then he patted the thigh of his bad leg and felt absolutely nothing.

"You need to tie me up again."

Shandra turned her head from side to side as if she were looking for something. "We aren't alone here."

Ted held out his wrists. "You can't let me hurt Lisa."

Her rifle was aimed at him with no pretence of anything otherwise. "I won't."

"Do it then."

She nodded and descended half a dozen steps to stand on the platform beside the exit to Level 6. Ted waited as she removed her backpack and rummaged inside, the rifle wavering in her one free hand and her eyes wavering with it. Pain flared instantly in his leg and despite himself, despite everything he intended and everything he wanted, he launched himself down the staircase.

His shoulder impacted her midriff before he could think, before he could even utter a word, the two of them crashing into the wall behind and then falling sideways down the next flight of steps in a furious series of impacts.

Ted was only vaguely aware of the stairs and ceiling clattering by, of the ringing in his ears as his head collided with concrete and the jarring pain in his elbow as it twisted the wrong way. Then it was all over, and he was lying on his back beside the door to Level 5 tasting blood and feeling broken.

Shandra!

She was there beside him, her body twisted in so many directions, blood leaking from a gash in her temple.

"Shandra?"

He tried to move and found that he could, albeit slowly and with more than a little pain. He crawled over to her on his knees and was relieved to hear she was still breathing, her chin slumped on the backl of her hand. He tried to shake her awake.

"Shandra?"

She wasn't waking up. He watched himself reach for the gun in her holster, felt the grip in his hand, the trigger under his finger. Felt it and then with a wrench, he swung his arm away and grabbed the barrel with his other hand.

"I will not!"

Perhaps his will was too strong or perhaps the nanomachines were working too hard to heal him of his other injuries. Either way they were at a standoff for control, a standoff that Ted felt he was slowly winning as he struggled to stand up and then walk away, step by step, back to level 6 and Shandra's discarded backpack. He kept on walking, winding his way up the staircase faster and faster, the reluctance in his joints giving way.

It was very possible that Shandra was dying, that the injuries caused by her fall could prove fatal. Ted knew she required immediate attention, but he could do nothing about it, not with the gun clutched tightly in his hand. Perhaps that was why he had won the fight to walk away, perhaps the nanotech had concluded their job done and were saving their remaining energy for his next victim, for Lisa.

He decided to stop, just stop, but found that he couldn't, not even for a moment. His progress was not as fast as before, not by any means, but it was constant and it was irrepressible. He tried to let go of Shandra's gun, just open his hand and let it drop.

He couldn't.

Level 7 gave way to Level 8 and then to Level 9 and all his willpower was for nothing. He couldn't stop himself climbing.

"Oh my God."

He was going to murder Lisa and there was nothing he could do to stop himself, nothing at all.

* * *

Lisa sat slumped against the wall in the corner of the ruined Commissary gasping for breath as she stared at the results of her frenzied handiwork. Most of the chairs were in pieces, tables dented, plates shattered. Food had been splashed over the floor and all over the walls and there was broken glass everywhere.

"Did that make you happy, Lisa?" Randall asked.

She didn't answer, she just sat there, her breathing slowly coming back under control as her rage subsided and turned into a thick and cloying hopelessness.

"What did you hope to achieve?" Randall asked. "How did that little display help you?"

She looked up, her eyes red and full of tears. "It didn't help at all."

"I know," Randall answered.

"Please," Lisa said. "Please Randall, I'm begging you, don't do it. Don't let everyone die."

"Everyone won't die."

"Randall, you can't."

"I'm sorry Lisa," he replied. "But it's the only way, the only possible way, the human race can survive. I've saved who I can. It's not within my power to do any more. I wish I could."

Lisa wiped her eyes. "It's not right."

"No Lisa," Randall said quietly. "It just is."

Around her the Commissary brightened and blurred as the tables banged out their dents, the plates and glasses became unbroken, the food returned to its serving stations and chairs became upright and whole.

Lisa shook her head in disbelief. "How?"

"I'm afraid you have achieved nothing, Lisa," Randall replied. "This place is only a layer of reality, a projection of my focal point. That focal point forces a refresh if the projection deviates too far from the source, overwriting whatever physical changes have been made. You can't hurt me here."

Lisa staggered to her feet and walked unsteadily across to one of the serving stations. Very carefully, she cut herself a slice of chocolate cake.

"A good choice, Lisa," Randall said. "Perhaps it will make you feel better."

She took her bowl and spoon and sat down at the nearest table.

"Do you have nothing to say?" Randall asked.

She swallowed some cake and licked her lips. "It's very good."

"My puppet is on his way to kill you, Lisa," Randall said. "He will be here very soon. What will you do?"

She dug in her spoon. "I'm going to finish my cake."

"Strange," Randall said. "Somehow that saddens me. I believe Dominic would be very upset that you gave in so easily, that you refused to fight."

Lisa looked up. "Why do you care if I fight or not?"

"I don't know."

She sat there, eating and savouring, letting the sweetness dissolve in her mouth, letting herself enjoy the cake. She felt tired, with nowhere to go and nothing to do. There was no point, she couldn't change anything or save anyone. At least Ted would be okay. She consoled herself with that thought. He was one of the remembered, and all the remembered had been chosen by Randall to survive. He would go on.

She found herself picturing his face, finding his smile, and hearing his laugh. She could recall him in the early morning light as he woke up beside her and tried to hide his pain. Ted would go on, Ted would live. She had hoped to carry on living with him, enjoying him, loving him, and perhaps later on when the time was right they could have created someone new to share and love together.

That was all gone, that possible future, all gone, dissolving in her mouth like so much sugar.

The door to the commissary opened and she didn't even look up. She didn't want to.

"Lisa?"

It was Gina. Lisa raised her head and saw the old lady being guided in by Webster, her hand tucked into the crook of his forearm.

"What do you want?" Lisa asked.

"Webster told me what happened," Gina replied. "You've upset him."

Lisa's eyes widened. "Upset him?"

The old lady took the seat beside Lisa, her spindly limbs shaking in the process. Webster held her forearm all the way, not letting go until she was settled and gave him a nod of thanks.

"Go away," Lisa said.

Gina reached over and pressed her hand down onto Lisa's fingers. "I'm sorry." The sensation was like ice. "But it's better that some survive than none at all."

Lisa pulled away. "And better yet if you're one of the survivors."

"Maybe," Gina said. "I don't know yet. It could be much worse."

Lisa turned to face her. "Worse than dying?"

Gina bowed her head. "The chosen will not go on as they are. We cannot. The Visshon will change us, absorb us. I don't know what that means."

Lisa gritted her teeth. "Would you rather be in my position?"

The old lady was silent.

"I thought not," Lisa said. "How will it happen? How will they 'cleanse' us?"

"Very carefully," Webster answered. Gina looked up at him and he took her hand and squeezed it gently. "I'll tell her."

"Then tell me."

"The part of us that resides in your frequency has almost cleansed your mining site. Afterwards we will travel across the desert to your dome and attack that too."

Lisa had a thought. "If you puncture the dome you would kill everyone, including your precious chosen ones."

"We don't intend to puncture your dome," Webster replied. "But we will enter, and we will consume all those not required for transformation. It is inevitable."

With a screech of her chair, Lisa stood up. "It's not necessary."

Webster straightened up to face her. "We've been down this road. Your people must die so mine can live. By saving the chosen we are being merciful. We don't have to save anyone. This way we are being kind, this way we are allowing you race to continue."

Lisa turned her back on him and marched off to the window. She felt his eyes on him as she did so. He wanted something and suddenly she knew what it was.

"You want me to admit you're right?"

"Yes," Webster replied. "Will you?"

Lisa leaned into the glass, staring out at the ghostly buildings and not seeing all the people she knew were there. The time for chocolate cake was over.

She turned around. "No, I won't."

The Visshon intermediary nodded. "Then I'm sorry."

"You're sorry, Gina's sorry, Randall's sorry. You know, you normally make an apology after you've done something wrong, not before."

Webster blinked. "I wish—"

"Whatever," Lisa spat. "You know what? Just send me home. Let me fight and die with everyone else. That's all I want to do. I don't want to be in this mad house anymore."

Webster sighed heavily. "I won't do that and besides, other arrangements have already been made..."

She stared at him.

"...But rest assured, it is a kindness compared to the end in store for the others."

"Kindness?"

"My people prefer to consume living food from the inside out."

Lisa's mouth opened.

Webster nodded solemnly and then turned towards the commissary door. "Holloway, you can come in now."

The door swung open again and a man entered, a pistol gripped in his steady hand.

Lisa shivered.

"Ted?"

* * *

When he reached Level 10, Ted was less than surprised to see that the thing resembling Jason Webster alive and waiting for him. The Grey Man seemed much healthier than the last image he had seen. There was colour in its cheeks and its hair was a shock of thinning red and grey hair rather than a washed out white. The environment suit was the same though, the same V in a reverse triangle logo. A suit issued from a ship long since dismantled. Beside it stood an old woman, the sight of her catching him by surprise. She was an ancient version of Gina Davies, the one time lover of Jason Webster who had died all those years ago on Old Earth.

"Yes, Ted," she confirmed. "It's me."

Ted had paused beside her, not of his own volition, but under the control of the nanotech Dominic had injected into his bloodstream. He wanted to speak to her, to ask how she survived and what she was doing here. He wanted to understand what the grey men was, how he could do what he could do, and why he shared Jason's face. He wanted to do so many things other than keep walking.

"Stay here," the Grey Man said. "I will call for you."

He was relieved even though he was trapped where he stood, Shandra's gun in his right hand, ready for use. He wanted to shout, to warn Lisa he was coming to kill her.

He wanted to scream.

He could do none of those things. All he could do was watch as the grey man and the old woman left him behind and walked towards a room marked with a circle and utensils. He shivered as the door swung open and they entered, leaving him to his silence and immobility.

He closed his eyes. Perhaps if he concentrated, he could regain some control. He had won the fight on the stairs after all, he could win again. With a grim determination he tried to move a leg, just a little bit. When that failed, he tried to wriggle one of the toes buried in his boot. He could feel that particular leg, he could feel that toe, but neither responded to his commands. He was being blocked.

But he could move his eyes, he wasn't sure why, but he could look from side to side, he could focus, he could even blink for all the good it did him. He experimented further, finding to his surprise that he could flare his nostrils, he could breathe faster, he could... There was an itch on the back of his neck. That was irritating. That was... his left hand moved, just a little, the fingers extended to execute a scratch. He was winning, but very slowly, very incrementally.

Would there be enough time?

"Holloway, you can come in now."

His legs started moving of their own accord despite his every mental effort to stop them. The gun in his hand was raised to head height, his grip on it tightening as his other hand slammed into the commissary door and pushed it open.

Gina and the other Jason were there, standing by the central table as he entered. Lisa was beside the window, her mouth dropping open as she saw him.

"Ted?"

His hand levelled the gun, his trigger finger poised to fire.

"What are you doing?" Lisa asked.

He didn't answer, he couldn't answer.

"Not you, Ted," she said. "Not you."

He was about to take aim, about to, until he did the one thing he had forgotten he could do with barely any effort at all.

He closed his eyes.

The gun hung there, for seconds or minutes, he didn't know which, his finger tightening on the trigger. Then without even seeing her, he fired, once and then twice more, the three bullets speeding on three separate and random paths.

A body thudded to the ground.

He pulled the trigger again and again, sending two more bullets into the darkness. He heard glass break, and screaming, but still he kept his eyes screwed up tight. There were still more bullets, and he didn't shy away from using them. He fired again and again and again until he could fire no more. The gun was empty.

"Ted," Lisa said.

He opened his eyes, afraid of what he would see, afraid of what he had done.

The old woman was on the floor, her white dress flowering with blood as the other Jason knelt beside her, his hand clamped down hard on her shoulder. Lisa was crouched by the broken window, the upper atmospherics of the parallel dome lifting her hair as she held fast to a table leg, her shoulders covered in glass.

"You're alive," he said with relief, his mouth working just briefly before the nanotech launched him towards her. She saw him coming and dived away sideways.

"Lisa," he cried. "You have to get away from me. I've got no control."

She was already up and running towards the centre table, jumping first onto a chair, then a tabletop and finally over his head. He moved to intercept her, a hand reaching up for her leg but not connecting. She landed just out of reach and shouldered her way through the door.

Despite his internal protest Ted made to follow her. He was going to hunt her down and murder her with his bare hands.

"Holloway, stop."

His body locked up as he stared into the eyes of the The Grey Man.

"Come here," the older Jason ordered.

Ted proceeded across the room to where Jason knelt nursing the old woman.

"She has a shoulder wound," Jason said. "Apply pressure while I get the medical kit."

Ted took Jason's place, one hand over the other pressing down upon Gina shoulder, pushing against a tide of escaping blood.

"I won't be long," Jason said and skidded out through the swinging door.

Ted found himself peering down at Gina, her face so much more crinkled than when they had met minutes before, and so much paler too.

She smiled up at him.

"Hello, Ted."

He couldn't reply.

"Well done for outsmarting the nanotech," she said. "They're programmed to assume the senses are permanently switched on. They forget about eyelids."

He said nothing.

"You are free to speak," Gina said.

His mouth moved again. "How could you be so cruel?"

"It wasn't my idea," she replied. "But Lisa needs to die somehow."

"Why?"

"She's in the wrong place at the wrong time."

Ted gritted his teeth. "That's not an answer."

"Webster wouldn't do it and he wouldn't return her to where she needs to be."

"So I'm here because he wouldn't dirty his hands?"

"He can't," Gina said. "He's a lifelong pacifist. Even letting you do it was almost too much for him. This is going to hit him hard."

"I don't care."

She grimaced in a sudden outburst of pain, her body shuddering under his hands.

"Are you going to die on me?" he asked.

"Not yet," Gina gasped.

"You should. You almost made me murder the woman I love."

"It needs to be done," Gina insisted weakly. "And this way it's a mercy, Ted, a mercy. You're one of the chosen - one of us. You're the only person we could use."

"Chosen?" He bared his teeth. "I didn't choose any of this."

"Only a select few will survive what is to come. You're one of them."

"You want to me to kill the woman I love and then happily get on with living?"

"Yes," Gina said and began to cough. "Her survival could jeopardise everything. The very future of our species is at stake."

Ted gritted his teeth. "You don't know what you're asking."

The old woman managed a stifled laugh between coughs. "Of course I do, you don't think I can't recognise my own grand-daughter? My own kin?"

Ted's eyes widened.

"The man I fought beside would understand. All those years ago, how many people did we willingly sacrifice for the greater good? How many tough decisions did we have to live with?"

He wanted to pull away from her then; he wanted to deny everything she was saying.

"You are that man," Gina said, and coughed again. This time she was coughing blood.

Ted gazed down into her gold flecked brown eyes. "I don't want to be."

The door swung open again and The Grey Man entered carrying a green medical kit.

"Get out of here," the older Jason Webster ordered. "Nanomachine Inhibitor protocol 8421 Delta, activate."

Ted felt his limbs return to his own control. He turned towards the man in the environment suit.

"Go away, Ted," The Grey Man said. "You've done enough damage."

Ted stood up uncertainly and then realised he felt no compulsion to run after Lisa, none at all. The Grey Man had freed him.

"Can you save her?" he asked.

"I don't know," the older Jason said. "Your bodies are so fragile. If any one part is damaged the whole system tends to fail. My people can lose up to 80% of our mass before we're compromised. Your design is seriously flawed."

"You're right about that," Ted agreed.

Webster was preoccupied with setting up a blood transfusion.

"Is there anything I can do?" Ted asked.

The Grey Man didn't look up. "I told you to go."

For a moment Ted stared at the old woman. She seemed so cold, so distant from the Gina he remembered.

"You are that man," she mouthed.

He turned and ran to the door.

Chapter Fifteen

Dominic settled into the flyer's cockpit and tried to remember how the controls worked. There were so many buttons, levers and switches, so many readouts and gauges, they all confused him. It hadn't been that long ago since he landed, he should have been able to remember. He should have been able to... He looked again, and the world spun.

He couldn't fly. He couldn't even takeoff.

"You all right up there?" Jason called from the cabin.

Dominic slumped back into the pilot's chair and took a deep breath. "No, I don't think I am."

"I can pilot," Thomas Jarvis offered.

"Thank you," Dominic replied and wrenched himself out of the seat and down the internal steps. In the cabin, Jarvis had already released his flight harness and sat up from his flight couch. He eyed Dominic with a sullen glare and then squeezed past him in the narrow space, his armour scraping Dominic's side

"The flight computer will let you plot a reverse course," he said.

"Got it," Jarvis replied without turning round.

Dominic watched him climb the steps and then sealed the internal cabin door.

"I think Thomas has a problem with you," Jason said.

Dominic shrugged as he strapped himself into the neighbouring flight couch. "All the enforcers hate me. I've never subscribed to their authority."

"You think you're above it?"

"Something like that."

"Hello Randall," Jason said.

Dominic shook his head. "Not quite."

"As close as it gets at the moment," Jason replied.

The flyer's engines started and a steady vibration ran up through Dominic's feet, up the flight couch, and into his back.

"I never wanted to be a part of your plan," Jason said, turning to face the avatar.

Dominic met Jason's eyes without blinking. "If it's any consolation, your death did cause a few issues."

"You made a promise to me."

"Which Randall kept," Dominic said. "He didn't bring you back."

Jason laughed softly. "You connived to get someone else to do it."

"The enforcers were presented with a problem and offered a possible solution. They reacted accordingly."

The Flyer was taxiing and picking up speed. Jason reached for his harness release button.

"Don't do it," Dominic warned. "We'll be in the air soon. I don't want you to hurt yourself."

With a grinding of teeth, Jason dropped his hand. "I wanted to hurt you."

Dominic managed a half-smile. "I'm more hurt than you could possibly imagine, old friend. My mind is breaking down."

"The Visshon," Jason said.

"Their presence tends to disrupt complex machinery, especially the Quantum linkages of a Biomesh brain. You and Jarvis are still carrying a part of them with you."

Jason turned over his hands and nodded.

"They are keeping track of you," Dominic said. "As soon as we arrive back at the dome they will dispatch their representative to return you to Gina."

"Gina?" Jason whispered.

Dominic's stomach lurched as the flyer attained upward motion. They were finally on their way.

"Together you will be the first to undergo the transformation," Dominic said. "The other chosen will follow soon enough."

"The Golden Realm," Jason mouthed. "What about you?"

Dominic raised an eyebrow. "I will perish along with everyone else."

"And Randall?"

"Him as well. Our nature is not compatible with the Visshon and our continuance was never an option."

"Don't you want to live?" Jason asked.

"I want to save the human race," Dominic replied and smiled wistfully. "Even more so because I have so enjoyed being human myself."

"I did wonder," Jason said.

"When Randall gave you this option, did you really think it was so he could survive?"

"He's Randall," Jason said simply.

"The Visshon were always going to wipe out the human race," Dominic said. "Our consumption of their life essences gave them no other option. This way, Randall's way, the human race will go on."

"But so many will die. So many!"

"That is the price that must be paid," Dominic said. "I do not pay it lightly."

"You just made the decision without giving anyone else the choice, you, the high almighty Randall."

Dominic sighed and then leaned forward in the harness as far it would go and peered across at his oldest friend.

"Part of me agrees with you, Jason. Part of me wants to save everyone, to fight even though the fight would be hopeless." He closed his eyes, aware that something new was happening. A reaction he had not experienced before.

Guilt.

He needed to explain, he needed to make Jason understand, because if Jason couldn't understand, no one would.

He opened his eyes.

"I don't have the luxury, your luxury, of making irrational and illogical decisions, and I wish I did, I wish... but without that luxury, without it, I'm constrained by probability, by statistical analysis, by everything in this world that is hard and unbending. At the end of the day... I don't have any choice either."

For a moment Jason just stared at him, chin raised, nostrils flared, sitting there in judgement. Dominic felt the cabin around them heave and sway more than ever before.

He had failed.

* * *

Jason was fuming. Randall the oath breaker was just sitting there explaining long and hard why mass murder was right and proper. It made him want to release himself and throttle the black suited man to within an inch of his life. It made him want to fight more than he had ever wanted to fight in his life. But then Randall wasn't really Randall at all, Randall was an avatar, a human puppet, endowed with Randall's memories and personality and yet separate from him. Beating Dominic would make no difference to the real Randall, no difference at all.

There was also something else, an almost desperate sincerity playing out on that human face, an implicit honesty. Dominic was suffering, his eyes dangerously bloodshot, his lips dry and his skin pale as death. Whatever Randall's plan, whatever the implications, it was completely unselfish, completely self sacrificing. Dominic and Randall were doing what they were convinced was right. They were saving some rather than losing all.

They had given up.

But then, so had he in his last life. That was why he made Randall promise not to resurrect him and why he had walked out into the desert with no intention of ever coming back. He looked down at his hands, the young smooth hands of a man not yet twenty-nine. Perhaps being young again made all the difference. Perhaps the testosterone was more concentrated, the hormones firing with more ferocity. Perhaps that was the reason he didn't feel like giving up this time. Perhaps that was why he had decided to fight.

He felt his anger towards Dominic dissipate. The emotion replaced with something new. Leaning forward, he turned towards the avatar.

"I'm here now, Dominic," he said. "For better or worse, I'm going to give you that choice."

The black suited man wiped his forehead with the back of his hand and nodded.

"You will try."

"Can you be repaired?" Jason asked.

Dominic smiled. "As I'm mostly biological, I prefer the term 'healed'."

"Can you be healed?"

"Perhaps I could recover given sufficient time and distance from the Visshon. I don't know."

"Then you don't need to die," Jason said.

"Optimistic."

Jason smiled. "Perhaps I can surprise you yet, machine head."

Dominic coughed loudly.

Jason turned his attention to the window on the far side of the flyer cabin. The amber glint of the dome was sparkling on the horizon. They were almost there, almost home. There was the spire of Randall's tower just penetrating the dome's surface. In a long ago conversation he had asked the machine mind why he needed to construct the AI stacks beyond the bounds of the dome.

So I can look out as well as in.

Jason sat in his stateroom on the Valhalla staring at Randall's monstrosity of engineering on his monitor.

"If you were human, I'd think you were making some sort of statement."

"Whatever could you mean?" Randall asked. Jason was sure there was a certain amount of amusement hidden in that deep mechanical voice.

"Never mind," Jason said. "Have we managed to shave off any power from those projections?"

"Designs of the city have been pared back so that there will be no internal transportation system. I'm afraid you humans will have to use your legs or worse, a bicycle."

"Healthy," Jason said. "Does that get us anywhere near the level of consumption the Visshon are willing to allow us?"

"Even with city, terraform station construction and mining development as frugal as we can make them?"

"Yes."

"We would need at least six decades more power than they are willing to give us."

Jason tapped his fingers playfully upon his desk. "Not so bad considering it was a hundred and twenty years over when I last looked."

"Indeed, but it's still not good enough."

"How are our pet scientists getting on?" Jason asked. "Have they discovered any way for us to theoretically defeat the Visshon should they attack?"

"No," Randall replied.

"But we process them all the time for the reactors."

"They allow that," Randall said. "They even initiate the chemical change by themselves."

"So we don't have a way to fight back if they decide to... melt us?"

"No," Randall replied. "And remember, they don't have a beneficial effect on me either."

Jason scratched the back of his neck. "I didn't want to order this but..."

"You want to dismantle the Valhalla and use its parts, reactors and fuel to lower power consumption cost."

Jason nodded. "Yes."

"That was the only logical choice remaining to you."

Jason drummed his fingers together. "I don't like it. At least if we kept the Valhalla operational, we could leave the planet if we needed to."

"We would not even make it to the next solar system," Randall replied.

"Not conventionally," Jason said. "But The Valhalla doesn't really need a crew for that sort of flight. As long as your memory drives remained uncorrupted, we could drift for thousands of years and still be returned to life."

"On Earth they would freeze the heads of the recently deceased and hope for that same outcome."

"It would be a chance," Jason said. "Admittedly, not a very good one."

"Moot, if the Valhalla is dismantled."

"What's the saving?" Jason asked.

"Maybe three decades, I would have to run a precise inventory."

"Then do it," Jason said and rose to his feet. "I'll go and see what my evil twin has to say."

"He appeared in the main lounge two hours ago," Randall said. "He finds light jazz relaxing."

"We'll make a human out of him yet," Jason added.

"I also noticed you said 'we' could be returned to life."

Jason frowned. "And you said it was moot."

"What about Gina?" Randall asked.

"I told you I don't want to see her," Jason replied "Assign her to one of the construction crews and keep her away from me."

"I refuse," Randall said. "If you saw her..."

"You can't make me," Jason answered.

"No I can't."

"Glad we agree," Jason said and walked across to the stateroom door. "I won't be bullied by you or by anyone."

"Indeed," Randall commented.

Jason slammed the release plate with his palm and the door slid open.

Gina was waiting for him on the other side.

*　*　*

Dominic felt the insides of his stomach squirming and threatening to climb up his throat. He swallowed the bile and dug his nails into the material of his armrests. The flyer was being buffeted again, the winds picking up as a new storm front moved in. Almost without thinking he recalled Thomas Jarvis's flight rating and found the word 'adequate' flashing ominously in his mind's eye. It was a rating that did not inspire confidence.

He leaned forward and vomited.

"Dominic?" There was concern in Jason's voice.

Dominic wiped his mouth with the back of his hand, smearing something disgusting onto the sleeve of his suit jacket.

"I'll be fine," he replied, "just a little flight sickness."

"I don't believe you."

It was a silly lie anyway. Dominic sat back and followed Jason's gaze to the cabin's far window. The dome was rapidly filling up the view, eclipsing the night sky. If Jarvis could remain 'adequate' for just a little while longer, they would be able to dock at the Tower's flyer port. After that it would be only a quick elevator ride down and then a short wait for Webster to arrive and take Jason to the Visshon.

Dominic could relax after that, his purpose at an end. He could even synchronise with Randall one last time and let Jarvis go his own way. The invasion was not so far behind. Jarvis could fight and die heroically with his fellow enforcers and Dominic could succumb quietly to the quantum sickness. Meanwhile Jason and Gina would be the first transformed by the Visshon and the rest of the chosen would swiftly follow.

It was all coming together exactly as he had planned.

Except, of course, Jason had hinted at some other way, a chance for the human race to continue without the need for bloodshed or transformation. Neither Dominic nor Randall had seen such a solution, but that didn't mean such a solution didn't exist. Dominic knew Jason far too well. Well enough to know he was not to be underestimated.

"I thought we were docking at the tower," Jason interrupted.

"That should have been the course laid in," Dominic replied.

"Not anymore."

Dominic agreed, the dome had filled up the window, but the tower was nowhere in sight. They were coming in to dock at the flyer station near the base of the dome. Jarvis was piloting them to the wrong place.

Dominic touched the cabin to cockpit intercom button on his armrest.

"Jarvis, why are you not following the pre-assigned course?"

There was a pause followed by a light buzz of background static.

"Flight control have ordered a course change override," Jarvis said.

"Ignore it," Dominic replied. "Proceed on the original course."

Again the light static.

"I can't do that," Jarvis said. "The order comes from Commissioner Chandler himself."

Damn him.

"He's the one who sent me to the mines in the first place," Jason said. "I'm guessing people don't normally come back."

Dominic nodded. "Any criminal element in such a carefully controlled environment cannot be tolerated. Chandler is very good at his job, but he is also very ambitious, and recently he exceeded his authority."

"Tell him that."

"Maybe I won't need to." Dominic pressed down on the button again. "Jarvis, my authority comes directly from Randall himself. Please ignore Commissioner Chandler's orders and proceed on our original course."

"I can't do that," Jarvis repeated.

"Jarvis, you will do as I say."

The intercom remained stubbornly silent without even the whisper of static. Dominic hit his harness release and almost hurtled towards the door that sealed the cockpit from the cabin. Despite his security codes, it didn't open. It was locked from the inside. It must have been locked ever since they had taken off from the mining site. Dominic resorted to punching it, giving the remains of his enhanced strength full reign. Even after a few satisfying and livid dents the door remained obstinately in place. It was designed to survive a crash impact, and unlike many human constructions, it had been built too well.

A hand clasped him on the shoulder. "Stop it," Jason said. "Save your strength."

Dominic heard him despite the loud blood pumping in his ears and took a step back, almost unaware that his knuckles were bleeding.

The flyer abruptly pitched sideways and sent them both careening into the nearside wall. Dominic took the impact with his shoulder, but Jason took it with his head. The avatar scrambled over his old friend. Jason's eyes were closed and there was a rapidly darkening welt just above his left eye.

"You stupid idiot!" Dominic shouted. "What were you thinking, getting out of your harness while we were in flight? What were you thinking!"

Jason slowly opened his eyes and groaned. "I'm fine, thanks."

Dominic's anger was still off the leash. "Don't you realise how dangerous that was?"

Jason struggled to sit up, "No more dangerous than what you did," he said. "My head aches and my ears are ringing."

Dominic leaned against the wall beside him. "I'm not surprised," he said, his breathing slowing down. "But then again, any brain damage might be an improvement."

Jason laughed too loudly. "You do have a sense of humour. Five thousand years and you finally tell a joke."

"Heat of the moment," Dominic replied and examined Jason's skull. "You'll live." He felt the violent lurch of descent in his stomach. "We're coming in to land."

Jason wiped his eyes and blinked. "There's something I need you to do for me."

* * *

The flyer landed with both of them still sitting against the wall, the engine vibrations building to a staccato as they reverberated up Jason's spine and into his skull, rattling his teeth. Beside him, Dominic was looking more than a little worse for wear. The avatar had spent his anger in a savage but pointless onslaught on the cockpit door. The way the metal had bent beneath the blows was more than a little frightening. Jason could only imagine what Dominic could do to a man if he had a mind for it. But the aftermath of the assault had apparently left Dominic weaker than ever before, his head drooped against his upper chest as if it was a weight his neck could not support.

The flyer shook violently one last time and then the engines were still. They had taxied to a halt. Jason struggled to his feet and then nudged Dominic's shoulder. The avatar glanced up without focussing his eyes before taking the offered hand. Jason lifted Dominic up with a heave and almost fell down in the process. The avatar was like a dead weight. Jason swallowed and braced him, one of Dominic's arms over his shoulder and one of Jason's arms around the avatar's waist.

"It's not as bad as all that," Dominic said. "I'm getting ready to deploy what I have left."

Jason nodded as the misshapen cockpit door banged within its housing. Thanks to Dominic's handiwork, Jarvis was trapped on the other side.

"Someone will get him out," Jason said.

"No hurry," Dominic replied.

Jason turned his attention to the airlock, the green light indicating pressure had normalised. As it opened two armoured enforcers filed in almost immediately, rifles aimed and at the ready.

"Don't move," one of them ordered, leaning forward to relieve Dominic of an ancient hand weapon.

Jason could barely shrug. With most of Dominic's weight bearing down on his shoulders the two of them were more likely to collapse than anything else.

Chandler followed the enforcers inside wearing the same suit as the day before.

"Good evening, gentlemen," he said. "Pleasant flight?"

"What is the meaning of this?" Dominic asked weakly. "Why did you divert us? You don't have the authority—"

"The city council voted to rescind Randall's security privileges exactly two hours ago," Chandler interrupted. "Your legal status is highly questionable, Dominic. You're not even human. I could have you shot where you stand."

"As if it matters how a few old men vote," Dominic said. "Randall's systems control everything."

Chandler pursed his lips. "My techs advise me his higher brain functions can be severed and his automated responses preserved. Cut off the head and the body will still function."

"You can't lobotomise a machine mi—" Dominic suddenly began laughing, his body shaking violently beneath Jason's arm. "As if it matters anymore... The end is coming."

"Your circuitry is obviously damaged," Chandler said and turned his gaze upon Jason. "You were important once. What threat do you pose now?"

"None," Jason said. "I'm not here to challenge anyone."

The Commissioner shook his head. "Randall brought you back to be our puppet leader, just like you were before. But it's too late, Webster, far too late."

"I don't think you understand," Jason said.

"Oh, I understand," Chandler glared. "You even destroyed my mine somehow, infected it. Now I have to nuke it from orbit and find a new site. But it won't save Randall, nothing will."

One of the enforcers raised a hand to his ear and then turned towards the Commissioner.

"Sir, Randall has deployed his defence drones, they've taken down three of our men and pinned down the rest of the security detail in the tower stairwell."

Chandler raised an eyebrow. "Order reinforcements. Now, where's Jarvis?"

Jason motioned to the cockpit door. "He's trapped."

Chandler briefly studied the warped metal and then turned to his enforcer. "Get these two into holding and then get a crew down here to cut him out. Perhaps Randall will be interested to know that I have his two puppets as my hostages."

The enforcer nodded and motioned his weapon towards Jason and Dominic. "Move it."

Chandler had already turned away and was walking back down the airlock.

"Well played, Commissioner," Dominic called after him. "A few days ago it might almost have mattered."

Chandler paused to flick something off his shoulder. "You shouldn't have threatened my family, machine head."

With those words he continued walking.

"Come on," the enforcer ordered, his companion circling around the cabin to stand directly behind Jason and Dominic.

"So, we're not dead," Jason said quietly.

"We just need a little more time," Dominic whispered back. "Webster will be coming for you soon and after that, nothing Chandler does will matter to anyone."

Chapter Sixteen

Lisa was running down the staircase too fast, the heel of a boot catching on a step as she neared Level 8 and almost sending her headlong into a wall. She collapsed, slowly regaining her breath and looking back the way she had come. There was no sign of pursuit, no sign of Ted. He had almost shot her - she couldn't get over that - and he had shot Gina.

The old lady was dead or hurting, and yet somehow had been complicit in the whole situation. Gina and Webster had wanted something from her, approval that what they were doing was justified. She hadn't given it. She would never give it. After her rejection they sent in Ted to execute her.

What had happened to him? She couldn't even begin to guess why he had agreed to kill her. But there was something odd about how at the last moment he had closed his eyes, closed them and fired blind. Perhaps he had been ashamed; perhaps he simply couldn't look her in the eye. But that very action had given her a chance to survive and she had taken it, ducking down under his line of sight and staying stock still as he filled the Commissary with bullets.

After his gun had emptied she escaped, not that she really had anywhere to go. If she left the tower, one or more of the Inishi would hunt her down, and if she stayed, Ted would do the same. Well, of the two options Ted was the easiest to face. She couldn't beat a monster, but she could beat a man, especially one as disabled as Ted. Except, another mystery, he had been walking normally and without physical support, walking as if his leg had never even troubled him in the first place.

She stood up slowly, brushed off her uniform, and looked down the centre of the staircase. It was not so very far to the bottom. With an upward glance she began descending again, this time more carefully, more slowly, and as silently as she could. Briefly, she tried to spot one of Randall's security sensors, but that effort was in vain. Microtechnology was incredibly difficult for the human eye to detect. As for Randall, the machine mind was keeping quiet and probably directing Ted directly to her location. He could arrive at any moment. It was on the descent from Level 7 to Level 6 that she saw something that put him to the back of her mind.

It was Shandra Broussard, lying on the Level 5 platform spitting blood.

"Shandra?" Lisa called, rushing down with no more pretence of stealth.

The female enforcer raised her rifle and Lisa stopped where she was, metres away, staring down the barrel of another gun.

"Shandra? What happened?"

The enforcer winced as she lowered the rifle. "I finally caught up with you."

Lisa closed the distance and kneeled down beside her, Shandra had a nasty cut on her forehead and her gums were more than just a little bloody.

"Did Ted do this to you?"

Shandra nodded slowly. "Sort of, it's complicated. Dominic injected him with some sort of nanotech to help him walk. Turns out the tech does a bit more than fix his leg, it lets them control him."

Lisa felt a hot flush of relief. "He didn't mean to do it."

Shandra coughed up more blood. "No, but then he didn't mean to shoot poor Steve either. I was stupid, I let my guard down."

Lisa looked around. "Steve's here?"

Shandra shook her head ominously and Lisa understood the meaning.

"All Ted wanted to do was find you," Shandra said.

Lisa leaned against the balustrade. "He took a few shots at me too."

"It's not his fault," Shandra said and indicated her rifle. "We have this."

Lisa looked down at the weapon covered in Shandra's sticky blood. She didn't know if she could use it on Ted. Not him. In retrospect she was sure he had tried his damndest not to kill her. She would do the same.

"Shoot to wound," Lisa said.

"Yeah," Shandra agreed weakly. "Backpack."

Lisa looked up and saw it on the Level 6 platform, one strap broken, but the contents still inside. She ran up and retrieved it.

"I have at least two broken ribs and probably a punctured lung," Shandra said as Lisa returned. "Deal with them quickly."

Lisa opened the pack and began to rummage through the contents.

"I don't know if Randall can see us here," Lisa said. "But we have to assume he can."

"No Ted yet," Shandra said. "But, what's that?"

Lisa looked up. "What's what?"

Shandra pointed to the wall by the nearest stair. "Holes. I'm sure they weren't there a minute ago."

Lisa saw them too. Seven bullet holes puncturing the concrete in a pattern she readily associated with automatic weapon fire. As she looked on, more holes appeared beside the seven with no obvious point of origin. She reached up and pushed her finger through, the dust spilling over the staircase.

"I haven't fired," Shandra said.

Lisa looked down at her finger and recalled how the commissary had repaired itself after her tantrum. It was then that she understood.

"The tower, the real tower, is being attacked and that damage is being translated here. Someone must be trying to kill Randall."

Shandra raised her head drowsily and then slumped back down against the wall. "Amen to that."

* * *

Ted closed the door to the Commissary behind him and looked up.

"Okay Randall," he said. "Where's Lisa?"

"I last detected her entering the main stairwell," the machine mind replied. "After that I have no idea. Many of my local surveillance feeds have been cut at our point of origin and those differences are translating here. The enforcers are attacking my tower even as we speak."

"Chandler?"

"Yes," Randall answered. "He swung the city council against me. It seems they would like me to be a little less controlling."

"It couldn't happen to a nicer machine head."

"It's all too late to matter, Ted," the voice boomed. "Far too late."

"We'll see," he replied, and ran down the corridor towards the staircase entrance. "Goodbye Randall."

He clattered down the stairs, passing level 9 in moments, level 8 even faster. He wasn't worried about how much noise he made, in fact, the more noise the better.

"Lisa!" He called without slowing

As he rounded Level 6 a bullet buried itself in the wall beside his leg. He halted abruptly and held up his hands.

"I'm not armed."

"Stay right where you are," Lisa ordered. She was hugging the wall on the bend in the staircase just above the level 5 platform, a rifle in both hands, aimed indelicately at him. Just behind her he made out the injured form of Shandra, her chest bandaged and her clothes bloody as her eyes stared deeply into space.

"I'm not a threat," Ted said. "Not anymore."

"Why should I believe you?" Lisa asked.

He bowed his head. "None of that was me up there, Lisa. I wasn't myself. I was being controlled."

"I know," Lisa replied, her aim unwavering. "But it doesn't change anything."

"It's me," Ted said. "Please believe that. No-one's controlling me anymore. It's just me."

He watched her bite her bottom lip. "I want to believe you, but..."

"I'm not going to hurt you," Ted said and took a step down despite the gun. "I would never hurt you."

She motioned to his leg. "The nanomachines are still working."

"Just enough for me to walk," Ted replied. He took another step.

"Please don't make me shoot."

He could see her eyes water. She was exhausted, they were all exhausted.

"I'm not going to hurt you," Ted said. "I would never—"

"What about Steve?" Lisa asked. "What about him?"

Ted was speechless.

"Disable him," Shandra interrupted. "It's the only way to be sure."

"Lisa?"

"Sorry, Ted," Lisa replied. "This is for your own go—"

The stair beneath her feet abruptly collapsed and sent the rifle flying.

Ted leapt forward. "Lisa!"

Her fingers had found a handhold on the remaining step beside her, but it was a tenuous grip at best. She was slipping.

Shandra knelt down and leaned across the gap, hooking her arms around Lisa's waist. "I've got you."

Three steps were gone, the powder and rubble indicating an explosion that they hadn't even witnessed. Ted rapidly closed the distance between them and took hold of Lisa's wrists, hauling her up.

"Thank God you're all right," he said, pulling her towards him. "I thought I'd lost you so many times."

Lisa met his eyes and breathed hard. "Ted?" All the sweat, tears and dirt made no difference, he was laughing.

"Come here," she said.

They kissed.

"Hey," Shandra interrupted as she stood up. The ground was shifting under her feet. "This could go any second."

Ted let Lisa go and held out his arms. "Jump across."

Shandra peered downward and gritted her teeth. "You better catch me."

"Of course I will."

Shandra jumped. Ted took the impact and fell backwards, cushioning her from impact even as the edge of a concrete step jarred into his spine.

"I owed you that," Shandra said.

"I know," he replied.

She peeled herself off him and stood up, wincing. Ted saw a few speckles of red forming on her bandages. He hadn't cushioned her enough. Swiftly he climbed to his feet and looked around.

"This place is falling apart."

"Look!" Lisa pointed down the centre of the staircase. The flickering rainbow colours of an Inishi creature had appeared at ground level were rising fast. As they watched two more followed.

"Someone must have bombed the lobby," Lisa said.

Ted nodded. "Those things will swarm the place. Come on." He pushed the two women in front of him and they ran up the staircase two steps at a time. It was becoming more unstable every second; great chunks of concrete vanishing without cause just as suddenly as rubble appeared from nowhere. Some sort of pitched battle was taking place; a battle with effect but no visible cause. This alternate reality stuff was giving Ted a headache, but he didn't have to understand it in order to run.

"Where are we going?" Lisa asked.

"The grey man," Ted replied, a sudden dent in a step underfoot almost knocking him off balance. Lisa caught his hand. "We can make him take us home."

Lisa nodded and they carried on. As they reached the platform for Level 9 the staircase abruptly terminated, literally vanishing before their eyes. Another second and they would have been standing on it. Ted looked down and saw an explosion of colour. The Inishi were gaining.

"In here," Lisa said, pulling open the door to Level 9. Ted stepped away from the edge and followed her and Shandra inside.

Level 9 appeared untouched, the potted plants ornate and undamaged at various points along its untroubled corridor.

"Will the door hold them?" He asked.

Lisa and Shandra carried a heavy plant pot over to the staircase door and lodged it in place under the handle.

"That should do it," Lisa said. "Webster told me they can't open doors, but this will make sure."

Ted nodded and leaned against the nearest wall to catch his breath. "Good." When he looked up, the plant pot had returned to its original position.

"Oh, come on!"

"The refresh rate is getting faster and faster," Lisa said.

"Whatever that means," Shandra added, her palm rubbing against her bandages. "What now?"

Ted looked around. "I think we should—"

"I was asking Lisa," Shandra interrupted. "No offence, Ted, but she's senior."

Ted rolled his eyes.

"We find somewhere safe to rest up," Lisa said. "Then we find Webster and go home."

Ted pointed at the ceiling. "He's just up there. We can—"

"Should we shout?" Shandra asked with her arms crossed.

Ted gnashed his teeth.

"Rest," Lisa said. "Let's find a room of limited strategic importance. Maybe it won't get shot up while we're in it."

"Okay," Ted said and motioned to the corridor. "Which way?"

Lisa looked left and then right, her lips moving silently. "Right," she said finally. "It's as good a way as any."

Lisa started walking. Ted motioned to Shandra. "After you."

"Thanks," Shandra said and reached for Lisa's arm. "Any chance you want to tell me exactly what's going on?"

"I'm not sure you would believe me," Lisa replied.

"Try me."

As the two female enforcers walked away, Ted took a deep breath. There was no point being angry, he had to go beyond that. He had to stop reacting and start thinking; he needed to remember his training. With a long exhale he pressed his hand against the staircase door. It moved ever so slightly within the frame. He truly hoped it would be enough to keep the Inishi out. He had to trust Lisa's judgment.

"Come on, Ted," she called from a few metres away. "I've got some things to tell you, and with that leg of yours working again, you've got no excuse to lag behind."

He ran to catch up.

* * *

On Level 9 they found six server rooms, the cooling fans too loud and the air too hot. Nevertheless all the rooms were untouched by violence, or even a power cut, the machines whirring away in a drone of unknown activity. Lisa concluded they were home to integral systems the enforcers wished to preserve rather than destroy. She decided to shelter in the largest of the rooms, and the three of them settled down at the centre of a cluster of server towers upon a cold hard floor, stopping to catch their breath.

Lisa was both tired and hungry and helped herself to a nutri bar from the backpack, chewing it slowly as the other two sat in silence.

On their way here she had tried to answer all their questions, tried to make them understand about The Visshon, Randall and The Chosen and exactly what was at stake.

She had listened to herself and wondered if she was going insane.

"How long are we staying in this place?" Shandra asked abruptly. The wounded enforcer was sweating in the heat and scratching at her bandage. It would need re-dressing very soon.

"Until I say so," Lisa replied. It was good to exercise authority again even if it was only to disguise the fact that she had no actual answer to the question.

"Yes ma'am," Shandra said, apparently satisfied.

Ted was sitting opposite, his gaze wavering on a point somewhere above Lisa's head. After their initial kiss he seemed to be avoiding eye contact.

"Ted?" she said, reaching a hand out to touch the toe of his boot.

"Sorry," he replied, snapping back to reality.

She patted the space beside her. "Come over here."

He managed a feeble grin. "Are you sure you trust me now?"

So, he was hurt and wanted attention and reassurance. Sometimes he could act like a typical man.

"Yes I do," she said. "Now come over here."

He did, sharing an odd glance with Shandra as he scrambled across. Lisa ignored it and reached for his hand. He smiled shyly as their fingers intertwined.

"Sorry," he said.

She leaned forward. "What are you sorry for?"

"You know."

"Yes?"

He raised his chin and laughed awkwardly. "For trying to shoot you."

"But it wasn't you."

He raised his other hand and stared at it. "It was still me, even if I wasn't in the driving seat. I..." He gritted his teeth. "How could they do that to me?"

She kissed him on the cheek. "I don't know."

He closed his eyes and bowed his head, the pressure on her fingers increasing. He was holding on very tight.

"I'm sorry for almost shooting you in the leg," she said. "I wouldn't have missed."

He laughed at that. "Only if you closed your eyes."

She frowned. "You were lucky."

He met her eyes. "I'm very lucky."

"Please!" Shandra interrupted.

Lisa grinned. "Sorry."

Shandra pointed to the wall. "Should I go next door?"

"I think we should stay together," Lisa said and reached into the backpack. "Have a nutri bar."

"I'm not hungry," Shandra replied and threw the bar back. "I just want to go home. I've had enough of this place."

"How are your ribs?" Ted asked.

"They still hurt."

"I'm sorry for attacking you."

"I know you are," Shandra said. "But it doesn't stop me from being angry."

"I'll make it up to you."

Shandra shook her head. "It's not you I'm angry with."

Ted nodded in understanding.

Lisa studied the two of them. Shandra's anger was easing but Ted still seemed anxious. She patted his hand and looked upward.

"Randall, are you there?"

Both Shandra and Ted stared at her in alarm. She ignored them. They needed help and Randall was their only choice.

"Hello, Lisa," the machine mind replied.

"Do you still want to kill me?" She asked.

"I don't want to kill anyone," the deep voice declared. "But some death is... necessary. However, considering Gina's failing health, the chosen may shortly require an emergency replacement. You could be that replacement, Lisa. It's what Gina would want."

Ted couldn't believe his ears. "After all that?"

"The end is almost at hand, Ted," Randall replied. "I am nothing if not pragmatic."

"No," Lisa said.

Ted turned towards her. "What?"

She looked up into the eyes and smiled. "I don't want to be one of the chosen."

His mouth opened. "But this way we can survive... together."

She reached up and gently cupped his cheek in her hand. "No, Ted, it's not right."

"But?"

"You didn't have any choice," she said. "But I do."

Her hand dropped away.

"What about me?" Shandra asked.

"Your status remains unchanged, Officer Broussard. But as I believed you were dead already, I am no longer in a position to do anything about it. Webster will decide what to with you as and when he arrives."

"Where is he?" Lisa asked.

"The damage to my tower demands he take a circuitous route. He will be with you shortly."

"Will he take us home?" Lisa asked flatly.

"He can," Randall replied. "If that is what he wants."

"I want to go home," Lisa said.

"You can only delay the inevitable," Randall declared.

"I have no problem with that."

"I'm not disappointed." Randall replied. "I wish you well. The Visshon in our home frequency have almost arrived at the dome. Very shortly my functionality will be compromised."

"Was this all worth it?" Lisa asked.

"I don't know, Lisa," Randall replied. "I will never know, but I hope so. If your species survive in one form or another then I wouldn't have it any other way."

"We will fight," Ted declared.

"You can't fight the Visshon," Randall said. "But neither will they harm the chosen. Ted, if you go back, you will witness the death of everyone around you, including Lisa. You won't be able to do anything to stop it."

He shook his head. "I don't believe that."

"Belief doesn't come into it," Randall replied. "A fact is a fact. Goodbye, Ted, you were the only one to come close to challenging Jason in my affections. I wish you could remember all our discussions, all our experiences together. Maybe a small part of me would live on if you did."

Shandra scrambled to her feet and savagely kicked one of the server towers. "Just die, machine head! Die!"

Silence...

Lisa felt Ted's arm curl around her shoulder. She closed her eyes.

"Good evening."

Webster was standing over them in his environment suit, having appeared from nowhere. Shandra, still enraged, threw herself at him in a feeble attack. The grey man caught her easily in both arms and eased her down to the floor, despite her writhing limbs.

"You're making your injuries worse, Miss Broussard," Webster declared. "Please calm down for your own good."

Shandra screamed angrily and tried to punch him.

Lisa pulled away from Ted. "Officer Broussard!"

Shandra stopped fighting, the anger still glistening in her eyes.

Lisa stepped forward and knelt down to squeeze Shandra's shoulder. "You have to keep it together."

She could see Shandra's anger had dissipated slightly even if the awful pressure remained.

"Please Shandra."

The injured Enforcer nodded slowly and Webster eased his grip. As he let her go she clutched her chest and silently began to cry.

"Shuush," Lisa soothed and stroked her hair. "It's okay. It's all okay."

Webster stepped back. "Did I hurt her? It wasn't my intention."

"No more than she hurt herself," Lisa replied. "She'll be fine."

"I apologise for startling you all."

Lisa stood up and brushed herself down. "Can you take us home?"

"I shouldn't," Webster declared. "I will be taking you back to die and that death will be much worse than a bullet. You should wait and take Gina's place."

"Then she is dying?"

"She doesn't have long," Webster replied quietly. "She asked that you take her place. She feels it is appropriate."

"I can't," Lisa said. "I won't. Will you take us home?"

Webster sighed deeply and wiped his eyes. It was only then that Lisa realised he had been crying. Did he care for the old woman that much?

"I can't make you take her place," he said. "Right now I should be retrieving Jason."

"Then take us with you," Lisa added quickly.

He frowned. "I won't be responsible for your death."

"But if you leave us here what will happen to us?"

The thing that resembled Jason Webster rubbed his jaw. "Eventually, my people will come for you."

Lisa met his eyes. "Then it doesn't matter what you do."

"Lisa, I don't..." he stared up at the ceiling. "I don't know anymore."

Chapter Seventeen

Dominic was feeling better, his tremors and sweats gone, his eyesight steady and his brain apparently more able to process coherent thought. Whatever had infested Jason's hands was not active enough to cause him pain and Dominic realised he was almost himself again. But even with all his faculties and physical superiority, he and Jason were still locked in a holding cell, still trapped. The exit was as implacable a barrier as the one between cabin and cockpit on the flyer. He could damage it, of that there was no doubt, and he could damage himself, but escape seemed doubtful. He needed to wait for the right opportunity. He needed to bide his time.

Jason was sitting on a bench on the other side of the cell, his head bowed in silent thought. Outside the reinforced transparent window, the dome had gone into night mode, the lighting reduced to a soft glow that illuminated objects but denied daylight detail. It was not the night that would have been experienced on the true exterior of the planet. That was a darkness that was so close to pitch black that even Dominic wouldn't have been able to see more than few metres ahead. No, the dome dwellers didn't really have any idea of what true darkness was. Only the remembered would have experienced anything close to it.

Beyond the cell door, the block corridor was empty. No visible guards or enforcers, no officialdom, all to give Dominic the sense that they had been locked up and forgotten. He knew that wasn't true. His surveillance filtering device had been removed so that sensors could track their vital signs, record their breathing and tabulate the slightest variation in body heat. Perhaps a man or woman sat behind a desk somewhere, monitoring and waiting, not knowing what to expect but expecting something. Beyond that, he hoped Randall was watching as well, watching and ready to help.

"So," Jason said abruptly. "Did the Visshon ever tell you exactly what this 'transformation' would mean?"

Dominic scratched the back of his neck. "Not exactly, only that it would allow you to conquer death, and to add your thoughts and feelings to Visshon society just as their thoughts and feelings would be added to yours."

"A merger," Jason said.

"Immortality and enlightenment," Dominic replied. "A new dawn for humanity."

"In the golden realm," Jason added quickly.

Dominic blinked. "Yes, they are very fond of that term."

"It's all very vague," Jason said.

"I'm sure it will all become clear once the process is complete."

"But you and Randall don't really know?"

Dominic stood up and paced across the room, his arms crossed. "We are machine minds, Jason. To be brutally honest, we don't know how you think at all. Those organic sponges you call brains defy analysis. My biomesh brain is an attempt at something similar, but I can't measure how similar it is. I can only make an informed decision."

"A guess?"

"Exactly, but a logical one. Humanity created the first machine minds and our thought processes follow some of the same rules as a result, but the Visshon are completely alien, we do not share any common ground. Yes, their emissary uses our language, but in this context language as a means of communication and relating ideas is a flawed medium. The Visshon may not possess the words required to adequately convey their meaning and may be attempting to use ill-advised substitutes."

Jason smiled. "I've missed this. You have a roundabout way of saying you don't know by explaining exactly why you don't know."

"Yes," Dominic replied excitedly. "You have always understood me, Jason."

Still grinning, Jason shook his head. "Never mind."

Dominic stood over him. "But you don't want to transform, do you?"

Jason licked his lips. "Maybe if I knew more about what it meant, but... no. There is a natural order of thing. I know that sounds strange coming from me. But, I think our way of life needs to be preserved and I will find a way to preserve it, even if it's from the inside."

"You disagree with Randall's solution?"

"I always did," Jason said. "But you and Randall were faced with an impossible situation and made the only decision you could. I understand that now, but I'm not limited by your logic."

Dominic paced back to his side of the cell. "No, I don't suppose you are."

Jason raised an eyebrow and then stood up and walked across to the cell door. "Come on, come on." He peered down the long corridor. "Where exactly is my evil twin when we need him?"

Dominic returned to his bench and sat down. Webster would be here eventually, he knew that. He closed his eyes and sifted through the minutiae, recalling each one of the chosen in turn. He saw men and women of so many different races, religions, caste systems, political affiliations, all sharing a common goal to help others with the unburdened creativity of the truly gifted. They were the best of the best, the best the human race could offer, and they would go on because Randall had dared to make it happen. He had dared to sacrifice.

It wasn't wrong, not when the alternative had been to lose everything and everyone. It wasn't wrong.

"You're sweating again."

Dominic opened his eyes and saw Jason's youthful and innocent face swimming in his vision twice over.

He knew what that meant.

"The Visshon are here," he declared. "The slaughter has begun."

Jason stamped his foot. "Damn it, where is he? I just need to get to them. I just need to make them see."

Dominic felt a ripple of cold dance through his shoulder and chest. It was far too subtle for a human to sense, but it wasn't beyond him, not yet.

"He's here."

Jason stopped and turned his head from side to side, looking for something he couldn't possibly see.

"Where?"

Webster appeared beside the window, transparent to solid in less than a second, the grey environment suit pressing out from the bulk of a man who appeared twenty years older and twenty pounds heavier than Jason. They could have been father and son, not representations of the same man, long gone.

"I'm here."

The light in the cell instantly changed from white to red as the whole block filled with an ear splitting siren. Dominic covered his ears. He did not find it pleasant.

Webster held out his bare hand to Jason and mouthed words that were too indistinct to understand. Dominic's eyes were not working well enough to lip read.

Jason nodded and then turned to Dominic briefly and smiled. So this was the final goodbye.

Dominic looked on as the two men linked hands and very slowly - and so gradually - began to fade away. Three enforcers ran down the hallway and halted by the cell door, weapons raised. But they didn't fire. They just stood and watched, frozen in place, frozen in awe. Seconds later Jason was gone.

Gone forever.

"Good luck," Dominic said.

There were two more words he had heard his humans use on such an occasion. Somehow they seemed appropriate.

"God Speed."

* * *

The Visshon intermediary was just as Jason remembered, an almost mirror image of himself. Yes, he knew he was younger now, the youngest he could possibly be, but that old weathered face on the Visshon simulacrum was how he truly saw himself. It was the face he wore inside.

As the sirens wailed louder than seemed possible, the ambassador spoke to him.

"Gina is dying. She needs to see you one last time."

Jason couldn't hear the sirens anymore.

You're so old.

Gina was standing there in the doorway of his stateroom, lips opens, her skin and hair a lustrous brown as those impossible gold flecked eyes bored into his very soul.

"What are you doing here?"

She smiled. "I wanted to see you."

He reached for the door control but it was too late, she had already inveigled herself inside.

"Get out."

She ignored him, walking around his space slowly and thoughtfully as she examined his bookshelves and mounted holoframes. One was currently displaying an old Earth painting of an Austrian village complete with mountain peaks and a boy tending a goat. She grinned thoughtfully at the image and then turned away. He fumed as she wistfully dragged her fingers over the surface of his desk and then slowly over his console keyboard.

"I want you to go right now!"

He moved to grab her arm but she darted away before his fingers could close around it.

"This isn't much better than the room we used to share in the refuge."

He blinked. He could barely remember that room. For him it was so many lives ago, so many millennia, but to her it was only yesterday.

"Neither you or I have ever shared anything."

She reached down onto the carpet and picked up a discarded sock. "Disgusting, you never were very tidy."

"Put that down."

She draped it over the top of his console screen and laughed. "That's a good place for it."

He stormed over and gripped her arms tightly. "Get out now!"

Angrily, he manoeuvred her into the doorway, only to find himself hurled into a wall and knocked onto his back. She was as quick and strong as ever. Stunned for a moment, he tried to get up, only for her foot to come crushing down upon his chest.

"I know I'm not Gina," she said. "Of course I know. The crew of this ship can barely look me in the eye, let alone talk to me. I remind them too much of the woman who died, of the woman I replaced!"

He looked up at her. "It wasn't because of me."

Her foot pushed down all the harder.

"Oh, I know that. Randall did it because he cares so much for you. A machine head, Jason, a machine head! They're the enemy."

"Not for a long time," he gasped. "We're founding a new colony."

"They killed everyone," she screamed. "They killed our families, our friends, they even killed us. They killed you and me both!"

She raised her hands and stared at them.

"I don't know what this is!"

With a push, he shoved her foot away and sent her careening into the side of the bed. Her head struck the metal frame and she toppled face down onto the carpet.

"Gina!"

He scrambled over to her body and rolled her over. She was breathing rapidly and her eyes were open, fixed and staring up at the ceiling.

"What am I?" She asked.

"You're Gina Davies," he said without hesitation.

She started to cry. "What am I?"

He leaned over her and peered down, the smell of her was so overpowering, so familiar, reaching in and exposing him to a thousand memories, a thousand snapshots of time.

"You're Gina Davies," he repeated. "You've lived hundreds of lives, all of them with me. You're my wife."

"I'm not her."

He kissed her lightly on the lips and pulled away, the taste melting into his mouth.

"Do you remember that?" he asked. "I do."

She wiped her eyes. "Jason?"

"You're Gina Davies, and..." He exhaled sharply and smiled. "I thought I'd lost you. I thought you were gone forever." He was the one crying now. "I thought..."

She reached up and encircled him in her arms; pulling him down.

* * *

The red light was still blinking but thankfully the alarm itself had been silenced. Dominic sat alone in his cell and calmly ran internal diagnostics. Physically he was fine, even a little better than fine. His body was the best it could be, his internal organs, his musculature, all exceptional by any human standard. But it wasn't his body he had to worry about, that was a prime product of genetic engineering. No, he had to worry about his mind. If only there was a way of shielding himself from the Visshon effect to keep his mind running without interference.

That was the problem when dealing with a life form that existed in multiple realities simultaneously. The way it communicated with itself interfered with every machine connection in the vicinity. Complex circuits broke down and quantum linkages only operated intermittently. He could only imagine the effect the Visshon were having on Randall. As far as machine organisms were concerned, Randall was the most advanced on the planet, and because of that, the one most susceptible to damage. His final death would be swifter and far more painful than Dominic's could ever be.

Dominic did not find this a fortuitous state of affairs, he had always hoped he would synchronise with Randall when the end came, that they could be one and face death together. Sitting there, he didn't even know if synchronisation was even possible anymore. Both he and Randall could already be too far gone. He didn't know, but he still had to try. Somehow he had to return to the tower. He had no choice.

Outside in the corridor the three enforcers stood to attention. Dominic guessed who was coming.

Sure enough, Neil Chandler, Security Commissioner, stood before the bars of his cell. Unusually, he was no longer dressed in a suit. Instead he wore the grey armour of the other enforcers, the grip of a gun quivering in its holster beneath his left hand.

"You look good, Chandler," Dominic said. "Almost as if you're going to get your own hands dirty for a change."

"Arrogant as ever," the commissioner replied and turned to one of his subordinates. "Open this door."

Dominic leaned back as the cell slid open and Chandler entered alone, the gun out of its holster and pointed directly at his head.

"I can dodge any number of bullets," Dominic said.

Chandler shook his head. "I don't think so, not anymore. Tell me how our reactor fuel can suddenly turn on us and attack the dome."

Dominic shrugged. "It's alive, it's defending itself."

Chandler pressed forward. "We've been using it for over half a century and it's never shown any sign of life before."

Dominic scratched his knees. "Of course it has. Jason and Randall negotiated a deal after the Valhalla landed."

"Where is Webster?" Chandler asked.

"The aliens took him."

"To negotiate?"

"He may try, but I doubt he'll succeed. The Visshon have come here to put you down."

Chandler snarled. "This is because I attacked Randall, isn't it? These... Visshon are his allies."

Dominic massaged his head; it was beginning to ache. "You know better than that, Neil. The Visshon inhibit our function. Isn't that why you placed Jason in the mines to begin with? This isn't about you or any reaction to what you've done. This was always going to happen."

Chandler turned away, pacing to the other side of the cell, the gun clutched ever more tightly in his hand.

"What do you want me to do?"

Dominic raised an eyebrow. "Do?"

Chandler slowly replaced the gun back in its holster and turned over her his hands. "How can I make amends?"

"I don't know what you mean."

Chandler took a step closer. "There are dozens of reported casualties. The Visshon entered via the sewage outtake and are sweeping through the dome killing everyone they come into contact with. Any barriers we erect only slow them down. They can melt right through them."

"Yes," Dominic nodded. "That's to be expected."

"I need your help."

"I can't help you," Dominic replied. "I'm going to die with everyone else."

Chandler stood over him, eyes narrowed. "There must be something you can do."

"I can only point out the obvious," Dominic said. "Evacuate everyone to the underground bunker. Seal it as you would for a reactor leak."

"The Visshon won't be able to get in?"

Dominic pulled himself to his feet. The muscle ache he felt couldn't possibly have been real.

"They will get in," he said, "eventually. But it will buy you a little time."

Chandler snarled. "Is that the best you have to offer?"

Dominic sighed. "Everything dies eventually, Commissioner. All you can do is fight against the inevitable for as long as you possibly can. Isn't that what you humans do?"

Chandler grabbed him roughly by the collar. "You're coming with me. I'll be interested to see if you have any more pearls of wisdom once the Visshon are melting your face."

Dominic allowed himself to be dragged to the doorway where Chandler pushed him into the arms of two of his subordinates.

"Get some men to my wife's office and my children's school," Chandler barked. "I want them with me as soon as possible."

Dominic brushed himself down. "Don't these men have wives and children too?"

The Commissioner turned to the nearest enforcer. "Escort this man to the bunker."

The enforcer saluted. "Yes, sir."

"Good," Chandler replied. "And..." He closed his eyes and took a deep breath. "All of you, contact what families you have and tell them to proceed to the nearest bunker entrance. You have ten minutes until I order a formal evacuation."

"Yes, sir!"

Dominic allowed himself a self-satisfied smile as the enforcers reached for their communicators.

* * *

The sky was a dim blue rather than a bright red, the starlight punctuated by infrequent bolts of lightning and the loud peal of thunder. The skeletal outline of the dome stood out before him, thin and intangible, barely visible in a place with so little light and even less warmth. It was hard to breathe. This was not any Redfern Jason recognised.

"Where are we?" He asked his companion.

"A reality far removed from yours or the one we seek," Webster explained. "The attack on Randall's tower necessitates a circuitous route if we are to return to Gina."

Jason squinted as more lightning seared his field of vision. "What do you mean?"

"The tower is translated across all quantum states," Webster replied. "Every change at source is copied down at varying speeds depending on how much change occurs and the distance from that source."

"I think I understand," Jason said.

Webster chuckled. "I don't think you do." He waved his hand. "This place is so far removed that the changes from the source will not be translated for at least another day. Where Gina sleeps the tower staircase has been all but destroyed, but in this place, that staircase still exists."

Jason nodded. "Lead on."

"We must be quick," Webster said as they set off again. "The other Visshon would prefer I not take you to see her at all. They want you now."

"I want to see them too," Jason said. "They need to call off their attack. I need to convince them of that."

"They won't," Webster replied. "Nothing you say can make a difference."

They stalked through a house and garden, apples in full bloom on the tree.

"I can't believe that," Jason said. "If I'm one of them, they have to listen to me."

"I'm one of them," Webster replied. "Do you think they listen to me? Look what they did." He patted his chest. "They turned me into you, but not even a you that can live in your reality without suffering degradation. I am exiled to the Inishi frequency. It's only there that I can live without pain, that I can be refreshed. I was made into a man and I cannot even live among them."

"What did you do?" Jason asked.

Webster stopped suddenly, his head swaying wildly on his shoulders. "I dared to question."

Jason looked into a copy of his own eyes as if they were wavering in melted glass. "What was the question?"

"Why do we kill each other?"

"The Visshon kill each—"

"The Visshon are more than you know," Webster said. "The golden realm is a conglomeration of all our thoughts, our love, our aggression, our doubts and our fears, all constantly at war with each other. I was one such doubt - I was excised."

Jason shivered as he realised the truth. "We used up the others."

"In your generators," Webster said. "You powered your dome with every individual that could have helped you."

"I still have to try," he said. "Maybe I can get through to them."

"No, Jason, you took all their compassion, all their kindness. There isn't anything left to appeal to. Those who were on your side sacrificed themselves so you could live. All that remains is coldness and cruelty. That is the Visshon now. That is our majority."

They marched again at a much faster pace, passing eerily through an office lobby. Jason's teeth began chattering and wouldn't stop.

"Tell me," he struggled to say. "What is the purpose of the chosen?"

"Diversity," Webster said. "The Visshon believe they can learn and grow."

"And what if they don't like how they learn and grow?"

"Your numbers are too small to make any real structural difference," Webster replied. "They will take what they want and overwhelm the rest. You cannot fight them from the inside, Jason. You will become them."

"We'll see," Jason declared. "I'm five thousand years old and no-one has ever overwhelmed me yet."

The tower came into view, a striking edifice in any reality. Randall had seen to that.

"What about Gina?" Webster asked. "In our short time together I have found her to be very persuasive."

"I'm too obstinate even for her," Jason said. "But if anyone could have changed me, she would have been the one."

"Come," Webster said, climbing up the path towards the tower's glass entrance. "I feel her time is close."

Jason followed the older version of himself into the tower.

"Take me to her."

Chapter Eighteen

They had been led through a dark blue world filled with bolts of pure light and anger until Webster let them go, leaving them in the open courtyard behind Randall's tower surrounded by mobilised enforcers. Ted didn't know who was more startled, his little group or the greater assembly of men, women and weapons that ringed Randall's home and fortress.

In answer, several guns were rapidly positioned, aimed and ready to fire.

"Where the hell did you come from?" An older female enforcer asked. Ted recognised her immediately as a colleague from his ancient past and one of the few to greet him on his resurrection.

"Gemma?"

The armoured enforcer frowned for a moment before delayed recognition set in.

"Holloway?"

"It's me," Ted replied and peered thoughtfully over her shoulder. "We come in peace."

She raised her hand. "Stand down, he's one of ours."

"And so am I," Lisa said, stepping forward. "Recognise the uniform?"

The older woman saluted. "Yes Lieut... ma'am, I apologise if we offended you, but you made quite an entrance."

Lisa stood up straight, head raised, and even though she was several inches shorter than the woman she was facing, Ted couldn't help noticing how her determined rigid posture made her seem so much more imposing.

The tricks of the military.

"Who's your commanding officer?" Lisa asked.

Gemma massaged the bridge of her nose. "Captain Neary, but he took a bullet pretty early on. Lieutenant Tarquin was second, but I think he just bought it, so..." she frowned. "I'm senior."

"Not anymore, Enforcer..." The nameplate on Gemma's helmet glinted beneath artificial starlight that was brighter than it should have been. "Howe. We need medical attention, some food, equipment and information. I need to know everything that's happened in the last two days."

"Yes ma'am, right away." She signalled to a nearby colleague. "Alessandri, do as the Lieutenant asks."

The enforcer saluted sheepishly and then ran but the other enforcers seemed in no hurry to disperse. Ted wondered how he would feel if three battered unknowns suddenly materialised in the midst of a combat operation, two dressed in civilian clothing and one in an operations uniform.

Suspicious would be an understatement.

Shandra was very quiet, the colour having all but drained from her face. Ted reached out to take her weight but she pushed him away.

"I'm fine."

"You don't look fine," Ted said.

She smiled wide enough to reveal clenched teeth.

"I was seriously thinking about attending your memorial service, ma'am," Gemma said quietly to Lisa.

The comment was met by a visibly raised eyebrow. "Thank you, Howe, but under the circumstances that won't be necessary."

"No," Gemma said. "Alessandri!"

The young enforcer dodged through a milling group of his colleagues and skidded to a halt by Howe's side.

"Please follow me," he said with a breathless salute.

Ted caught Gemma's eye and felt the heat of her inquiring glance. He offered a brief reassuring nod and hoped that was enough. They had served on many combat missions together on old Earth, enough that mutual trust had been earned the hard way. Even so, he knew it was only a matter of time before she reported their presence to Chandler. He could only guess at what action the Commissioner would take and did not relish the prospect of being returned to a cell.

Surely there wasn't time for such nonsense. The Visshon were here.

Alessandri escorted them to a medical tent at the perimeter of a security cordon. There were more wounded than Ted would have expected, the surgeons working in close quarters on enforcers whose armour had been shredded by drone fire. In one corner alone he counted ten sealed body bags lined up in a row.

This was worse than anything he had seen on Redfern before, worse than anything he had seen in this life before. On Redfern the main concerns were drunks, rapists, murderers or small groups. What he was seeing was more like the hell he had come from. More like Earth during the war.

After some shouting from Alessandri, Ted found himself in a makeshift cubicle as a junior doctor cut away the bandages from his wounded side. The cuts themselves were livid but almost superficial, and had already begun to fade. Ted wondered how much that rapid progress was down to the nanomachines infesting his blood and how close they were to expending themselves.

"How did this happen?" The doctor asked.

Ted shrugged nonchalantly. "A bear escaped from the zoo?"

The doctor didn't believe him but started working anyway.

Ted laid back and looked across at the neighbouring cubicle and watched Lisa's silhouette as it resisted medical examination. On the outside edge a figure stood apart, hands gesturing madly. "-lost his legal status, ma'am," Alessandri advised. "We were sent in to secure the tower so the techs could do their work."

Ted was surprised, somehow Chandler had seized power away from Randall, no easy feat, after which the Commissioner had used all the means at his disposal to mount an attack.

"I've cleaned it up," the doctor told him abruptly, "and re-dressed the wounds." The medical officer removed his rubber gloves with a ping. "You'll have some scars but you won't need stitches."

"Thanks," Ted said, and swung himself off the bed. "Let me get out of your way."

"You should stay off duty," the doctor said.

"I would if I could," Ted replied. "But you know how it is."

Thinking it best to leave Lisa to her briefing he found Shandra two cubicles over shivering beneath her bed covers. Her clothes had been unceremoniously cut away and all that remained were rags at Ted's feet.

"They just left you like this?" He asked in disgust.

She peered up at him, her eyelids quivering, halfway closed. "Hello, Ted."

He reached for one of her exposed arms. It was hot to the touch.

"What's going on?"

She yawned. "They're transporting me to a proper hospital. Something to do with giving me the best possible care."

Ted frowned. "You just needed patching up."

"It's a little bit more serious than that," she replied. "My lungs... I think I'm out of it."

He clutched her hand and knelt down. "This is my fault."

She nodded. "Yes, it is." She turned her eyes upwards, one pupil much larger than the other. "Am I going to die in my sleep?"

"Of course not," Ted said. "The Doctors will sort you out, you'll see."

Her teeth collided loudly. "No, that's not what I meant. Am I going to die in my sleep?"

Ted understood and squeezed her wrist reassuringly. "We will stop the Visshon."

"Good," she slurred. "Because I'm not all fancy and chosen like you. I was born here and I'll die here." She turned her head and faced him. "But I don't want to die yet."

"I know," he said and patted the back of her hand. "I promise, you will wake up."

Her head lolled to one side and she began mumbling words he couldn't understand. He stood up slowly, carefully placing her arms beneath the bed sheets and then pulling those sheets up to her chin. The mumbling stopped and she almost looked peaceful.

A few metres away the tent flap peeled open and an enforcer was outlined against the night time glow, rifle clutched in both hands.

"Anyone who's able, come with me," Howe shouted. "There's an invading force of... something, coming through the sewage disposal plant."

So, the Visshon were finally on the offensive. As Ted watched, wounded men and women reached for their discarded, and in some cases, heavily damaged armour when they shouldn't have been moving at all.

"Wait!"

It was Lisa. She was standing beside her cubicle curtain still clad in her operations uniform.

"People are dying ma'am," Howe said. "We have to go, now."

Lisa folded her arms. "No. Get everyone assembled outside, Howe, quick as you can, I'm going to speak."

"I have my orders," Howe said, turning to go.

"Stop right there," Lisa ordered calmly. "You can't fight these creatures using conventional weapons. We need another way. What's the fallback position?"

Howe shrugged. "The bunker."

"Good," Lisa said. "Assemble the enforcers, Howe."

Ted couldn't make out Howe's face in the gloom. He had no way of reading her.

"Yes, Lieutenant," she replied finally. "Five minutes."

"Make it two," Lisa said and then turned her eyes on Ted. "Officer Holloway, please be so good as to find us some effing armour. I don't want to look like a complete desk jockey out there.

Ted stifled a laugh and saluted stiffly. "Yes ma'am."

* * *

The armour was too big for her and was punctured just above her left hip, sticky with someone else's blood. The helmet was a better fit, except with the strap over her chin, enough of her hearing was cut off to make her feel both distant and isolated while amplifying every breath she took. It was not the best position for a commanding officer but she needed to look the part. She needed to inspire confidence.

Of the fifty enforcers who had attacked the tower, eleven were in body bags and seven were on the critical list. That left Lisa with thirty-two able officers standing before her on the green, nine of which were nursing injuries they barely acknowledged. She admired the fact they wanted to fight even though some of them could hardly stand. Their anger only required direction. She would provide it.

"Enforcers," she began, her voice sounding quieter than she expected. "The dome is being attacked by a new and deadly enemy. It is not an enemy we can reason with or shoot or wrestle to the ground. It's an enemy that can murder with a single touch. It's alien, a sentient liquid, and a certain machine mind not very far from here has been trying to find a way to kill it for decades." She stopped and narrowed her eyes. "It failed. Randall – failed."

"So what do we do?" Someone shouted from the back. "Take it out for dinner?"

There was laughter in the ranks and Lisa smiled to herself. A joker was good for morale and that was why she had Ted standing at the back.

She waited for the laughter to subside and then held up her hands.

"Everyone in this dome is that thing's dinner," she shouted. "But we are going to make it work for that meal, and at the very least, give it the most almighty, awful and painful bout of indigestion any man or beast will ever suffer."

Two enforcers cheered and that cheering spread rapidly. More than one set of armoured gauntlets collided in a pounding of high fives.

Lisa cocked her rifle for effect. "We won't stop until it's dead, or we are!"

Despite the helmet, the cheers were almost deafening. She motioned to Howe on her right. The newly promoted sergeant came running.

"Where are the attackers now?" she asked.

"Last report has it heading north-west towards the park and the Justice Building."

Lisa frowned. "Last report? Where's my surveillance?"

"Sensors are down," Howe replied. "This stuff does come from the mine."

"Of course," Lisa replied. "We're going to have to do this the old-fashioned way. We'll need a team of relay runners for communication, also..." She paused thoughtfully. "Incendiaries, water cannons, construction equipment. We need to setup a defensive barrier between the aliens and the bunker. Get Ted to help you."

Howe nodded. "I'll lead the runners myself."

"No," Lisa snapped. "I need you with me. Choose half a dozen of the fastest from what we have left."

The older enforcer turned to leave only for Lisa to grab her forearm.

"Don't let them keep their weapons or armour."

The sergeant seemed less than pleased. "Ma'am?"

Lisa didn't understand why it was always necessary to explain herself.

"With this enemy, speed is all that matters. Everything else is for show."

Howe nodded grimly and offered a belated salute.

"Find me as soon as we're ready to move," Lisa added and then turned back to the crowd. "ALESSANDRI!"

The young enforcer was nearby talking to three colleagues. At her shout he came running.

"Ma'am," he saluted.

"I need to speak to the commissioner," she said. "Get him on the line, somewhere private."

"Yes ma'am," he motioned to a nearby tent. "This way."

She peered across at the large number of enforcers milling about. "You lot!" Lisa shouted. They didn't all turn at once. "Enforcers! ATTENTION."

Training took over and they assembled themselves rapidly under her glare.

"Report to Sergeant Howe and Enforcer Holloway immediately," she ordered. "There's work to be done. Dismissed!"

The enforcers saluted and she let them be. It was not good for a leader to micromanage.

"Alessandri," she said. "Communications, now please."

The young enforcer hurried her to the tent and held the flap open. Inside she saw a mobile communications array complete with cameras and an upright flat screen mounted to a desk. Without a second thought she swept the flat screen onto the grass and stamped on it with the heel of her boot.

Alessandri was startled. "Ma'am?"

She disconnected the cameras and threw them into a corner.

"What are you doing?" Alessandri asked.

"The equipment was damaged during the siege," Lisa said succinctly. "Connect the commissioner to my earbud, code CarLHH3."

She waited, aware of Alessandri's questioning hesitation and ignored it. Finally he sat down at one of the desks and began operating a console. She relaxed. The reason for destroying the equipment was simple enough. She didn't want to see Chandler or for him to see her. She had experienced firsthand his unique way of unsettling people. With half the sensory information denied, the conversation would go a lot easier.

"I have our commanding officer requesting urgent communication with the commissioner," Alessandri said. There was a short pause and then he gave Lisa the thumbs up.

"Captain Neary?"

It was Chandler's voice all right, but it was off, frayed at the edges. Lisa could sense panic stalking the periphery.

"Captain Neary is dead, sir, as is Lieutenant Tarquin," Lisa said.

"Well who is in-"

"Lieutenant Lisa Carmichael, sir."

"You? But you're de—"

"No sir. Not yet. I'm in the process of organising a defensive barrier at Morganstern Avenue. I take it you will shortly be organising an evacuation to the bunker?"

"I was just about to announce it, Lieutenant." There was a long pause. "What exactly are your plans for this 'defensive barrier'?"

Lisa took a breath, now or never, she had to convince him.

"We're going to burn them sir, with as much heat and flame that we can bring to bear, and if that doesn't work, they should be weakened enough for us to wash them back into the sewers with our water cannons."

Another pause, she could almost hear him thinking.

"I can spare ten men to transport fuel from the flyer depot," Chandler said finally. "You seem to have everything else in hand, Lieutenant."

"Thank you, sir."

"I'm very interested to know exactly what happened after your disappearance."

"It will be in my report, sir," Lisa said.

"Yes, a report..."

"Sir?"

Chandler hesitated for a moment. "Lieutenant, after all the civilians are evacuated to the bunker I will have no choice but to seal it off. With the effect the Visshon have, I probably won't be able to contact you."

"Understood, sir."

"Good," Chandler said and exhaled sharply. "I believe at their present rate of movement the Visshon will be at Morganstern Avenue..." She heard him click his fingers at some unseen aide. "Fifty minutes. Is that long enough?"

"Yes, sir."

"I have work to do," Chandler said. "The evacuation drill last year took seventy-five minutes. I'm sure we can do better."

Lisa nodded. "I'm sure you can."

"Good luck, Lieutenant," Chandler said. "My thoughts are with you and your officers. I know your father would be proud."

"Thank you, sir."

The channel reverted to static and then to silence. Lisa turned to Alessandri. He had removed his helmet and dropped it on the grass, his face as white as a ghost.

"You were listening in," she concluded.

He ran a hand through short-cropped brown hair. "I'm sorry ma'am. I know I shouldn't have."

"I would have," Lisa said, shouldering her useless rifle. "Do you have a family, Alessandri?"

"Huh?" he was staring down at his console.

"Alessandri, do you have a family?"

"Just my parents and my sisters," he answered, his eyes focussing somewhere else.

"Civilians?"

He nodded.

"Then they'll be safe in the bunker. What about a partner?"

"No. No, not yet."

She stepped over to him and patted him on the shoulder. "Come on."

He stood up only to motion towards the smashed flat screen.

"Why did you do that?" He asked.

She grinned lopsidedly. "Chandler creeps me out."

* * *

The corner of Morganstern Avenue was just over five hundred metres from the main entrance to the bunker, sitting between two of the oldest and largest trees in the dome. Beside each of them were two low buildings that served as bicycle storage and did not encroach on the tree roots. As enforcers battered the wide intersection with pickaxes and spades a steady stream of civilians filed past clutching suitcases and precious valuables. Ted watched them as he caught his breath. A mixture of the old and the very young moving fast enough to trip over their own feet. He could feel their eyes on him in return, a mixture of fear and resentment looking for a target. Their way of life from the day before and the day before that was suddenly over and they were barely coping.

He ignored the stares and stabbed again at the asphalt with his shovel, fragmenting it into layers and sending the material flying back over his head. This wouldn't be a deep trench; there wasn't enough time for any real depth. It would be more of a depression, just somewhere to slow the Visshon down and make them face the fire.

"Ten minutes," Howe called out as she inspected the line. Ted felt his bad leg for the first time in hours, the pain announcing its impending return. He guessed the nanomachines were not reacting well to increased muscular activity and were most likely dying in their thousands within his bloodstream just keep him going. It didn't matter, he needed only a little more time. Only a little...

"What do you call that?" Howe asked. She stood over him, hands behind her back, appraising his efforts.

"The best I can do," Ted said.

Howe eyed his bad leg. "Not good enough. Nine minutes and then we pour in the fuel. You need to match this travesty up with the holes around it or it will just cause a blockage."

"Yes, sergeant," he replied breathlessly.

"Oh, get out of the way," Howe ordered. "I'll do it myself." She snatched away his shovel and left him reeling. "Keep the count and make sure this sorry excuse for a trench is half decent."

He stood back for a moment and watched as she attacked the path in his stead. Her strikes were cleaner and more forceful than he could hope to match.

"Eight minutes," she said. "Go!"

He wiped his forehead again and almost collapsed. He was so hot. Recovering himself, he limped down the line looking for things that were obviously wrong. He even called out a few men and women for the sake of it, asking for adjustments that weren't really needed just to make them angry and work harder.

"Five minutes," he called out. "Put your backs into it!"

It was so much easier to be the person shouting rather than digging although he wasn't so exhausted that he didn't feel a little guilt. He had flown a desk for too long.

Traversing the trench a second and third time, he saw it was finally smoothing out, becoming an ever so slight depression running down an even slighter hill.

"Two minutes!" He shouted.

A few more tired strokes from the digging team and that was as good as it got.

"Rest!" He ordered.

Lisa had setup camp on the roof of a nearby sports hall and without thinking Ted found himself looking up in that direction. There she was, a short figure at the centre of three taller ones, moving in a frenzy of unknown activity. He wondered what she was doing. Behind him fuel was flowing down the makeshift trench, filling it up, the noxious toxicity burning into his nostrils.

Someone tapped him on the shoulder. It was Gemma Howe.

"Not long now," she said. "You should go and join Lisa."

He looked up at that figure, all the easier to recognise as the morning continued to brighten. Beside her one of the men beamed a coded sequence by signal lamp.

"She doesn't need me," he said.

"Well, you're not going to be much use to me down here," Howe said. "You can barely walk anymore."

He nodded reluctantly and patted his bad leg. There was a quiver of pain, nothing like he was used to, but his increased mobility was almost gone.

"I'll go," he said.

"Good," Howe replied, "one less thing for me to worry about. Jason really did a number on you didn't he."

Ted gritted his teeth. "Yes, he did."

The sergeant squinted at the repeating coded signal.

"She wants me to get ready," Howe said. "I have to reply. Sorry Ted, just get out of here."

He nodded as she ran towards her signalman at the top end of the trench next to the fuel tank. She was right, he wasn't going to do anymore good down here.

He limped away, walking down a side street and then cautiously up a metal fire escape to where Lisa was waiting. As he struggled across the roof, she smiled and then her mouth opened as she registered his limp. Perhaps coming here had been a mistake, he didn't want to be a distraction.

"Alessandri," Lisa barked. "Help him."

The young enforcer ran to his aid and propped him up.

"Have you been injured, sir?" Alessandri asked.

Ted shrugged. "A long long time ago, and don't call me, sir, we share the same rank."

There was a momentary register of surprise on the boy's face and then it was gone.

"I'll still call you sir, if that's okay?" Alessandri said. "Makes it easier for me."

Ted nodded and took his place at Lisa's side. He was standing awkwardly, trying to balance out his weight without seeming too obvious. He missed his cane.

"Sorry," Lisa said, pulling away her binoculars. "No chairs."

"I can always sit on the floor," Ted replied.

Lisa smiled absently and raised the binoculars again. "Damn it!"

"The Visshon?" Ted asked.

Lisa handed him the binoculars. "Look for yourself. Clarke! I need you to signal Howe. We have civilians."

Ted peered through the glasses, and sure enough there they were, a young couple with a toddler and a little girl, running down Morganstern Avenue. He flicked his view back to the trench. Howe had thrown away her helmet and was running towards them.

"What's she doing?" He asked.

"Give me those." Lisa snatched back her binoculars. "No, Howe, send someone else! You're meant to be in charge down there."

Alessandri offered his own pair of binoculars which Ted took gratefully. Down below he saw green liquid melt through a wall and pursue the young family down the avenue. It was moving faster than they were, the children slowing the parents down as the liquid closed in.

"They won't make it," Lisa commented. "Clarke, signal whoever the second is to be ready to light that fuel."

"Yes, ma'am," the enforcer replied. Ted didn't turn round, he was watching as the liquid sped closer and closer. The mother was screaming and the little girl was crying.

"Come on, Howe," he said under his breath.

The female enforcer abruptly caught them up and slung the little girl over her shoulder. The father grabbed the baby from the mother and overall their speed increased. Ted let himself hope they would make it.

Then something happened that surprised him. Somehow Gemma landed a foot badly and fell down, rolling with the girl still wrapped safely in her arms. The parents, unaware, kept going, not even realising that the green liquid had caught Howe and was engulfing her.

"No!" Ted shouted.

"Not now," Lisa said and placed a hand on Ted's forearm.

"But, Gemm—"

"No, Ted," Lisa interrupted. "Clarke, on my mark."

Ted watched as Gemma's thrashing armoured form sunk beneath wave after wave of green liquid. He couldn't stop watching.

Closer to the line, the rest of the family had crossed the trench and were being held back by three enforcers. The Visshon were still coming.

"Now!" Lisa ordered.

Ted turned to see a tall enforcer click a final signal and then watched as the trench flowered into flame and thick black smoke.

"Gemma!"

He realised that like him she had been remembered. That meant she was among the chosen. That meant she should have been spared.

He raised the binoculars back to his eyes and scanned for her through the smoke. With a sigh of relief he caught sight of her sitting among the asphalt, stunned but apparently unharmed. Randall had been correct, the chosen were left alone. He peered closer and saw she was holding something close to her breast, her mouth opened wide in a silent scream.

"Oh no."

The little girl was gone and Gemma was hugging nothing more than the charred remnants of infant flesh and bone.

Ted pulled the binoculars away and handed them back to Alessandri.

"I've seen enough."

Chapter Nineteen

Jason followed as Webster tirelessly and relentlessly climbed the undamaged tower staircase. Even clothed within a heavy environment suit, the alien was easily outpacing him. In fact Jason suspected it was slowing down just to let him to keep up. The situation could have been worse, the muscles of his newly reset body allowing him much more stamina than he was used to due to the fact they were still attuned to the slightly heavier gravity of old Earth. There had been little chance for them to soften yet.

Recalling his previous life, he felt stronger and fitter than he had in decades. The man who had walked out into the desert to die had been replaced by someone else. He wasn't sure he was even thinking the same way, and despite the memories, there was a growing distance between what he was and what he had become.

Youthful arrogance?

He recognised it easily enough. It was a trick of his body's true age fighting the weight of hundreds of combined memory grafts. He was Jason Webster, but not the same one. All those sins, all those mistakes, all those murders and resets, belonged to someone else. He was innocent and this time he would get it right. This time... He clutched the handrail tightly and paused. He had believed that before.

I'm pregnant Jason.

They were lying in bed together in their new house in the dome, his arm around her, pulling her close.

"What?" He asked sleepily.

"We're having a baby," Gina said.

He was suddenly awake. "But..."

"Randall gave me permission to have the coil removed," she replied. "The human race is settled now, we're building a new world." She laughed. "There's no holding back anymore."

He found himself laughing too, and kissed her furiously.

"We've never had a child before," he said. "In all that time, all that space." He gazed deeply into the ceiling.

"Don't zone out on me now Millennia man," she said, her fingers pulling on his chin. She kissed him again.

He smiled with a satisfaction he had never felt before, that he had never even dreamt of before.

"It really is going to be different this time," he said.

"Of course it is," Gina replied. "You're going to be a father, and it doesn't have to stop at one. We could have half a dozen."

He gripped her thigh. "Hold on."

"We can watch them grow up, even have children of their own. We can be grandparents."

"My god," he said. "Is this really happening?"

"Yes," she answered with a laugh. "It's really happening."

"Change," he said finally.

"It's what we've always wanted," Gina said. "Do you remember that? Can your mind go that far back?"

He could, but it was like a dream. A conversation, like this one, but in a much smaller bed, buried underground during a war that could never be won.

He turned over and stared into her young and hope-filled eyes. "I remember."

She brushed away a strand of his thinning red hair. "I know it wasn't me really, any more than it was you. But I think... I think they would be happy for us."

"I am happy," he said. "How long until...?"

"Seven months," she replied.

"That seems like an eternity now."

"No," she disagreed. "It's just the blink of an eye."

He kissed her lightly on the nose.

I want you

That was a strong one, the strongest yet, enough to stop him dead in his tracks and send a tear trickling down his cheek.

"Are you all right, Jason?" Webster asked from half a dozen steps above.

He unclamped his hand from the rail and wiped his eyes. Damn memories! He didn't want them. He didn't need them.

"Jason?"

He tried to smile. "Just the past making itself known."

"Your memory graft?" Webster asked.

Jason rubbed his sinuses. "More like memory torture. There's so much buried there, it's like..." He couldn't quite find the words. "Sometimes things get dislodged and rise to the surface."

Webster nodded solemnly. "We must hurry, Jason, time is against us."

"Yes," he replied and felt a growing wave of trepidation rising in his stomach. Gina was waiting for him, Gina, the mother of his child.

They passed Level 11 and then finally walked out into the gloomy corridor of Level 12. Webster marched down the passageway and opened a door at the far end, beckoning Jason inside.

It was as large as Jason's former stateroom, a small single bed standing empty in the corner with a red and blue patterned duvet neatly draped over two similar pillows. Beside it stood a tall maroon wardrobe and beside that, a painting, a real painting, of the Valhalla, the great hawk-nosed ship with its wingspan spread wide, traversing deep space. He almost fell over at the sight of it.

More paintings littered the walls, lifelike illustrations of the Valhalla crew, leaping out from the stippled brushwork. There was Holloway and Howe, the infrequent husband and wife, and next to them, Gina and himself, together and smiling in eternal youth.

"I don't understand," he said.

Webster stepped inside behind him. "This is Dominic's room, but its twin also serves Gina. Take my hand."

Jason reached out and clasped it by the palm. Almost immediately the room brightened and the bed was no longer empty. A shivering form was nestled in the red and blue sheets that were much more red than they should have been.

"Gina?" He asked tentatively.

She turned over and faced him. A wrinkled, dried out woman he could barely recognise.

"You're so old," he said before he could stop.

"Jason," she smiled and reached out a gnarled hand. "You came back."

He knelt down by her bedside, and something slammed down inside of him. "I never should have left."

She touched his face, her rough fingers tracing his smooth face. "He looked like you."

"Who?" He asked, trying not to flinch from her touch.

"Our son," Gina whispered.

He smiled. "Is he here somewhere?"

Her eyelids closed slowly. "No, he died and without you, I couldn't stay. I couldn't."

He clasped her frail hand. "I'm sorry. I..." He felt a loss he didn't understand. "I would like to have met him."

She licked her lips. "He was a leader like you. He even became the security commissioner for a time, changed his name just to be his own man."

"How did it happen?"

"An accident in the mines."

"An accident?"

"A stupid and pointless accident," she replied. "Sometimes that's all it takes."

He waited, but that was all she was going to give him.

"I never meant for you to be alone," he said finally. "I'm sorry. I thought you would at least have the child."

"I did," she answered. "He even had a child himself."

Jason felt renewed hope. "A grandchild."

The old woman turned towards the ceiling. "She was here, briefly. I was going to... Can you forgive me?"

"Forgive you for what?" Jason asked.

"I was going to have her killed, to spare her the touch of the Visshon."

"You were going to do what?" He pulled away.

She smiled thinly. "But the bullet found me instead."

"Why wasn't she chosen?" Jason demanded.

A strong hand clasped his shoulder.

"Be gentle, Jason."

He nodded and took a deep breath. "Why, Gina?" He asked, softer this time.

"How could I make Randall choose her," the old lady replied, "knowing that someone else would have died in her place? I don't have that right."

He understood. She had always been better than him.

"Where is she now, can I meet her?"

"I returned her to the human frequency," Webster said. "She insisted on fighting the Visshon."

Jason smiled. "My brave girl." Then he looked down at Gina and took her hand. "This isn't how it was meant to be," he whispered. "We were meant to raise our children together, play with our grandchildren together. Grow old and die together."

"You walked into the desert."

He bowed his head and buried it in the bed. "I know, I know. But I can't take it back. I can't."

Her hand went limp.

"Gina?"

Fingers that were much like his own, gripped his shoulder again. "She's gone, Jason."

"But..." He looked up at her still form, her face frozen in that thin smile. "She never heard me forgive her."

"She didn't need your forgiveness."

Jason turned and looked up at the being that shared his face. "But I needed hers?"

Webster took a step back. "What will you do now?"

Jason rose to his feet and then carefully pulled the duvet over the body, his hand lingering over the shape of it.

"I will do what's expected," he said finally. "I will go to the Visshon and finish this."

Webster nodded. "You will be the first human to enter the golden realm. It has been so long for me, so very long. How I envy you."

Jason glared in response.

"Don't."

* * *

Dominic was marched into the Justice Building basement and then led into one of the many evacuation tunnels that connected with the bunker. The air was damp and moisture dripped down from a ceiling inches above his head with alarming regularity. The two enforcers who were escorting him flicked on their helmet lamps, the feeble light enough to illuminate the rocky path underfoot but could enough to truly penetrate the darkness.

Dominic willed his eyes to adjust quickly, but all it did was allow him to observe all the small writhing creatures that were best left unseen, the ones that otherwise would creep up and crawl through his hair and down his neck. He shook at the very thought of it and ran a hand through his hair at the slightest imaginary sensation. The ceiling was so low, the walls so close, and he could barely breathe for all the cloying moisture. He could barely breathe!

"Are you claustrophobic, Dominic?" The closer of the two enforcers asked.

He was pleasantly surprised to hear the enforcer use his name.

"I didn't think so," he replied, "until now."

The other enforcer laughed loudly enough to cause an echo. "Well, you better reprogram yourself not to be."

"If only it were that simple," Dominic said. "But I can't reprogram myself anymore than you can stop eating and sleeping."

"Do you want us to stop here for a minute?" the first enforcer asked.

Dominic took the opportunity to study them both. The older one, a little unkempt, a little fatter around the waistline was friendly enough. The younger one, slim and smooth was like a sharp instrument ready to cut him at the slightest opportunity.

"We keep going," the thin one said.

"What's the rush?" The older man asked.

"Babysitting this machine head wasn't my idea. I want to get out and see some action."

Dominic smiled. "I don't think you want to see that action. It would be the last thing you would ever see."

"Just get moving," the thin one ordered, nudging the barrel of his rifle into Dominic's back. Dominic did as he was told.

"Here," the older man said as they walked, pushing a canteen into his hand.

Dominic considered it. "No thank you, I think perhaps it's wet enough down here already."

"Well," the older man replied with a wink. "That might dry you out."

Dominic understood his meaning and opened the canteen. The fumes were noxious enough and he drank thankfully.

"Faster, you two," the thin one said.

"Hey," the older man retorted. "You can order me around when you outrank me. But you don't outrank me yet."

Dominic handed back the canteen. "Thank you."

He felt better, not just because of the alcohol warmly penetrating his insides but because, with so much rock between him and the Visshon, he was recovering again. In the end it was a ping pong game, back and forth between illness and health without any control of the outcome. Dominic didn't like it. He didn't like it all.

Finally the tunnel came to an end and they emerged into a huge man-made cavern that was so well lit it hurt his eyes. There were three levels, all connected by a sloping infrastructure cut deep into the rock. On the level he entered were rows and rows of bunks, stretching a few hundred metres across. On the slope below were showers, wash basins and lavatories all gloriously open and exposed. On the level above were tables, chairs and the hatch to an inner kitchen. It was a huge survival chamber, connected by a vast network of tunnels threading down from various strategic points above. A last refuge for humanity should the worst ever happen.

And the worst was happening.

A few hundred people were already in occupation and watched him with a mixture of curiosity and fear. A large number sat by the tables above, children playing and adults engaging in panicked conversation. On the sleeping level, more families gathered and a child cried so loudly it raked at Dominic's insides. There were so many more to come of course, thousands in fact, and when the bunker was full, the claustrophobia he had felt in the tunnel would be just the beginning.

"Over there," the thin enforcer said, pointing to one of many unoccupied bunks. Dominic complied and sat down uneasily.

"What happens now?" He asked.

"You stay right there," the thin one said. "Don't move a muscle. I'm going up top, Costigan, he's all yours."

"You're meant to stay with me," the older enforcer said. "Those were our orders."

The young enforcer smiled bitterly. "You can order me around when you outrank me, but you don't outrank me yet."

Costigan frowned. "Do what you want then, get yourself killed, why should I care?"

"Just get a good nap, old man," the thin one said. "I'll see you later." With a last look at Dominic, he turned around and ran towards a nearby tunnel.

"He'll be dead in an hour," Dominic declared.

Costigan leaned his rifle against the bunk and put the canteen to his lips. He took a long swallow and then handed it to Dominic with a self-satisfied grin.

"An hour you say? Then I think I'd better stay here with you."

"We might last three," Dominic replied. "It all depends how long it takes the enemy to melt through solid rock."

Costigan pulled off his helmet, his white hair glistening beneath the harsh light. "Three hours, is that all?" He glanced from side to side and then rubbed his eyes. "Maybe you should keep that to yourself."

Dominic leaned back. "I wasn't planning on making an announcement. What are you going to do?"

Costigan hefted up his rifle. "I think I'll find out what they're doing for breakfast. You coming?"

Dominic was surprised to be given the choice, not that he couldn't overpower the old enforcer if he wanted to, he just didn't see the point.

"I am a little hungry."

* * *

"You will need my environment suit," Webster said. "The atmosphere of your dome does not bleed into the golden realm as it does other frequencies."

Jason nodded as he followed the intermediary out into the hallway, closing the bedroom door behind them with a numbing finality.

"Helmet and gauntlets?"

"Wait here," Webster said, and walked into the neighbouring room. Jason leaned against the nearest wall and closed his eyes. He felt sick and exhausted, all his newfound youth dissolved in an instant. He was the old man again and there was nothing more to give. He cupped the back of his neck and squeezed, revelling in the pain.

Webster returned minutes later, the environment suit removed and folded in his arms, the helmet and gauntlets resting on top. In its place he wore jogging pants and a Team Valhalla shirt with a wide-nosed caricature of its captain. Jason almost laughed at the lack of formality. It was the same shirt he had worn on the day of his first encounter with the Visshon, right down to an exact copy of the bad artwork.

"Is this amusing?" Webster asked.

"No," Jason said and sat down on the floor to remove his shoes. "How long have you been wearing all that?"

"It does not require washing," Webster replied. "It is part of the body template which is fully restored each time I return to this frequency."

Jason held up the heavy suit. "This is part of your body?"

"In a way," Webster replied. "Put it on."

Jason rubbed his fingers against the fabric weave. It felt like an environment suit.

"It is functional," Webster said. "Let me help you."

Jason bit his lip and cooperated, letting himself slowly be sealed into the alien's skin. Finally with the helmet in place, he felt dizzy. The atmosphere inside the suit was so much more richer than the one circulating inside the tower that he felt drunk on the oxygen.

"Take my hand," Webster said.

Jason remembered the last time he had breathed like this, the time when he had walked out onto the surface never to return.

Where are you going, Jason?

The comms channel was open and resisted all attempts to close it. Randall had overridden his control.

"Go away, Randall," he said.

"You need to come back, Jason."

"No," he replied and kept walking. It was an upward march, the ground underfoot rising at a shallow elevation that was enough to put a strain on his knees. His old body was letting him down.

"Jason?"

He looked up. The stars in the night sky were so much brighter than he remembered on Earth. The atmosphere on Redfern was thinner, so much more exposed, it almost made him think he could take a running leap and jump right out into space.

"Jason, you must return. Your suit only has two hours of air remaining."

"I don't want to go back," he replied.

"You're being illogical."

"Yes, I am," Jason said. "That's what happens when you ask me to murder thousands of innocent people."

"It isn't murder, Jason."

"Of course it is," he shouted and staggered on. "Don't you ever get tired of playing God? I am."

"We never played."

"I wanted my son to grow up, Randall."

"He will."

Jason shook his head. "With no hope for the future? Whatever he builds will be destroyed, whatever children he has, will die. He won't even get to live a full life."

"But he will live," Randall said. "He can even be among the chosen if you wish."

"How would you know if he fulfilled your criteria?" Jason asked.

"He's your child," Randall answered. "Of course he does. Come back, Jason."

"You made a promise to me."

"I remember."

"Will you keep it?"

"I will."

Jason laughed bitterly. "I don't believe you."

"It doesn't matter," Randall replied. "I can save your son, Jason."

The slope was getting steeper and his heart was pumping faster. "All those people..."

"We don't have a choice," Randall replied. "The power requirements are too high. In just under seventy years the Visshon will turn on us. This way we can save a few."

"To become what?" Jason spat. "They won't be human anymore."

"Humanity will survive in one form or another," Randall said. "It is enough."

"No, it isn't! Being human is about living as a human. We hope, we fear, we love, we create, and we die. That is being human. What the Visshon offer, it's worse than death."

"I disagree," Randall said. "Come back, Jason, Gina is getting anxious."

He was struggling forward on his hands and knees. "I can't face her. I can't take responsibility for what you want to do."

"But I don't want to do it," Randall replied. "I have to do it."

He stopped and rolled over onto his back. "There has to be another way!"

"There isn't."

Jason exhaled sharply. "I let them believe we could build a home here. I let them hope for a normal life, I let them have children." He closed his eyes. "How could I let them have children?"

"In seven decades most of the original settlers will be dead anyway," Randall countered. "Isn't it best to let them live with that hope, with that illusion? They can be satisfied, they can enjoy their children, enjoy their lives."

"But we will be sacrificing the future."

"But thousands of humans will get to live who would never have lived if not for us. They get to live, Jason."

"And then die," Jason said.

"They will die anyway," Randall replied. "That is the inevitable conclusion of the human condition."

"But—"

"Will you come back, Jason?"

He felt tears on his cheeks. "I murdered the crew of the Valhalla so many times, resetting them whenever Gina tired of me; wiping out their entire existence just to preserve a lie."

"It was a beautiful lie."

"No," Jason protested. "It was anything but."

"They would never have survived the five-thousand-year journey anyway," Randall said. "Periodic resets were required."

"But I reset them when it wasn't required," Jason answered, "because of a lie. If I told Gina what I did, do you think she would ever forgive me?"

"I don't know."

He closed his eyes. "I can't live a lie anymore, Randall. I can't see their faces everyday and know I condemned them to death so many times. I won't condemn their children."

"Please, Jason, come back."

"No."

"But I don't know if I can do this alone. Jason I..." Randall paused. "I need you, Jason. I need you."

"No..."

No!

"Another memory?" Webster asked.

Jason was leaning heavily against the wall, his head bowed and his teeth chattering.

"I'll be all right in a minute."

"It must be strange to remember so many lives and know that none of them were really your own?"

Jason took a deep breath. "Sometimes I think like that. It makes it easier to cope."

"Only sometimes?"

Jason looked up. "Randall had a saying, 'Continuity is everything'. He was right, my continuity is unbroken. I am the one and only Jason Webster."

"Then I pity you," the alien said. "It is a burden none of your kind should bear."

"I never had a choice."

Webster held out his hand again. "Take it."

Jason straightened up and willed his breathing back to normal. He would be calm, he would be focussed. This was it.

He reached out.

The golden realm was waiting…

Chapter Twenty

Full artificial daylight finally arrived as Lisa kept her binoculars zeroed in on the trench, watching for any sign of the Visshon.

"So far, so good," she said.

The smoke from the flames was drifting up towards her, interrupting the view, the blackened air biting painfully into her lungs.

Ted was standing beside her, most of his weight on his good leg, arms dropped to his sides, coughing hoarsely.

"Ted?"

"Howe's still out there," he said. "She survived, but the child she was carrying..." He coughed some more.

"We can't think about that now," Lisa said, ignoring the acrid taste in her mouth. "Clarke, can you still contact our people down there?"

"I can't see them," the tall enforcer said. "The smoke is too thick."

"Damn! Alessandri, I might need you to run down there."

"Yes ma'am," the enforcer said.

"If the Visshon made it..."

Ted coughed. "We're probably breathing in what's left of them this very minute."

Lisa shook her head and kept the binoculars trained on where the trench should have been. It couldn't be this easy, not if Randall gave up.

"Cleanse with fire," Alessandri said.

"What?" Lisa asked.

"Just something I read once," the enforcer said. "Never mind."

She ignored him and concentrated on penetrating the smoke. She needed to see. Finally, it seemed like the smoke was clearing, the fuel for the flames was running low.

"Fingers crossed," Lisa said. "Let's hope we've— NO!"

The green liquid had emerged from the trench without even changing colour. As she watched, it began to pick up speed again. She scanned for her men and found the signalman frantically beaming a message up to her position.

"Did you get that, Clarke?"

"Fire ineffective, request orders."

"Signal them to retreat behind the water cannons. Signal the cannon crews to fire as soon as our people are clear and the enemy is in range."

"Yes ma'am."

"What's going on here?"

Startled, Lisa turned to see Commissioner Chandler emerging from the fire escape. His armour did little for him other than to accentuate a wide waist, thick arms and a bullish face.

"Sir? I thought you were staying in the bunker."

Two other enforcers followed the commissioner onto the roof, weapons ready. Chandler stared at her.

"Report, Lieutenant."

Lisa composed herself. "Fire didn't work so we've moved on to the water cannons. I'm hoping it will break the enemy down."

"Good," Chandler said, eyeing Ted with clear distaste. "Enjoying the view, Holloway?"

Ted craned his neck. "No, sir. Not at all."

Chandler grunted in response and then stood to the other side of Lisa gesturing to Alessandri.

"Sir?"

The commissioner snatched the young enforcer's binoculars and surveyed the trench.

"What a mess."

"I'm sorry it didn't work," Lisa said.

"It was a good effort," Chandler replied quietly. "And at least if we lose I'll never have to face the civic committee about it. They can be a right bunch of bastards."

Lisa wasn't used to him speaking so plainly, "Why are you here, sir, if you don't mind me asking?"

Chandler removed the binoculars and faced her. "It's not my job to cower in the dark."

"But your family, sir."

"I can protect them better here."

Lisa frowned. "Are you taking command, sir?"

Chandler eyed Ted again and Lisa reminded herself that the Commissioner really didn't care for the remembered.

"Not yet. Carry on, Lieutenant Carmichael."

Lisa turned her attention to the two water cannon emplacements two hundred metres south of the trench. They were stationed by the park gates, pumping the water directly from the hydroponic aquifer. The Visshon themselves appeared to be making no attempt to avoid them, in fact they were purposely heading in that direction.

They really wanted to kill everyone.

"Seven casualties," Clarke reported. "Everyone else is clear."

"Fire when ready," Lisa ordered.

"Confirmed."

Chandler turned to the tall enforcer and inspected the lamp and shutter with a grin.

"So, this is what we've been reduced to now."

"Technology doesn't work around the enemy, sir," Lisa said. "Three of our men have had semaphore training."

"Interesting," Chandler commented and addressed Clarke. "What made you take you up the semaphore, enforcer?"

The tall enforcer hesitated. "It seemed easier than applied anatomy, sir."

Chandler touched the shutter. "I don't think it is."

The water cannons fired, sending a thick stream of clear white spray down into the Visshon. The green liquid exploded in all directions.

Alessandri cheered. Ted sat down to watch.

With her binoculars, Lisa could see more than they could, enough to know that almost as quickly as the green liquid separated it welled back together in an attempt to reform. The cannons were not watering it down, instead the water was either being rejected outright or consumed in a cloud of acidic heat.

"It's not working," Chandler said.

"Give it time," Lisa said. "It has to work."

The cannons kept firing, the spray spreading as far as the sports hall roof. It helped to rid Lisa's nostrils of the burning smell of smoke.

"What's next?" Chandler asked.

Lisa took a deep breath. "This is it. I thought about liquid nitrogen, but there was no time to get anyone to the university."

"A good idea," Chandler commented. "Pity it couldn't be put into practice."

"The cannons were meant to wash them into the sewers," Lisa said. "Send them back the way they came."

"How long will the water pressure last?"

Lisa checked her wrist. "Damn it, my watch isn't working," She bit her bottom lip. "At a guess, another twenty minutes until hydroponics is exhausted."

"Enough time then," Chandler said and motioned to his personal guard. "We're going."

"Where to, sir?" Lisa asked.

"The bunker is designed to survive a reactor leak," Chandler said. "Maybe the Visshon aren't. I'm going to arrange one."

"Sir?"

Chandler saluted. "It's been a pleasure, Lieutenant."

"Thank you, sir," Lisa said and returned the salute.

The Commissioner grinned. "You weren't expecting noble self-sacrifice, were you Carmichael?"

"No, sir," she answered before she could stop.

Chandler laughed. "I just don't want to face the civic committee."

"Sir."

He saluted each enforcer in turn until finally he was standing over Ted. "Enjoy what time you have left, Holloway."

Ted looked up but said nothing.

"Your time is all borrowed anyway," Chandler added. "Consider yourself lucky."

Ted nodded slowly and Lisa watched Chandler march off towards the fire escape without further comment, a man determined.

Briefly she returned her attention to the water cannons, their pressure undiminished and their operators undaunted.

Stalemate.

Pulling away her binoculars, she sat down beside Ted and leaned into his shoulder.

"So, not a bad man, considering..."

"Considering," Ted repeated, reaching out to grip her knee.

"Do you think he'll make it?"

Ted exhaled sharply. "Maybe. If he does, I won't have to worry about being chosen anymore."

"No."

"But, if the Visshon survive the leak and penetrate the bunker, the radiation will kill everyone down there as well."

"No more chosen," Lisa said.

"At all."

With a sinking feeling, Lisa realised there was no way Chandler could succeed.

"The Visshon aren't that stupid."

"No," Ted said. "I don't think they are."

The water cannons continued their pounding.

* * *

Randall's tower was the only structure standing in the darkness; alone without even the ghost of a building beside it or of the dome rising above it. The red sand was all, carpeting the landscape and careening through the air, tearing into anything so bold as to be unprotected. It was there that Webster, his skin cut in so many places, pointed towards the yellow glow of a distant horizon. Jason nodded slowly and then watched his twin with a morbid fascination as each new wound blossomed into glorious crimson. Finally, damaged enough, Webster patted the ruined picture on his shirt and waved.

He was gone before Jason could wave back.

Blinking at the sudden disappearance, Jason realised he was standing alone against the howling wind, his environment suit all that stood between him and oblivion. It was not a pleasant thought.

He activated comms. "Can anyone hear me?"

Harsh static made his ears ache and he switched off almost immediately. It seemed there was no talking to anyone or there was no one to talk to. He turned his attention to the horizon, noting the yellow glow Webster had pointed out was in the wrong direction to be a rising sun.

The golden realm?

He started walking towards it, pushing into the wind and then struggling to keep his balance as it changed direction and buffeted him from side to side. He had enough air for five hours, more than enough time to reach that distant point if he didn't tire. He concluded it was easier than the last time he walked in the desert. He was younger this time, fitter, and he had purpose. He would not be swayed by something as innocuous as wind and sand. He would not be swayed by anything.

The sand grew thicker and he wiped his helmet visor with increasing frequency, his feet sinking more and more with each step. It was as if the world was building a barrier to keep him in one place, the loose sand gathering together as far up as his knees. He wondered how long the suit could repel the onslaught, because if it couldn't - that was it.

Ahead, the yellow glow wasn't getting any closer. Instead, it was a fixed point always moving away, like a pot of gold shimmering at the end of a rainbow.

Jason Webster.

A whisper in his ear, no more, the howling of the wind penetrating the confines of his helmet.

Welcome.

Was he imagining it? The glow was still so far away and the sand was getting thicker, turning each step into a climb.

You are very tenacious.

"Where are you?" He called out in frustration. The sand was piling up past his waist, burying him. He tried to keep going, tried to force it to part and give way.

You are a worthy addition to the Visshon.

"Show yourself!" Jason shouted. His comms abruptly reactivated and white noise screamed into his ears.

"Randall?"

You will succumb eventually. You have to.

The red sand was up to his shoulders, and then beyond. He couldn't lift his arms and his visor was almost completely obscured.

He was being buried alive.

"Did you bring me all this way to kill me?"

The sand built up above his helmet and he felt the weight of it pressing down, pushing in. Was his visor beginning to crack?

Gina's visor had cracked.

The golden realm is all around you, Jason Webster. Prepare yourself.

The visor's plexifibre glass shattered, the sand rushing in, plugging up his nose, stinging his eyes and forcing its way in between his lips. His teeth crunched down in an effort to block it, but there were too many gaps. He couldn't breathe anymore. The sand was filling him up.

He couldn't even move enough to accommodate the spasms that followed.

* * *

The water cannons were losing pressure fast and the Visshon were reforming almost without impedance. Ted glanced in the direction of the dome's reactor complex situated in the north-east corner. There was no mushroom cloud, no evidence of a reaction. Was Chandler still on his way or had he been stopped? Lisa paced the roof anxiously behind him, Clarke and Alessandri waiting for whatever orders she would give.

What orders could she give?

One water cannon stopped firing completely, its supply exhausted, and the Visshon responded accordingly, forming up into a vicious wave that rose up and engulfed the emplacement. Ted heard the screams and put his hands over his ears.

Lisa leaned out over the edge of the building and stared, no longer even bothering to use her binoculars.

"That's it."

The second water cannon ran dry seconds later and the wave rose again.

"Signal a retreat," Lisa said to Clarke, "every officer for themselves. My last order - stay alive."

Clarke swallowed. "Yes ma'am," and began signalling.

When he finished, he turned to Lisa and licked his lips, the sweat running off his forehead.

"Get yourself out of here," she ordered. "You too, Alessandri." She peered again over edge. "The main wave has gone. The two of you can get behind it."

Alessandri nodded. "What about you, ma'am?"

Ted looked up, awaiting her response. She met his eyes and smiled wanly.

"Officer Holloway can't run and I don't want to. We'll be staying here."

"Ma'am?"

She clapped Alessandri on the shoulder. "We'll be fine, you and Clarke get going."

Alessandri didn't move.

"Go," Lisa ordered and then snatched the semaphore lamp from Clarke's hands. "Go."

The two junior enforcers stared at each other for a moment before running head first for the fire escape. Ted turned to Lisa, he didn't know what to do or what to say. He just knew what her staying behind meant. In response, she smiled and then eased herself down to sit beside him, her head resting on his shoulder.

"Nothing to do now but wait."

He squeezed her thigh affectionately. "You did make the Visshon work for their supper."

"But it wasn't enough," Lisa said.

"It was the best you could do."

"I lost most of my officers."

"Casualties of war," Ted said.

"How long do you think we have until the Visshon come for me?"

Ted shrugged. "Minutes, hours, I don't know. It will take a while for them to break through to the bunker, maybe longer to hunt everyone else down. They won't be coming back this way anytime soon."

She kissed him, her lips tasting of smoke, grit and treated water. "I think I'll just stay here with you."

He nodded and then thought of Howe and the dead girl in her arms. He knew the same would happen to Lisa and him. He didn't know if he could live with that.

"I need a gun," he said.

She reached down and pulled her pistol from its holster, handing the gun over to him.

"A mercy killing?"

He weighed the weapon in his hand, when the Visshon arrived he could it use on Lisa and then on himself.

"No, Ted," she said, reading his intention. "I want you to live."

"What about you?" he asked.

She bowed her head. "Throw the gun away. I don't want you to be the one who does it. If they want to kill me then let them kill me. But it shouldn't be you, Ted, not you."

His grip on the gun momentarily tightened and then he pulled his elbow back and hurled it over the edge of the roof.

It was gone.

"Stay with me, Ted," she said, her cheek resting against his. He glanced down and saw her eyes were closed.

Putting his arm around her, he closed his eyes too.

* * *

Lisa smelt the fire escape burning and opened her eyes, wondering how long she had slept.

"Ted?"

His head was still leaning against hers, his eyes closed and a sad smile upon her lips.

"I'm awake," he said. "I was just listening to you breathing."

She kissed his forehead and turned her attention the burning smell. A cloud of acid vapour was rising from the fire escape, and as she watched, green liquid seeped over the last metal rung onto the rooftop.

The Visshon had arrived.

Ted sat up in alarm. "Lisa!"

She looked up at him. "I know, I can almost taste them."

"You need to go," he shouted, reaching to pull her up.

She didn't want to move. "Let them come."

He ignored her, and despite his leg, stood up and in one move flung her over his shoulder, carrying her like a rag doll. It was far from dignified.

"Put me down, Ted," she ordered. "There's nowhere to go."

He struggled to limp to the far side of the roof, as far as he could go before being faced with a drop.

Her fists pounded into his back. "Put me down!"

He lurched to the ground, his bad leg deserting any pretence of support and Lisa broke free, punching him in the arm for his trouble.

"Why did you do that?" She screamed.

He rubbed his arm. "I was just trying to..."

She gritted her teeth. "I was ready, Ted! I was ready!"

His face reddened. "Well I wasn't!"

She stopped. She couldn't deal with this anymore. She didn't want her last emotion to be anger. "Ted?"

He struggled to his feet and planted himself between Lisa and the encroaching green liquid.

"You can't have her!" He shouted. "I won't let you have her!"

The liquid paused as Lisa pulled at his arm.

"Stop this!"

"Leave us alone!" Ted ordered the Visshon. "Just leave us alone!"

The green liquid began moving again, this time faster than before. Ted held his arms out wide as if somehow they could shield her.

She knew they couldn't.

This isn't how I want it, Ted," she said slowly. "Please stop."

She clambered to her feet and took hold of his arm, pulling him around to face her. His cheeks were tear-streaked.

"I'm sorry, Ted," she began and leaned into his shoulder. "But this is my choice." Closing her eyes she breathed in the smell of him and tried to lock it in her memory.

She didn't want the moment to end.

* * *

The golden light was so bright it spilled in under his eyelids, rousing Jason from his deep sleep. Without thinking, he opened his eyes only to instantly close them again, the brief exposure spawning ghostly afterimages, swimming upon his retinas.

Hello, Jason.

The environment suit was gone and so were the clothes he had worn beneath it. He was suspended horizontally, his bare skin burning under the yellow light.

"What are you doing to me?" He asked.

Purifying you.

"Why does it need to hurt so much?"
Soon, nothing will ever hurt you again.
"What is this place?"
It is the inner mind of the Visshon.
"Just one mind?"
Made up of many component parts, but yes, essentially I am one.

His right foot stung and then his left foot followed suit. He couldn't feel his toes.

"What's happening to my feet?" He asked
You don't need feet.

Jason squinted, trying to see down the length of his body. Trying to see... Oh. His feet and ankles were gone.

"What have you done?"
Your body is not required.
"My body is what makes me, me."
But soon there will be no you. There will only be me.

Jason tried to move, lifting his arms to wave them around an empty space. He was not lying on anything, he was floating, and there was nothing to grab onto.

"I don't think this is what Randall had in mind," Jason said.

The concepts were fully explained. I will become humanity and humanity will become me.

Jason's fingertips were tingling and he watched as they split apart particle by particle, drifting upward. What remained of his hands swiftly followed.

"I want to make a deal with you," Jason said quickly.
We already have an agreement with the quantum being.
"I have a new proposal."
What?

"Stop attacking my people and allow us to complete the terraforming process. After that we won't need you to power our reactors anymore. We can live simply and in peace."

It is too late for that. All available donations have been made. If I allowed you to continue, you would eat into the very heart of me.

"Then let us only use the material already processed. We will not use any more of you."

Your people would die.

"But we would not be murdered."

It is too late. I want to end your people myself. I believe I will find that satisfying.

"You mistake me," Jason said. "I'm not begging, I'm giving you a chance. If you don't agree, I will destroy you."

Destroy me? How do you plan to do that? You no longer have arms, you no longer have legs. Soon you will not even have a nervous system, or internal organs, or eyes or ears. You will not even have a mouth to speak with.

"Don't make me do it."

You can do nothing, so why not just surrender and become a part of me? We can learn so much from each other.

"You're running out of time."

No, you are. You invaded my planet, and little by little, you consumed me to survive. As you humans say, 'I am simply returning the favour'.

There was a pain in Jason's stomach as more of him dissolved and streamed upward, the process accelerating. He found himself remembering the war, remembering Randall, the Valhalla, and Gina loving and hating him in equal measure. He remembered the human race and a desire to fight for it, to win at any cost.

He remembered asking a weak and sickly Dominic to reactivate the combustible in the back of his head.

Ah, Jason, there is a foreign object located in your skull. What is it?

It was all so simple, so very simple.

Is this what you threaten me with?

He opened his eyes fully and stared up into a light as bright as any sun.

Soon you will not even remember existing.

"Valhalla," Jason said, his tongue sliding comfortably over the syllables. "VALHALLA!"

And the light grew brighter than ever.

* * *

Silence.

Ted felt the heat of the dome on his head and the steady breeze rifling through his hair. He felt the arms of the woman who held him, supporting him and keeping him upright because he couldn't stand without her.

But all he could hear was her breathing mixing in with his own.

"Lisa?" He whispered.

She opened her eyes and stared into his. "I'm alive."

He nodded. "You are." He tried to turn around but she stopped him.

"It isn't moving," she said.

"What?"

"It isn't moving," she repeated, this time louder and with certainty.

They turned together, and he saw the green liquid had become a stretched out and isolated puddle. His mouth opened.

"What the?"

She let him go and he staggered uncertainly as she rushed to collect her binoculars from where they had been dropped.

"What's going on?" He asked.

She stared out across the dome, running from one side of the rooftop to the other, scanning again and again.

"Lisa?"

She put down the binoculars and ran into his arms, laughing.

"I think the Visshon are dead."

He didn't understand. "How?"
She kissed him on the lips.
"We won."

Epilogue

The doors to Randall's tower were bent and smashed beyond repair and there was a crater at the centre of the reception area. Dominic stepped around it and considered the staircase. The door was gone and the opening enlarged. Stepping through, he couldn't actually see any stairs at all, just fragments of concrete lining the scarred and pockmarked walls. There had been a fierce battle here, and more than one body was rotting away beneath the rubble. He held his nose and picked at the remains of a combat drone. The enforcers had given as good as they got.

He considered the possibility that Randall had been destroyed and then summarily dismissed the notion. He had been trapped in the bunker for two days before a signal had reached them from the dome. On emerging into the outside world, the air still seemed fresh, the temperature stable and the daylight steady. If Randall was dead the entire life support system would have been in chaos. No, Randall was alive and whatever damage had been done to the tower was superficial at best.

He looked up, trying to zero in on a working sensor.

"Randall," he called out. "Can you hear me?"

There was no answer, and he reached out with his own wireless systems, searching for a connection. There it was, a weak signal emanating from a damaged relay in the ceiling.

- *Randall, can you hear me?*

Yes, of course. I am gratified you still function, Dominic. One of my elevators remains undamaged. I will send it down for you.

- *Thank you.*

The Visshon no longer affect me. I take it the same is true for you.

- *It is.*

The elevator on the right hand side pinged open and Dominic marvelled that it was still intact. Of course the enforcers would avoid the elevators, but leaving one working was a small miracle in itself. He stepped inside and felt a heavy vibration as he began the ascent. Briefly he wondered how safe he actually was.

Do you know what happened?

- Jason happened.

How?

- I re-enabled his combustible. I think it's safe to say he used it.

He always was tricky.

- And now he's finally gone.

The elevator doors pinged open at the top floor. Dominic walked out and made for the chamber overlooking the curve of the dome. Redfern's true sun was setting.

Strange you should say that. My tower in the golden realm registered a signal from the neural sensors of an environment suit just before it was destroyed.

- A neural scan of Jason?

Yes, he was wearing a close approximation of one of the suits specially made for him. I suspect it belonged to Webster.

- Then he can live again.

We should synchronise, I would like to know everything that's happened to you.

Dominic looked out over the glittering amber skin and the desert of red stretching into the distance. He took a breath.

- Do you mind if we don't?

Why?

Dominic swayed on the balls of his feet and gripped the side of the window frame.

- I think it's time I was separate.

You no longer wish to be my avatar?

- I...

He disengaged the wi-fi connection and turned away from the view of the outside.

"Dominic?"

He peered upward at the speaker. "The last few days I've had trouble deciding where you end and I begin. I've been mixing us up in my mind."

"The Visshon have damaged you," Randall declared. "We will run a full diagnostic and instigate repair."

Dominic shook his head. "It's more than that. I... I need to be separate."

There was a pause.

"I think I knew," Randall replied finally. "The last time we synchronised, I wanted to be you. I wanted to open my eyes and walk out onto the grass barefoot, just like I did before."

"You did?"

"I didn't know who I was either."

"Then you agree?" Dominic asked. They had always agreed.

"No," Randall replied, "but I understand. What will you do now?"

The former avatar turned back to the window and looked down below. "I will live among them. Perhaps then I will find out where I belong."

"You can come back whenever you wish," Randall declared. "I am your friend."

Dominic smiled. "As I am yours."

"And as a being no longer bound by the promises I made, there is one thing you can do that I cannot."

* * *

The remembrance ceremony took place in the park outside the Justice Building. A framed picture of each and every fallen enforcer lined up before the central podium. Ted was in his dress uniform, neatly pressed, his cap on straight and his new stripes emblazoned on his arms. He was in the fifth row of twenty, far enough away not to be confused with the families of the departed, but close enough to hear the new Commissioner make her speech.

"-And we also remember Steve Miles, Thomas Jarvis and most of all Neil Chandler, who sacrificed themselves in the line of duty so the rest of us could live. Please, all of you, stand for a minute's silence so that we can honour those who gave us their lives."

Ted braced himself with his cane and stood with the rest, his head bowed in contrition.

...

"Thank you, everyone," Lisa said, her eyes delving deeply into the crowd. "It has been a trying few days, but we have survived. We have survived and yes, we will rebuild everything that has been destroyed. We will make this colony of ours the paradise it deserves to be. Together we are strong, together we can do anything."

She took a breath.

"My father, the late Commissioner Andrew Carmichael, used to say 'continuity is everything'. Well I think he was wrong. I have faith that in the end, the very end, we can do more than just continue, more than just survive. We owe it to ourselves to do more and be more. Together we can live as we were meant to live, on our own terms and in own way."

She smiled as the crowd erupted into a wave of deafening applause. When it had almost subsided, she raised her hand.

"Thank you everyone for what you have done and what I know you will do. The future is ours now, it's our time and we will succeed. We don't have any other choice."

She looked up, her eyes lost far away, and Ted became aware of the reverential silence stretching out across the park. They were all waiting for her to speak again.

Finally, she straightened up and faced her audience.

"Please don't go anywhere," she said. "There will be a short reception to follow."

The clapping began again as Lisa stepped off the podium and carefully walked across to the far side. Belatedly, Ted realised she was going to shake the hand of every single person in attendance. He lined up with the others, shuffling along with the crowd until finally her hand was clenched in his.

"Thank you for your service," Lisa said.

He shook her hand and saluted. "Thank you ma'am, and congratulations on your appointment, it is thoroughly deserved."

She eyed him seriously. "Don't go far, Ted."

"Yes ma'am."

He left her to face the rest of the line and found his way to a champagne glass and a seat by a table.

"Sergeant Holloway."

It was Lieutenant Gemma Howe. He tried to get up but she placed a hand on his wrist.

"Don't bother," she said. "I just want to sit with my old friend."

He nodded and signalled to an attendant for another glass.

"Thank you," Gemma said.

She took a sip as he studied her. There were black bags dragging under her eyes.

"Have you been sleeping?" He asked.

She hesitated. "I have nightmares. The little girl..."

Ted nodded.

"How did we win?" she asked. "Nothing we did could stop them."

"There are rumours," he replied. "One of the remembered managed to get through to where they were vulnerable and activate his combustible."

"*His* combustible?"

Ted blinked, he had said too much.

"It was Jason."

Gemma did not seem surprised and lightly touched the back of her own skull. "I had my combustible removed. How about you?"

"Years ago, I never felt very happy about walking around with a bomb in my head."

Gemma nodded and then raised her glass. "To Jason."

"Jason," he said, their glasses chiming.

Howe turned towards the distant needle of Randall's tower rising into the heavens.

"What's Lisa going to do about him?"

Ted drank some more. "Nothing, for now. We need him to keep everything going. He's a necessary evil."

She leaned in. "You don't sound too pleased about that."

He smiled. "Did the whole 'necessary evil' thing give it away?"

"One day we won't need him anymore."

He stared long and hard at her. She was perhaps a decade older than he was, the beauty he remembered so well, long since faded.

"I'm sure on Earth we were the same age."

"I'm not that old," Howe said, "and more than a match for you."

He shrugged. "Dominic told me I lived many lives. I wonder if we…"

She laughed suddenly and then punched him in the arm. "Don't drink so much."

"I just meant—"

Gemma laughed.

"Ted?"

He looked up and saw Shandra standing over them. She was wheezing quietly.

"Join us," Ted offered without hesitation.

Shandra glanced across at Howe uncertainly and then took a seat.

"Lisa will be here soon," Ted declared. "If she ever gets away."

"I hear she wants to cut down on surveillance," Shandra said.

Howe finished her glass and reached for a new one. "She has a meeting with the civic committee tomorrow."

Ted puffed out his cheeks. "That should be fun."

* * *

Deep within the bowels of The Revival Centre, the reconstruction mainframe accessed a stored physical file and a recently acquired neural scan, running a comparison. It then combined the data into a new digital file and siphoned the required matter into the reconstruction matrix.

Two hours later...

The process completed.

The End

About the Author

G.D. Tinnams has worked as a barman, a call centre operator, an IT support analyst, and a software tester. But during all this time he was also an insatiable reader of science fiction and fantasy books like Susan Cooper's 'The Dark Is Rising Sequence', Orson Scott Card's 'Ender's Game', Robert Charles Wilson's 'Blind Lake' and Greg Egan's 'Permutation City'. He is very fond of weird, mind-bending stories and decided quite early on to try writing some. 'Redfern' is his third novel.

Available from Amazon in both e-book and print formats:

Threshold Shift
(2012)

"I will hurt you more than you hurt me. Death will be a long time coming."

On the frontier planet of Threshold a hard won truce exists between the native inhabitants and the human settlers. When a murder puts this truce in jeopardy, Marshal Jacob Klein must try to see justice done, whatever the cost.

But Klein has his own problems - an addiction to a fatal narcotic, a disenfranchised son, and a dark secret he has been hiding for over two decades.

For there is a greater threat to Threshold than just a petty civil war. An ancient presence has invaded the planet for its own purposes and Jacob Klein is in no shape to stop it.

Five Byte Stories
(2012)

Andy Hopkins awakes from cryo-sleep to find his colony ship being pursued by an alien craft and his commander determined to destroy it.

"An assassin that can't be touched or hurt, who can go anywhere and kill anyone? You think that follows due process?"
Michael Armitage is a ruthless assassin who cannot be stopped. When Michael starts to develop a conscience his controllers are

not happy.

John is the clone of a convicted serial killer created for scientific research. The man that created him is determined to make John a killer too.

Davey Weis was involved in a car accident that destroyed part of his brain and prevented him making any decision. When revolutionary neural surgery repairs his brain he is far from normal. But what is normal anyway?

Jacob Landers has ruled the Earth for a thousand years. He has ended war and hunger and set the world onto a path of continuous happiness and prosperity. He is very bored.

Aliens, Assassins, Clones, Cyborgs, Dictators...
Five dark science fiction stories to enjoy.

Hunter No More (2014)

-ATTENTION-

The Hunter Class Spacecraft designated 'The Amberjack' disappeared during a routine mission to Seek, Locate and Destroy the enemy Machine Mind contingent known as 'The Ochre'.

Conclusion: It was either destroyed by the Ochre or went rogue for reasons unknown. If sighted, approach with extreme caution.

On the planet Borealis, a violent revolution forces Samantha Marriot and her parents to flee their home for the relative safety of 'The Rainbow Islands'. Once there, Sam discovers a secret her father has been keeping from her all her life, a secret that will change everything. Meanwhile, The Machine Mind Hierarchy of Earth dispatches a ship to rid themselves of the planet's troublesome human population.

The only hope of a defence lies with a damaged binary Hunter unit that has long since abandoned both its programming and weaponry. In order for the unit to succeed it must call upon the aid of an ancient enemy, and prove, once and for all, it is a Hunter no more.

Printed in Great Britain
by Amazon